"I need a husband,"

Casey announced. "I'm willing to marry the first unattached man who's got the guts to stand with me against my family."

With an overwhelming sense of hopelessness, she sold herself in the only way she knew how.

"I'll live with you. Cook your food. I'll even share your bed."

A sound came out of the shadows. She squinted, trying to see, and then, when she did, she felt an overwhelming urge to run. The man had *don't care* in his walk and the coldest eyes she'd ever seen. He was tall and handsome, his clothing worn and ragged. In response to Casey's plea, he stood without flinching and answered, "About the only thing I have to my name is guts. If that's all you need, I'm your man."

"What's your name?" Casey asked.

"Ryder Justice."

Justice! Casey took it as a sign. Justice was exactly what she'd been searching for.

Dear Reader,

It's no surprise that Intimate Moments is *the* place to go when you want the best mix of excitement and romance, and it's authors like Sharon Sala who have earned the line that reputation. Now, with *Ryder's Wife,* Sharon begins her first Intimate Moments miniseries, THE JUSTICE WAY. The three Justice brothers are men with a capital M—and they're about to fall in love with a capital L. This month join Ryder as he marries heiress Casey Ruban for reasons of convenience and stays around for love.

Popular Beverly Barton is writing in the miniseries vein, too, with *A Man Like Morgan Kane,* the latest in THE PROTECTORS. Beverly knows how to steam up a romance, that's for sure! In *Wife, Mother...Lover?* Sally Tyler Hayes spins a poignant tale of a father, a family and the woman who gives them all their second chance at happiness—and love. *Reilly's Return* also marks Amelia Autin's return. This is a wonderfully suspenseful tale about a hero who had to fake his own death to protect the woman he loved—and what happens when she suddenly finds out he's really still alive. In *Temporary Marriage,* Leann Harris takes us to the jungles of South America for a tale of a sham marriage that leads to a very real honeymoon. Finally, Dani Criss is back with *For Kaitlyn's Sake,* a reunion story with all the passion you could wish for.

Let all six of these terrific books keep you warm as the winter nights grow colder, and come back next month for even more of the most excitingly romantic reading around, right here in Silhouette Intimate Moments.

Yours,

Leslie J. Wainger
Senior Editor and Editorial Coordinator

Please address questions and book requests to:
Silhouette Reader Service
U.S.: 3010 Walden Ave., P.O. Box 1325, Buffalo, NY 14269
Canadian: P.O. Box 609, Fort Erie, Ont. L2A 5X3

SHARON SALA

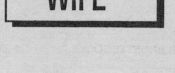

RYDER'S WIFE

Published by Silhouette Books

America's Publisher of Contemporary Romance

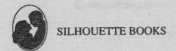

SILHOUETTE BOOKS

ISBN 0-373-07817-X

RYDER'S WIFE

Copyright © 1997 by Sharon Sala

This edition published by arrangement with Harlequin Books S.A.

® and TM are trademarks of Harlequin Books S.A., used under license.
Trademarks indicated with ® are registered in the United States Patent
and Trademark Office, the Canadian Trade Marks Office and in other
countries.

Printed in U.S.A.

SHARON SALA

is a child of the country. As a farmer's daughter, she found that her vivid imagination made solitude a thing to cherish. During her adult life, she learned to survive by taking things one day at a time. An inveterate dreamer, she yearned to share the stories her imagination created. For Sharon, her dreams have come true, and she claims one of her greatest joys is when her stories become tools for healing.

Magic comes to us in myriad forms. There is magic in the beauty of a sunrise, in the reflection on a dewdrop hanging from the petals of a rose. A mother's touch is magic when it soothes a crying child. And laughter is a magic that no medicine can match.

There have been many magic moments in my life that are mine alone to keep. But I would like to acknowledge two people who have made their own kind of magic in helping me create this world in which I write.

To Meredith Bernstein—an agent extraordinaire who stands behind me faithfully and does not know the meaning of the word "no."

To Jan Goldstoff—a publicist with a golden touch, whose visions are exceeded only by her persistence.

Prologue

Heat penetrated the black void of unconsciousness in which Ryder Justice was drifting. Even in the depths from which he was trying to escape, he smelled the hair burning on the backs of his arms and knew another level of fear. He moaned, and the movement of air through his lungs yanked him rudely into the now. Gritting his teeth against the pain racking his every breath, he struggled to sit upright. Acrid smoke drifted up his nose, mingling with the coppery taste of fresh blood as he fumbled with the latch to his seat belt. That which had most probably saved his life was now holding him hostage.

A sheet of rain blew in the broken window to his left and into his eyes. It was as effective as a slap in the face. Cognizance returned full force.

Just beyond the crumpled cockpit, he could see flames licking at the metal and eating their way toward him, and he remembered being up in the sky, and getting caught in the storm. A stroke of lightning lit up the night sky and he flinched as he remembered another bolt of lightning and how the plane had shuddered, then rocked. And afterward, the sensation of an electric free fall.

An instinct for survival pushed past the misery of broken ribs and bleeding cuts, past the bone-jarring ache that came with every movement, every breath. He'd survived being struck by lightning. The plane had crashed and he was still alive to tell the tale. By God, he would not sit here and burn to death when he still had legs to crawl.

And at that moment, he remembered he was not alone. He turned.

"Dad?"

Another streak of lightning snaked across the sky, momentarily illuminating what was left of the cabin. After that, Ryder had only the encroaching fire by which to see, but it was more than enough. Stunned by the horror of what the crash had done to Micah Justice, he refused to believe what his mind already knew.

The straps holding him in place suddenly came free and Ryder struggled to get out of his seat. Ignoring wave after wave of pain-filled nausea, he freed his father from the seat and managed to get them both out of the wreckage and into the falling rain.

Sometimes crawling, sometimes pushing, he dragged himself and his father's lifeless body until he found himself beneath some sort of overhang.

Shivering from pain, shock, and the chill of rain-soaked clothing, he scooted as far back as he could get beneath the outcropping of rocks, pulling Micah's body with him, then cradling his father's head against his chest as he would have a sleeping child.

A gust of wind cornered the overhang, blowing rain and a peppering of hail on Ryder's outstretched legs, and at that moment the fuselage blew, erupting into the night in an orange ball of fire. Ryder closed his eyes against the blast, and held his father that much tighter, refusing to accept the motion as wasted effort.

"Dad?"

Again, Micah Justice did not answer. There was no familiar, sarcastic chuckle, no awkward pat from a strong man's hands for comfort. Ryder buried his face against the back of his father's shirt and took a long, aching breath. He knew, but his heart wasn't ready to face the truth.

"Dad…come on, Dad. You can do this. You've told me time and time again that it takes a hell of a lot to put a Justice man down."

Thunder rumbled across the sky, and the deep, angry rumble sounded like his heart felt as grief began to settle. His arms tightened around his father's body, and for the first time since the accident had happened, tears began to fall, mingling with the raindrops clinging to Ryder's scorched and battered face.

Holding his father close, he began to rock, muttering beneath his breath and in his father's ear, although Micah Justice had already moved beyond the sound of his second son's voice.

"Please, Dad, talk to me." Ryder's voice broke. "Dad…Daddy, don't do this," he pleaded. "Don't leave us. We need you. All of us need you. Roman will go to hell without you on his case…and Royal, think of Royal. What will happen to the ranch and Royal if you don't wake up?"

A second explosion followed on the tail of the first— smaller, but still powerful in intensity. Bits of burning metal shot up into the sky and then fell down upon the ground nearby. Another flash of lightning, this time closer, revealed more of the truth Ryder Justice had been trying to deny. Micah was dead. Probably upon impact. And he was left with an inescapable fact. His father was dead, and he'd been piloting the plane. This time, when thunder rumbled overhead, it drowned out the sounds of Ryder Justice's grief.

Chapter 1

July—Ruban Crossing, Mississippi

"Casey, darling, you should never wear black. It makes you look like a crow."

Before Casey could take offense at what her half brother, Miles Dunn just said, he took a seat with the rest of the Ruban family, who were gathering for the reading of Delaney Ruban's will.

She picked a piece of lint from the skirt of her black silk dress and tilted her chin, reminding herself that she wasn't going to cry. Not now, and especially not in front of Lash Marlow, her grandfather's lawyer. Although he was sitting behind his desk and watching each arrival with a focused, predatory gaze, Casey was aware that he was also watching her every move. And it had been that way with them for more years than she cared to remember.

In spite of her love for her grandfather, Delaney Ruban, and in spite of Delaney's hopes that she and Lash might someday marry, Casey had been unable to bring herself to comply.

She'd been a willing student of Delaney's tutorial with regards to the Ruban empire, but she refused to give up what passed as the personal portion of her life. It didn't amount to much, but it was all she had that she could honestly call her own. Even more important, she didn't love Lash Marlow and had no intention of spending the rest of her life with a man who measured the value of a person by monetary worth.

She shifted nervously in her seat, wishing this day to be over. As Delaney's closest living relative and the heir who had been groomed to take over the vast Ruban holdings, she knew the task that lay ahead of her, right down to how many family members would be looking to her for sustenance.

Not for the first time since her grandfather's stroke six weeks ago did she wish her father and mother were still alive. And, if Chip Ruban hadn't taken his wife, Alysa, to Hawaii for their tenth wedding anniversary, they might still be. But he had, and they'd drowned in a boating accident off the coast of Oahu, leaving their only child, six-year-old Casey, as well as Alysa's ten-year-old twins from a previous marriage, to be raised by an absent and overbearing grandfather who quickly pawned off those duties to someone else.

Alysa's mother, Eudora Deathridge, was moved into the mansion and given full authority and responsibility of her daughter's children. And although she was Casey's grandmother as well, Casey found herself grasping for space in a lap already too full for one more small, six-year-old girl.

With the instinct of a child who knows where she is loved, she turned to Joshua Bass and his wife, Matilda. The butler and the cook. The kitchen became the center of her universe. In Tilly Bass's loving arms, she learned to trust and love again. On Joshua's shoulders, she saw the world in which she lived from a new and different angle, and in doing so, learned not to be afraid of reaching for the stars. They became the surrogate parents she had needed, and now, twenty years later, they were the anchors that kept her life on a straight and honorable path.

And while Tilly and Joshua nurtured and loved her, at thirteen years old, Casey suddenly became the focus of Delaney Ruban's world. He had looked up one day and realized that he wasn't getting any younger, and since Casey was his son's only child, she was, of course, to be his heir.

He looked for the child he'd all but ignored and found a girl on the brink of womanhood. Elated that she'd grown up so well without much of his effort, he decided that it was time she branched out past the familiarity of her school, her friends and Tilly Bass's kitchen.

And so it began. The treat of accompanying him on business trips became the first step in a lifelong education. Before long, Casey was spending all of her summers with him at his office. At first, she blossomed under his tutoring. Her grandfather had never given her anything but presents, and now he was sharing his time with her. It took the better part of Casey's teenage years before she realized Delaney's reasons for spending time with her were selfish. Someone must step into his shoes when he was gone. He'd decided it would be Casey.

And now, at twenty-six, Casey was about to become CEO of a multimillion-dollar corporation with holdings in everything from cotton mills to racehorses. Thanks to the last ten years of Delaney's coaching, she was more than up to the task.

A low murmur of indistinguishable voices hummed behind her like a worn-out motor, rising and falling with the advent of each new person to enter the room. She closed her eyes and took a deep breath. It wasn't the job that daunted her. It was those who were gathering. They were the ones who would be waiting for her to fail.

Someone else touched her on the shoulder. She looked up. It was her sister, Erica.

"Nice dress, Casey darling." Erica's eyes glittered sharply as she fingered the fabric. "I suppose it has a silver lining, too. Just like your life."

"Erica, really," Eudora Deathridge said, and gave her eldest granddaughter a none-too-gentle nudge as they moved past Casey to take their seats.

Casey let the comment roll off her shoulders, and as the women passed by her Eudora squeezed Casey's arm. It was nothing new. Miles and Erica had begrudged Casey everything from the day she was born—from being a Ruban, to being the one Delaney had chosen to follow in his footsteps. In all their lives, they had shared a mother, but little else.

Lash Marlow cleared his throat, well aware that the sound

added to the building tension. "I believe we are all here now. Shall we begin?"

Casey's pulse accelerated. She gripped the arms of the chair, focusing on the man behind the desk and was struck by an odd, almost satisfied smile on Lash's face. Reluctantly, she accepted the fact that he was privy to secrets about their lives she wished he did not know. It made her feel vulnerable, and vulnerability was a weakness Rubans were not allowed to feel. She watched as Marlow shifted in his seat and straightened the papers in front of him. It was the will. Delaney's will.

Fresh tears spiked her lashes as she struggled with composure, trying to come to terms with the fact that Delaney was dead. He'd been such a large and vital man that overlooking his age had been simple. But nature had not been as kind. Despite his ebullient personality and lust for life, the past eighty-two years had taken their toll. And no matter how hard he had tried to ignore the inevitable, he had failed.

Ultimately, Lash began to read and Casey's mind wandered, only now and then tuning in on his voice as it droned into the ominous quiet of the room. Once in a while a low murmur of voices became noticeable behind her, and she supposed Miles and Erica were voicing their opinions of the bequeathals being read.

"And to my beloved granddaughter, Casey Dee Ruban..."

Casey shook off the fugue in which she'd been hanging and focused.

"...the bulk of my estate and the home in which she's been residing since her parents' death, as well as the controlling reins of Ruban Enterprises. But to inherit..."

Startled, her gaze slid from the papers in Lash's hands to his face. What did he mean...to inherit? Have mercy, what has Delaney done?

"To qualify for the entire aforementioned inheritance, my granddaughter, Casey Dee Ruban, must marry within forty-eight hours of the reading of my will, and must live with her husband, in his residence and under his protection, for the duration of at least one year, or she will forfeit her birthright. If she chooses not to adhere to my last request, then the bulk of my estate will be deeded to my step-grandchildren, Miles and Erica Dunn."

Casey stood. Rage, coupled with a shock she couldn't deny made her shake, but the tremor never reached her voice. She looked at Lash: at his cool, handsome face, his blond, wavy hair, his pale green eyes. Her eyes darkened as she leaned forward, bracing herself against his desk.

"Surely I cannot be held to this!"

To his credit, Lash's gaze never wavered. "I'm sorry, Casey. I know this must come as a shock, but I can assure you it's legal. Your grandfather was of sound mind and body when this was written. I tried to talk him out of such an unreasonable clause, but..."

When Lash shrugged, as if to say it was out of his hands, she looked away.

Someone choked in the back of the room. Casey didn't have to look to know that it was probably Miles, reveling in his unexpected windfall.

A red haze swam before her eyes and she willed herself not to faint. Marry? She hadn't seriously dated a man in over five years. The only man who persisted in being a part of her life was...

She looked up. The expression on Lash's face was too calm, almost expectant. How long had he known about this? Even worse, what had he and Delaney planned?

She swayed, staggered by the idea of being bound to Lash Marlow by law, as well as in the eyes of God, even for so much as a year.

Lash stood. His voice was low, his touch solicitous as he tried to take her in his arms.

"Casey, I'm here. Let me help you—"

She stepped back. The selfish glitter in Lash's eyes was too obvious to ignore.

Damn you, Delaney, damn you to hell.

She walked out of the room, leaving those behind to wonder what the outcome might be.

Hours later, the sun was about to set on the day as a low-slung black sports car rounded the corner of an unpaved road down in the flatlands. The trailing rooster tail of dust was evidence of how fast the car was traveling. The skid the car took as it cornered was proof of Casey Ruban's desperate state of mind. She'd been driving for hours, trying to think of a way out of her dilemma without having to acquiesce to the terms of her grandfather's will.

By naming Miles and Erica as the recipients of his estate should she default, Delaney had been certain Casey would comply. He'd been well aware of her disdain for the syco-phantic life-style her half brother and half sister had chosen to live. They were thirty years old. Both had college degrees. Neither saw fit to use them.

Therefore, he had surmised that Casey would ultimately agree to his conditions. And he also knew Casey had no spe-cial man in her life, which would most certainly make Lash the prime candidate to fulfill the terms of the will. But he hadn't counted on Casey's total defiance, or the wild streak of rebellion that had driven her deep into the Mississippi Delta.

A short while later, the sun was gone and it was the time of evening when the world existed in shades of gray, faded by distance or muted by overlying shadows. Ahead, Casey could just make out the blinking lights on what appeared to be a roadhouse.

The fact that Sonny's Place was in the middle of nowhere was of no consequence to her. What mattered were the number of cars and pickup trucks parked outside the building. It stood to reason there would be a large number of men inside.

Blinking back a fresh set of angry tears, she gritted her teeth, focusing on the decision she'd made. As she accelerated, her fingers gripped the steering wheel until her knuckles turned white.

She turned into the parking lot in a skid, slamming on her brakes and barely missing a truck parked beneath the wide-spread limbs of an ancient oak. Gravel spewed, spit out from beneath the wheels of her sports car like a bad taste.

Casey killed the engine and was out of the car before the dust had time to settle. There was a defiant tilt to her chin and determination in her stride as she started toward the entrance, yet when she stepped inside, a moment of unrefined terror swamped her. Dank air, thick smoke and the scent of stale beer hit her in the face like a slap. And then Lash's smirk flashed in her mind and she let the door swing shut behind her.

Ryder Justice sat with his back to the wall, nursing the same beer he'd bought over an hour earlier. He hadn't really wanted the drink, he'd just wanted a place to sit down.

The months and the miles since he'd walked out on his family and his business had long ago run together. He didn't know what day it was and didn't really care. All that mattered was staying on the move. It was the only way he knew to stay ahead of the memories that had nearly driven him insane.

A few words with the man at the next table had assured him he'd be sleeping on the ground again tonight. He was too far from a town to rent a room, and too nearly broke to consider wasting the money.

A grimy ceiling fan spun overhead, stirring the hot, muggy air without actually cooling it. He lifted the long-neck bottle, intent on draining what was left in one swallow when the door flew open and the woman walked into the room. Her appearance was sudden, as was the swift jolt of interest he felt when she lifted her hand to her face, pushing at the black tangle of her windblown hair that had fallen across her forehead.

She was taller than average, and the kind of woman who, at first glance, seemed on the verge of skinny. Except for the voluptuous curves of her breasts beneath the black, clinging fabric of her dress, she appeared shapeless. And then she turned suddenly, startled by the man who came in behind her, and as she did, the dress she was wearing flared, cupping slim, shapely hips before falling back into loose, generic folds.

Ryder's interest grew. It was fairly obvious that she wasn't the kind of woman who frequented places like this. Her movements were short, almost jerky, as if she were as surprised to find herself here as the men were to see her. And although he was some distance away, he thought she looked as if she'd been crying.

Who hurt you, pretty girl? What drove you into the flatlands?

The beer forgotten, he leaned forward, studying her face as one might study a map, wondering what—or who—had backed her into a corner. And he was certain she'd been backed into a corner or she wouldn't be here. He knew the look of desperation. It stared back at him every time he looked in a mirror. And like every other man in the place, he sat with anticipation, waiting for her to make the first move.

A half dozen dirty yellow lightbulbs dangled from a sagging fixture in the middle of the room. Only four of the bulbs were burning, cloaking the fog of cigarette smoke and dust with a sickly amber glow.

Heads turned and the understated rumble of voices trickled to a halt as Casey's eyes slowly adjusted to the lack of light. When she was certain she'd seen the location of every man in the place, she took a deep breath and sauntered into the middle of the room, well aware that each man was mentally stripping her—from the black silk dress flaring just above her knees to the opaque black stockings on her legs.

Behind her, she heard the bartender gasp then mutter the name Ruban. She'd been recognized! Her lips firmed. It would seem that even down here in the Delta she was unable to escape the power of Delaney Ruban's name.

Smoke drifted, burning her eyes and searing her nostrils with the acrid odor, yet she refused to move away. She turned slowly, judging the faces before her, looking for a man who might have the guts to consider what she was about to ask.

The bartender interrupted her train of thought.

"Miss, is there something I can do? Are you having car trouble? If you are, I'd be more than glad to call a tow truck for you."

There was nervous fear on the bartender's face. Casey knew just how he felt. Her own stomach was doing a few flops of its own. She shivered anxiously, and at that point, almost walked out of the room. But as she turned to go, the image of Lash Marlow's face slid into her mind. It was all the impetus she needed. She turned again, this time putting herself between the men and the door.

"I need something all right," Casey said, and when she heard her voice break, she cleared her throat and took a deep breath. This time when she spoke, her words came out loud and clear. "I don't need a tow truck. I need a man."

The bartender grabbed a shotgun from beneath the bar and jacked a shell into the chamber as the room erupted.

Wide-eyed, Casey spun toward the sound.

The appearance of the gun was enough to quiet the ruckus she'd started, but only momentarily. When the bartender began to speak, she knew her chances of succeeding were swiftly fading.

"Hold your seats, men. That there is Casey Ruban. Old Delaney Ruban's granddaughter, so unless you're real tired of living, I suggest you suck it up and stay where you're at. This shotgun won't do nearly as much harm to you as the Rubans can."

"I heard he's dead," someone muttered from the back of the room.

"But the rest of them aren't," the bartender said.

Casey spun toward the men in sudden anger. "Let me finish."

At that point, they were so caught up in what she'd said, they would have let her do anything she asked.

"I need a husband."

Someone cursed, another laughed a little nervously.

Casey chose to ignore it all. "I'm willing to marry the first unattached man who's got the guts to stand with me against my family."

When no one moved or spoke, hope began to die. This was a crazy idea, as crazy as what Delaney had done to her, but she couldn't bring herself to quit. Not yet.

With an overwhelming sense of hopelessness and a shame unlike anything she'd ever known, she lifted her head, selling herself in the only way she knew how. She started walking, moving between the tables, staying just out of reach of the daring men's grasp.

"I'll live with you. Cook your food. I'll even share your bed."

Total silence reigned and Casey could hear their harsh, rasping breaths as they considered taking her to bed and suffering the consequences. If this hadn't been so pitiful, she would have smiled. It would seem that Delaney was going to win after all.

A sound came out of the shadows. The sound of chair legs scraping against the grit and dirt on the old wooden floor, and the unmistakable rap of boot heels marking off the distance between Casey and the back of the room. She squinted against the smoke and the harsh, overhead glare, trying to see, and then when she did, felt an overwhelming urge to run.

The man had *don't care* in his walk and the coldest eyes she'd ever seen. Their deep gray-blue cast was the color of a Mississippi sky running before a storm front. An old, olive drab duffel bag hung awkwardly on the breadth of his shoulders, as if it had to find a place of its own somewhere between the chip and the weight of the world.

He was tall, his clothing worn and ragged. But it was the still expression on his tanned, handsome face that gave her pause.

Before she had time to consider the odds of winding up facedown and dead in a ditch at some murderer's hands, he was standing before her.

Casey took a deep breath. Murderer be damned. Her grandfather had already signed her fate. At least she was going to be the one who controlled the strings to which it was attached.

"Well?" she asked, and surprised herself by not flinching when he reached out and brushed at a wild strand of hair that had been stuck to her cheek.

Ryder Justice was surprised by the vehemence in her voice. He'd been around long enough to know when someone was afraid. From the moment she'd walked into the room, her fear had been palpable, yet just now when he'd touched her, she hadn't blinked. And the power in her voice told him there was more to her backbone than the soft, silky skin obviously covering it. He also knew what it felt like to be backed into a corner, and for some reason this woman was as far in a hole as a person could get and not be buried. And, he was tired of running. So damned tired he couldn't think.

"Well, what?" he asked.

Casey's breath caught on a gasp. His voice was low and deep and an image of him whispering in her ear shattered what was left of her composure. Hang in there, she warned herself, then lifted her chin.

"I asked a question. Do you have an answer?"

Ryder touched the side of her cheek and felt an odd sense of pride when, once again, she stood without flinching.

"About the only thing I have to my name is guts. If that's all you need, then I'm your man."

"Hey, man, you don't know what you're getting yourself into," the bartender warned.

Ryder's gaze never wavered from Casey Ruban's face. Once again, his voice broke the quiet, wrapping around Casey's senses and making her shake from within.

"I know enough," he said.

"My name is Casey Ruban," she said. "What's yours?"

"Ryder Justice."

Justice! Casey took it as a sign. Justice was exactly what she'd been searching for.

"You swear you are free to marry?"

He nodded.

"My grandfather always said his handshake was as good as his word," Casey said, and offered her hand.

Without pause, Ryder enfolded it within the breadth of his own and once again, Casey felt herself being swallowed whole. Her gaze centered on their hands entwined and she had a sudden image of their bodies in similar positions. She bit her lip and stifled a shudder. Now was not the time to get queasy. She had an empire to save.

"Come with me," she said shortly. "We have a little over twenty-four hours to get blood tests, apply for a license, and find a justice of the peace."

At the mention of haste, his gaze instinctively drifted toward her belly partially concealed beneath the loose-fitting dress.

Once, being an unwed mother might have horrified Casey. Now she wished that was all she was facing.

"Wrong guess, Mr. Justice. It's just that I've got myself in a race with the devil, and I don't like to lose."

Ryder followed without comment. He'd been on a first-name basis with the old hound himself for some time now. He never thought to consider the fact that the devil was giving someone else a hard time as well.

The room erupted into a roar as they stepped outside, and Casey found herself all but running toward her car. Only after she slid behind the wheel and locked them in did she feel safe. And then she glanced toward the man beside her and knew she was fooling herself.

His presence dwarfed the sports car's interior. He scooted the seat as far back as it would go and still his knees were up against the dash. The duffel bag he'd had on his shoulders was now between his feet, and Casey imagined she could hear the rhythmic thud of his heartbeat as he turned a cool, calculating gaze her way.

"Buckle up, Mr. Justice."

He reached for the seat belt out of reflex, then gave Casey another longer, calculating look.

"I have a question," he said.

Casey's heart dropped. *Please stranger, don't back out on me now.*

"I have one for you, too," she said quickly.

"Ladies first."

She almost smiled. "Do you have a home? Do you have a job?"

His expression blanked, and Casey would have sworn she saw pain on his face before he answered.

"I don't have an address or a job. Does it matter?"

She thought fast, remembering the conditions of the will. She had to live in her husband's residence and under his protection. This was good news. It was something she could control.

"Do you have a driver's license?" she asked.

He nodded.

"Good, then you're hired."

He cocked an eyebrow as Casey started the car.

"Exactly what have I been hired to do?"

"You're going to be the new chauffeur for the Ruban family. You... I mean...we...will live in the apartment over the garage on Delaney's...I mean, on my estate."

Ryder frowned. "Lady, I have to ask. Why marry a stranger?"

She backed out of the parking lot, the tires spinning on loose gravel as she drove onto the road, heading back the same way she'd come.

"Because I will be damned before I let myself be forced into marriage with a man I can't abide."

He wondered about the man she'd obviously left behind. "You don't know me. What if you can't abide me, either?"

Her gaze was fixed on the patch of road visible in the twin beams of her headlights.

"Living a year with a total stranger is better than living one night under Lash Marlow's roof. Besides, I don't like to be told what to do."

So, his name is Lash Marlow. This time Ryder did smile, but only a little.

"Casey."

Startled by the sound of her name on his lips, she turned her gaze from the road to his face.

"What?"

"I think you should try calling me Ryder. I've never gone to bed with a woman who called me Mister, and I don't intend to start now."

Gone to bed with…!

Almost too late she remembered what she was doing and swerved to avoid the ditch at which she was heading. By the time she had the car and herself under control, she was too desperate to argue the point.

First things first. Marriage. Then rules. After that, take it one day at a time. It was the only way she knew.

Chapter 2

There was something to be said for the power of the Ruban name. It had gotten Casey and Ryder through blood tests without an appointment, gotten a court clerk out of bed and down to the county courthouse in the middle of the night to issue a marriage license, then dragged an old family friend out of bed before sunrise to perform the impromptu ceremony. The waiting period most people would have experienced was waived for Delaney Ruban's granddaughter.

"You all take yourselves a seat now," Sudie Harris said, and pulled her housecoat a little tighter across her chest. "Judge will be here directly."

Casey dropped into the nearest chair, well aware that Harmon Harris's wife had taken one look at Ryder Justice and found him lacking in both worth and substance. When Ryder refused a seat and walked to the window instead, something about the way he was standing made her nervous. What if he was already sorry he'd gotten into this mess? What if he was thinking about leaving? Nervously, she got up.

"Mr. Justice, I—"

He turned and she choked on her words. He was so big. So

menacing. So much a stranger. What in God's name had she done?

"What did you call me?" he asked.

She swallowed and the lump in her throat seemed to be getting larger by the minute. Oh, Lord. "Ryder. I meant to say, Ryder."

His eyes narrowed thoughtfully. Casey Ruban was on the verge of a breakdown. She might not know it, but he recognized the signs. Her eyes were feverishly bright and the knuckles on her fingers had gone from red to white from the fists that she'd made. Add to that, a breathing pattern that was little more than a series of short, quick gasps, and he figured it wouldn't take much for her to fall apart.

"That's better," he said shortly. "Now sit down before you fall down."

Casey did as she was told and then tried not to look at his backside as he turned away. It was impossible. In a few short minutes she would be tied to this man as she'd never been bound before, not only by law, but in the closest of proximities. Wife! Dear God, she was going to be that man's wife.

She watched as he shrugged his shoulders in a quiet, almost weary gesture, rubbing at his neck and massaging the muscles with long, brown fingers. She couldn't quit staring at his hands. Out of nowhere a random thought came barreling into her sleep-starved mind. *I wonder if he's a gentle lover.*

Startled, she shuddered and looked away, wishing Judge Harris would hurry. She doubted there was little about Ryder Justice that was gentle, and the tension between them was making her crazy.

Torn between the fear that she was jumping into a worse mess than the one she was already in, and fear that at the last minute he wouldn't go through with the ceremony, she wanted to cry. Instead, she closed her eyes. All I want to do is go to bed and sleep for a month, then wake up and find out this was all a bad dream, she thought.

Somewhere in another part of the house a clock chimed five times. Startled, she glanced at her watch. Five o'clock! In a little over an hour the sun would be up. Footsteps sounded on the stairwell behind them. She stood and turned to face the man who was entering the room.

From Harmon Harris's expression, he was none too pleased to see who awaited him. "Casey Dee, what on earth are you doin' here in the middle of the night?"

"Getting married, and it's not the middle of the night, it's almost dawn."

Regardless of whether it was night or day, Ruban women did not sneak around to get married, and Harmon knew it. He stared at the man near his living room window, then glared at Casey.

"Not to him?"

She gritted her teeth, preparing herself for a fight.

"Yes sir, to him. We have blood tests and the license right here." She thrust the papers into the judge's hands.

When he noted the dates he frowned, staring at her hard and long, from her head to the middle of her belly. Like Ryder before him, Harmon was assuming the only reason a woman would rush into marriage was to give a bastard child a name.

"Hell, girl, the ink is hardly dry on this stuff. What's the big rush?"

"You can get that look off your face," Casey muttered. "I'm not pregnant. I haven't even been exposed."

Bushy eyebrows lowered over his prominent nose as Harmon Harris laid the papers to one side and took Casey by the arm.

"I've known you a long time, Honey, and this isn't like you. Before I perform any ceremony, I want an explanation."

Casey's gaze never wavered. "If Delaney were alive, you could ask him yourself. All I know is, I had forty-eight hours to find myself a husband or forfeit my inheritance to Miles and Erica."

The judge's eyebrows rose perceptibly. "You're joking!"

Her shoulders slumped. "I wish I were."

He glanced over her shoulder to Ryder. "I don't understand."

Then his voice lowered. "Why not marry Lash Marlow? You've known him nearly all your life. Why this man?"

"Because he's not Lash."

The judge didn't comment. He didn't have to. Casey's answer pretty much said it all.

"Who is he?"

"His name is Ryder Justice."

"I know that," the judge said. "It says so on the papers. What I'm asking is *who* are his people?"

Casey shrugged. "I haven't the faintest idea, and quite frankly I don't care. What I do know is I will not be coerced, especially by a dead man, into marrying someone I do not even like, never mind the fact that I don't love him. Do you understand that?"

Suddenly Casey and Harmon realized they were no longer alone.

"Is there a problem?" Ryder asked.

There was something about the look on the big man's face that made Harmon Harris release his grasp on Casey's arms.

Harmon sighed. "No, I don't suppose there is. Casey is of age and enough of her own woman to do as she chooses." He turned. "Sudie, go next door and wake up Millard Shreves. We're gonna need ourselves another witness."

Casey relaxed as Judge Harris's wife hurried to do his bidding. It was going to be all right.

"It will take Millard a bit to get out of bed," the judge explained. "If you two want to freshen up before the ceremony, the guest bath is down the hall on your right. However, you're going to have to excuse me for a bit. I'm going to be needing some coffee."

Having put the wheels in motion, he left Casey and Ryder alone in the Harris parlor with Sudie's crocheted doilies and silk flower bouquets.

Casey put a hand to her hair, feeling the disarray. She started to the bathroom for a quick wash then remembered Ryder. Was it safe to leave him alone, or would he bolt at the first chance he got? She glanced back at him, and to her dismay realized he was watching her. It was almost as if he'd read her mind.

"Go on," he said. "I'll be here when you get back."

There was something compelling about this man, something she couldn't quite name. There was a strength within him that a couple of days' worth of whiskers and a faded T-shirt and jeans could not hide. Right now his eyes seemed blue, although at first they'd seemed gray. Their color was as changeable as the weather. She hoped his disposition did not seesaw as well and knew she was staring, but she couldn't help it. Although she was afraid of what he might tell her, there was something she needed to know.

"Why did you agree to go along with this madness?"

His expression hardened. "Don't dig too deep, Casey. You might find worms in the dirt you're taking out of the hole."

Startled, she pivoted and headed for the bathroom, telling herself it was exhaustion that was making her shake, and not the implied warning in his words.

"...pronounce you man and wife. What God has joined together, let no man put asunder."

Judge Harris's clock began to chime.

Once. Twice. Three times it sounded.

Casey exhaled slowly.

Four times. Five times. Six times the gong echoed within the silence of the room.

She went limp, and were it not for the firm grip Ryder had on her arm, she wouldn't have been able to stand. But she'd done it. It was over! The Ruban empire was safe, but dear God, could she say the same about herself?

"Congratulations. You may kiss your bride," Harmon added, although he doubted, considering the reasons for the ceremony, there was much to celebrate.

Both Ryder and Casey stared, first at Judge Harris who'd just granted permission for something neither had been prepared to act upon, then at each other as they contemplated the deed.

To Casey's dismay, her vision blurred.

Ryder had intended on holding his ground until he saw her tears. It was her weakness, rather than the bulldog determination with which she'd gotten them this far, that made him do what he did next. He'd entered into this farce without giving a thought for consequences, much the same way he used to go through life. But that was before he'd killed his father and lost his nerve to fly.

Intending only to assure her, he cupped her cheek with the palm of one hand, gentling her much in the same way his brother, Royal, tended the horses on his ranch, giving them time to adjust to his presence.

"Easy, now," he said softly, and when he felt her pulse beginning to slow, he lowered his head.

Casey saw him coming. Her lips parted. Whether it was to voice an objection or to ease his way, Ryder didn't know and didn't care. His focus was on her mouth and the woman who now bore his name.

Casey's breath caught at the back of her throat and this time, had Ryder not been holding her up, her legs would have given way. Whatever her intent had been, it stopped along with her heart when Ryder Justice kissed his wife.

It should have been awkward—their first joining—but it wasn't. The ease with which they touched, then the gentleness with which the kiss deepened felt right, even familiar. At the point of embracing, the judge's voice broke their connection.

"Well, now," he said, and made no attempt to hide a yawn. "I suppose you two are as hitched as a couple can be."

When Ryder moved away, Casey felt a sudden sense of loss, and then reality intruded and she felt nothing but dismay. She had no intentions of pursuing the intimate part of a marriage and the sooner Ryder Justice realized that, the better off they would be. She stepped back, then turned away, unwilling to let him see how deeply she'd been affected by what he'd done.

"It served its purpose," she said shortly, and started looking for her purse. "What do I owe you?"

While she was fumbling for cash, Ryder was dealing with uneasiness of his own. The kiss was supposed to have been nothing but a formality. He hadn't expected to feel anything because it had been months since he'd allowed himself the luxury. But something had happened to him between the time her breath had brushed his cheek and their point of contact. Left with nothing but a lingering dissatisfaction he couldn't identify, he, too, turned away. It was almost as if he'd left something undone. He hadn't been prepared for what the kiss had evoked—what it felt like to hold someone close, the pleasure that comes from lying in a willing woman's arms.

He inhaled slowly and considered the woman who was now his wife, if in name only. He had agreed to marry her and no matter what, he was a man of his word. But he didn't want to like her. There was already a time limit on their relationship. God forbid his feelings should ever go deeper.

Casey said something that made the judge laugh and Ryder turned to see what was funny. Instead of an answer, he found himself watching as Casey peeled five twenty-dollar bills from a wad of cash in her handbag and handed them to the judge. He frowned, then looked away, uncomfortable with the fact that a woman was paying his way for anything, and more than a little bit anxious as to how he was supposed to fit into her life. He had already suspected she came from money. Her car and her clothes had given her away, and the money she stuffed back in her purse only confirmed his suspicions.

For the first time since he'd run away, he thought about what he'd left behind, yet not once did he consider confessing his true background and identity to Casey.

She thought she'd married a bum, a no-account drifter without a penny to his name. His eyes narrowed as he stared out into the burgeoning dawn. Part of it was true. He didn't have two quarters with him that he could rub together. At this point, the fact that he owned four airplanes and a helicopter, and that his charter service had been in the black for nearly eleven years didn't matter. Nor did the fact that the deed to nearly fourteen hundred acres of prime real estate on the outskirts of San Antonio was in his name.

Sick at heart from an accident he couldn't forget, he'd walked away from it all. Things of monetary value had become unimportant to Ryder. If he could have, he would have given up everything just to have his father back alive and well.

But there would be no trading with God...or the devil. Micah Justice was dead and buried, and no matter how far Ryder went, he couldn't outrun his guilt.

Someone cleared their throat. He looked up. It would seem that Sudie was patiently waiting to lock them out. Casey held the front door ajar. Her posture and the tone of her voice gave away her impatience.

"Are you ready to go?" she asked.

Something inside him snapped. The quiet in which he'd encompassed himself over the past few months suddenly seemed too confining. Sarcasm colored his answer.

"I don't know, Mrs. Justice, are you?"

Her bossy, managerial attitude disappeared like air out of a punctured balloon. He had the satisfaction of seeing her pale as he walked past her and out the door.

The air was muggy, a promise of another long, hot July day. Sweat was already rolling down the middle of Casey's back and there was a snag in her stockings. Since yesterday when she'd made her exit from Lash's office, her hairdo had been windblown and finger-combed a dozen times. The last time she remembered putting on makeup was right before she'd gotten out of the car to go into the office for the reading of the will. She felt like hell and figured she looked a shade or two worse. She was exhausted and couldn't wait to get home and into a bed.

But thirty minutes outside of Ruban Crossing, Casey's plans were about to change. The flashing red-and-blue lights of a Mississippi highway patrol were an unwelcome addition to the events of the day. She had expected complications, but not quite so soon, or from the state police. She looked at Ryder, then began pulling over to the side of the road.

"I wasn't speeding," she said.

Ryder glanced over his shoulder, then started unbuckling his seat belt. The highway patrolman was already out of his vehicle with his gun drawn, and although the air conditioner was on and Casey's car windows were up, they could hear him shouting for them to get out of the car.

"I don't think that's the problem."

"What do you mean?" Casey asked, and turned. There was a gun pointed straight at her head.

"Get out of the car!" the patrolman shouted again. "Do it! Do it now!"

Stunned by the order, Casey began fumbling with her seat belt, but couldn't seem to find the catch. The harder she tried, the worse her fingers shook, and the longer she delayed, the louder and more insistent the officer became.

"Let me," Ryder said, and to her relief, the latch gave way, freeing her from the straps.

She opened the door. "Look, Officer, I don't know what…"

"Get out and put your hands on the hood of the car! You!" he shouted, pointing the gun at Ryder. "On the passenger side! Come around the front of the car with your hands in the air!"

Ryder didn't argue. He'd learned years ago never to argue with an armed man, especially one wearing a badge.

By now, Casey was out of the car and furious. "What's the meaning of this?"

Handcuffs snapped. First one on her right wrist, then the remaining cuff on her other.

"Sit down," the officer ordered, pushing Casey none too gently to a seat beside the rear wheel of her car before proceeding to cuff Ryder in the same smooth manner. He hauled Ryder off to the back seat of his patrol car and shut him inside while Casey watched in disbelief.

"This better be good," Casey said, as the officer returned and helped her to her feet.

"You're driving a stolen car and the woman who owns it has been reported missing."

Casey couldn't believe what she was hearing. "*I* am not missing, and *this* is my car."

The officer took a long, slow look at the disheveled woman in black and didn't bother to hide a smirk.

"That car belongs to Casey Ruban. Her family reported her missing when she didn't come home last night."

"I repeat, this is my car, and I didn't go home because I was out getting myself married," she said.

"Excuse me?" the officer asked.

She closed her eyes, counted to ten, then glared at the patrolman, derisively enunciating each syllable.

"Married. Capital *m*—little *a*—double *r—i—e—d*...Maaried. Last night...no, actually it was early this morning that we got married. You might say I've been on my honeymoon and you..." she frowned against the glare of early morning sun, peering at the name tag on the front of his uniform "...Officer Howard, have just stuffed my groom in the back of your patrol car. I want him out, and I want the handcuffs taken off both of us now, or I swear to God I will have your badge and all that goes with it."

Her adamancy startled the cop, and for the first time since he'd pulled them over, he began to consider the possibility of having been wrong in his first assumption. But he'd been so focused on being the one to get a lead on the missing heir that he hadn't followed protocol by asking for their identification first.

"I'll need to see some identification," he said.

"It's in my purse in the front seat, along with a copy of my marriage license. Want to see that, too?"

He unlocked her cuffs and opened the door. "No funny business," he said shortly, as Casey leaned inside.

She handed him the marriage license, her driver's license, as well as the title to her car. "There's nothing funny about any of this, and when I get home, I'm going to have someone's hide for this."

The officer looked long and hard at the picture on the driver's license and then at Casey. There was little resemblance between the cool, composed woman in the picture and the fiery-eyed hellion standing before him.

Casey could see he still wasn't buying her explanation, but she wasn't about to explain the mess she was in, thanks to her grandfather's will. She opted for something he would probably believe.

"Oh, for God's sake," Casey snapped. "I've been on my honeymoon, okay? You try a wedding night in the back seat of a car and see how good you look!"

The patrolman flushed with embarrassment as he began to realize the seriousness of his situation. Unless he made peace with this woman now, he could be in big trouble. The Ruban name carried a lot of clout.

"Sorry, Miss Ruban...I mean uh..."

"Justice," Casey said. "The name is Justice." She pointed toward the cruiser. "About my husband..."

Moments later, Ryder found himself standing by the side of the road, watching as an officer of the law did everything but crawl as an excuse for his overzealous behavior.

"Thank you for being so understanding," the officer said, as Casey brushed at the dirt on the back of her dress.

"We'll call it even if you just don't notify my family," she said. "I want to surprise them on my own."

"Yes, ma'am. I'll just call this in to headquarters so you won't be stopped again."

"Fine," she said, and didn't bother to watch as he drove away. When she glanced up at Ryder, he was grinning.

"What's so funny?" she asked.

"You're hell on wheels, aren't you, wife?"

"Don't call me that," she said, and slammed herself bodily into the seat behind the wheel.

Ryder was still grinning when he took the seat beside her. "Want me to drive?" he asked. "After all, I'm going to be your chauffeur."

Her bottom lip slid slightly forward as she started the car, leaving the side of the road in a flurry of flying dust and gravel.

"I guess not," Ryder drawled, and then settled back into the passenger seat. The longer he was around this woman, the more he liked her. She reminded him a little bit of his brother, Roman, who chose to believe that laws and rules were made by men with too much time on their hands.

There was a pasty white sheen on Lash Marlow's face as he hung up the phone. He glanced at the clock over the mantel and swiped a shaky hand through his hair. It was almost noon. Time was running out.

His thoughts were jumbled as he considered the possibilities of where Casey might be. Damn Delaney for insisting on that forty-eight hour time frame. He'd told him from the start it wasn't a good idea, but Delaney had insisted, claiming he knew his granddaughter better than anyone. He'd sworn she would never adhere to the terms of the will unless pushed.

Lash felt sick. It seemed obvious that he and Delaney Ruban had pushed too much.

"Any news?" Eudora asked, and not for the first time wished she'd sat beside her youngest granddaughter during the reading of the will. She was still convinced she might have been able to soften the blow Casey had received. If she had, maybe they wouldn't have spent a sleepless night expecting the worst.

Lash shook his head and reached for another antacid. Instead, his fingers closed around the rabbit's foot in his pocket, and he rubbed it lightly, making a bet with himself that everything would be all right.

Taking comfort from his superstitious gesture, he decided to forego the antacid. It probably wouldn't help anyway. He was long past worry and far past panic. From the way his gut was burning, he was either starting a new ulcer or about to have a heart attack. He'd expected Casey to be difficult, but he hadn't expected this. If she didn't show up soon, it would be too late.

Miles lounged near the window overlooking the tennis courts, contemplating the party he would throw when he got his hands on the money. He was sick and tired of pretending to be worried about Casey. As far as he was concerned, she could stay gone. For the past six years, even if she was his sister, she'd been nothing but a judgmental little bitch, always harping at him and Erica to get jobs of their own.

Eudora paced back and forth, fanning herself with a dampened handkerchief. "I just can't bear this suspense. Oh dear. Oh dear."

Miles rolled his eyes. "Oh, let it rest, Grandmother. She'll come home when it suits her."

Eudora frowned as she fanned, although the small square of fabric did little to stir the air. "I'm just sick about this. What if something awful has happened?" When no one echoed her concern, she sank into a nearby chair, dabbing at her eyes. "Poor, dear Casey."

"Poor, dear Casey, my ass," Erica muttered, and sloshed a liberal helping of Jack Daniel's into her iced tea and sat down near her twin. Ice clinked against crystal as she swirled the liquid before lifting the glass to her mouth.

Lash glanced at his watch and dug his own handkerchief from his pocket, mopping at a fine line of perspiration that kept breaking out across his brow. Time was running out. If she didn't show soon, his worst fears would be realized. Miles and Erica would be in control of the Ruban fortune and Lash's dreams to resurrect the Marlow estate to its former glory would be dashed. At this moment he didn't know whom he hated worse—Delaney for causing the fuss, or Miles for the possum-eating grin he'd been wearing all day.

Never one to let a good silence extend itself, Eudora tucked her handkerchief into her cleavage and rang a small bell near her chair.

Moments later a tall, dark-skinned man dressed in virgin whites entered the room. Still straight and handsome at sixty, the only evidence of Joshua Bass's age was the liberal dusting of gray in his hair.

"Yes, ma'am?"

Eudora pointed toward a nearby table. "Joshua, we're all out of tea."

"Yes, ma'am."

He picked up the tray and started out of the room when Eudora remembered.

"Oh, Joshua!"

He paused. "Yes, ma'am?"

"Have Tilly put some lemon in the tea this time. I do believe lemon helps cut the miasma of July."

Casey entered on the tail of Eudora's order, countermanding it with one of her own. She took the tray out of Joshua's hands and set it down, then to the continuing dismay of her family, gave him a huge, breathless hug, which he gladly returned.

Casey smiled up at Joshua, taking comfort in the love she saw there in his eyes. "Forget the tea, Joshie. Bring a bottle of Delaney's best champagne instead. We're going to toast my marriage."

Joshua looked startled, and his first thought was what his Tilly was going to say. Casey was as close to their hearts as if she'd been born of their blood and here she was about to drink to a marriage they knew she didn't want.

Miles's face turned an angry red. Erica choked on a piece of ice, and Eudora clasped her hands to her throat and started to cry.

As for Lash, he went weak with relief. Not only was Casey back, but she seemed willing to celebrate their upcoming union with no remorse. He went toward her with outstretched hands.

"Casey, darling, I'm so glad you..."

And that was the moment they realized Casey had not come alone. The unexpected face of a stranger at Casey's back, never mind his trail-weary appearance, startled them all into sudden silence.

"Everyone...this is Ryder Justice." She glanced at Ryder. To her surprise, he seemed calm, almost disinterested. "Ryder—my family." She pointed them out, one by one, starting with Eudora. "This is my Gran." She glanced at Miles and Erica and the expressions on their faces said it all. She sighed. Some things never change. "The two beautiful blondes with the fabulous scowls are my brother and sister, Miles and Erica."

As she smiled at Joshua, her voice softened. "And this is Joshua Bass. He and his wife, Tilly, helped raise me."

Ryder nodded. "It's a pleasure, sir," he said quietly. "And, I'd say you and your wife have done a fine job. Casey is quite a woman."

She gave Ryder a quick look of surprise. The praise was unexpected.

Joshua grinned, pleased to have been recognized as part of the family.

"Casey, really! He's one of the help," Eudora said, and then flushed, embarrassed that she'd been put in the position of having to remark upon the differences in their stations in life.

Casey's chin jutted. "Unlike the majority of this family, Joshua has a job. I have a job as well. I fail to see the difference." Then she softened her rebuke by winking at Joshua. "Joshie, hurry and bring that champagne. We have some celebrating to do."

Lash had more on his mind than sipping champagne and social niceties. He glanced at his watch. There were a million things to do and so little time.

"Casey, dearest, we've been so worried. When you didn't come home last night I even called the state police. We all realize the will came as a terrible shock to you, but if you'd just waited a bit, I could have saved you from all this turmoil. You know how I feel about you. It was only a matter of time before you came to your senses and did what was best for everyone."

When he reached for her hand, Casey took an instinctive step back, right into Ryder's arms.

"Easy," Ryder said softly, and Casey shivered. That was what he'd said earlier, right before he'd kissed her.

"I don't need saving," she told Lash. "And I've already come to my senses. I saved myself."

A nerve jerked at the side of Lash's eye, causing it to twitch. "What do you mean?"

Although Ryder was no longer touching Casey, she knew he was still behind her, and, oddly enough, it was his solid presence that gave her the courage to say what had to be said. She pulled the copy of their marriage license from her purse and handed it to Lash without batting an eye.

"Ryder and I were married this morning. I suppose you'll need this to confirm the legalities and finalize the edicts of the will."

"Married?"

The shriek came from across the room. Casey wasn't sure whether it was Miles or Erica who'd come undone, and she didn't much care.

The paper fell from Lash's fingers and onto the floor as shock spread across his face. Speech was impossible. All he could do was stare at the woman who'd dashed his last hopes. She seemed calm, even smug about what she'd done, and as he looked, he began to hate.

At this point, Joshua came back into the room with an uncorked bottle of champagne and a tray full of glasses. Casey took it from his hands.

"I'll pour while you go get Tilly. This won't be official until you two are in on my news. Also, will you please tell Bea to get the apartment over the garage ready. When it's cleaned, have someone move my things out there, okay?"

Joshua left with an anxious glance.

"Why on earth would you be doing such a thing?" Eudora asked.

Before Casey could respond, Ryder stepped to her side. For a moment, Casey had the sensation of what it would be like to never stand alone against this family again.

His voice was cool, his manner calm and assured. "Because a wife lives with her husband, and as of yesterday, I'm your new chauffeur, that's why."

Miles's snort of disbelief was echoed by his sister. "My God, Casey, marrying some ne'er-do-well is bad enough, but a chauffeur? Have you no shame?"

Ryder's expression underwent a remarkable change, from calm to quiet fury. He never took his eyes from Miles. "I don't care if he is your brother—do not expect me to like that little pig."

Casey almost laughed. The look of shock on her brother's face was priceless.

"You don't have to," she said, and then felt obligated to add, "but you can't hurt him."

Ryder gave Miles another cool stare, then took the champagne Casey handed him. "There's more than one way to skin a cat," he drawled, and gave Miles a cool, studied look. Then he lifted the glass toward her in a silent toast, pinning Casey with a stormy gaze that left her stunned.

"To justice," he said, letting them decide for themselves what he'd meant.

Chapter 3

After the family accepted the shock of Casey's news, there was one more person Casey needed to see. While Ryder was prowling through the garage and the cars that were to be under his control, she slipped into the kitchen in search of Matilda Bass. The need to lay her head on Tilly's shoulder was overwhelming. She hoped when she did, that she would manage not to cry.

And Tilly wasn't all that hard to find.

"Come here to me, girl," Tilly said, and opened her arms.

Casey walked into them without hesitation. "You didn't come drink champagne with me."

Tilly ignored the rebuke. She had her own idea of her place in this world and in spite of the money the Rubans had, she wouldn't have traded places with them for any of it. She had more self-esteem than to socialize with people who chose to look down on her because she cooked the food that they ate.

"Well now, what have you gone and done?" Tilly asked.

Her sympathy was almost Casey's undoing. "Saved us all, I hope," Casey replied.

Tilly frowned. She'd already heard through the family

grapevine what a burden the old man Ruban had heaped on her baby's head.

"If you ask me, that old man needed his head examined," Tilly mumbled, stroking her hand gently up and down the middle of Casey's back.

Casey sighed. "Well, it's over and done with," she said.

Tilly stepped back, her dark eyes boring into Casey's gaze. "Nothing is ever over and done with, girl. Not while people draw breath. You be careful. I don't know why, but I don't like the feel of all this."

Casey managed a laugh. "Don't go all witchy on me, now. You know what Joshie says about you messin' with that kind of stuff."

Tilly sniffed. The reference to her mother's and grandmother's predilection for voodoo did not apply to her. "I do not indulge myself in the black arts and you know it," Tilly huffed.

Casey grinned and then gave Tilly a last, quick hug. "I know. I was only teasing." Then her laughter faded. "Say a prayer for me, Mammo."

Casey hadn't used that childhood name in years. It brought quick tears to Tilly's eyes, and because it was an emotion in which she rarely indulged, she was all the more brusque with her answer. "Knowing you, I'd better say two," she said, and gave Casey a swift swat on the rear. "Now you run on along. I've got dinner to fix before Joshua and I go on home."

Casey paused on her way out the door. "Tilly?"

"What, baby girl?"

"Have you ever regretted staying on here as cook? You and Joshua are so smart, you could have done a lot of other things besides wait on a small, selfish family."

Tilly turned, and the serious tone of her voice was proof of her sincerity. "Maybe I could have, but not my Josh. You've got to remember, he only hears good in one ear. That handicap lost him a whole lot of jobs early on in our marriage. By the time we landed here with your grandfather, he was glad to have the work. And Mr. Ruban was more than fair. Our pay is good. We have health insurance, something a lot of our friends do not. And, because your grandfather did not like change in his household, the incentive he gave us to stay on was to set up trusts for our retirement. Actually, we're better off than some other members of our family who have college degrees.'' And then she smiled. ''Besides, I like to cook, and who else would have raised my baby if Josh and I hadn't been here?''

This time, Casey didn't bother to hide her tears. She wrapped her arms around Tilly's neck. ''I love you, Mammo.''

''I love you, too, girl. Now run on home. You've got yourself a man to tend.''

Startled, Casey did as she was told, and after that, the day went surprisingly well.

Although Miles and Erica no longer had any hopes of attaining control of the Ruban fortune, their circumstances were still the same. Before, they had come and gone as they pleased, spent and slept at Delaney Ruban's expense. For them, nothing had changed.

As for Eudora, she'd sacrificed much for her dead daughter's children. Years ago she'd given up a suitor who could have made her golden years something to remember. She'd left her home on Long Island and came to Mississippi with the best of intentions. She refused to consider that she'd contributed to the ruination of her eldest grandchildren by coercing Delaney to leave their upbringing in her care when he'd begun to focus his attention on Casey.

She hadn't meant to make them so dependent on others, but it had happened anyway. And now that their life-styles were pretty much set in stone, she felt it her moral obligation to see that their comfort level stayed the same.

Yet when it came to sacrifices, it was Casey who'd sacrificed the most. Whatever dreams she might have harbored with regard to her personal life were gone. She was married to a stranger, and for the next twelve months, had resigned herself to the fact.

At her demand, Ryder had been sent into Ruban Crossing with a handful of money and orders as to what to buy, while she went in to the office. There was a merger pending and an entire factory of workers in Jackson, Mississippi who were waiting to learn if they still had their jobs. She didn't want another day to pass without assuring them. In fact, everything was running so smoothly it should have been the warning Casey needed, because when the sun went down, tempers began to rise.

Casey climbed the stairs leading to the garage apartment and tried not to think of her spacious bedroom across the courtyard; of her sunken bathtub and the cool, marble floor, or of her queen-size bed and the down-filled pillows of which she was so fond. Her stomach growled and she wondered what feast Tilly was concocting across the way for the evening meal. At this point, she began to consider the benefits she was losing by having to live under Ryder Justice's roof. Who would cook? Where did she put her dirty clothes?

Caution forbade her to use any of the services available across the way. From the expression on Lash Marlow's face when he'd left the house this morning, she knew his anger would not easily disappear. It would be just like him to try and catch her cheating on the terms of the will.

Oh, well, she thought. I can always order takeout and take my clothes to the cleaners.

She took out her key to open the door then found it already unlocked. Her pulse skipped a beat. That meant *he* was home. Quietly, so as not to alert the "tiger" who lurked within, she shut the door behind her and then stood, absorbing the sight of what was to be her home for the next twelve months.

The entire apartment consisted of three small rooms, the accumulation of which were still not the size of her bedroom inside the mansion. But it was clean, and blessedly quiet. For today, it was enough.

Just when she was beginning to relax, she noticed a man's shirt draped over an easy chair and a pair of dusty, black boots on the floor nearby. Reality set in.

Never one to put off what had to be done, she reminded herself that the sooner the confrontation began, the sooner it would be over. She sat her briefcase by the door and looked toward the bedroom. Since he wasn't in here, he had to be in there.

She walked inside. Several pairs of blue jeans lay on the bed, along with a half dozen white long-sleeved shirts, a new sport coat and a broad-brimmed black Stetson. A pile of her best lingerie was on the floor next to the dresser. She frowned, wondering why her things were on the floor.

She stared at the clothes. Where were the uniforms she'd told him to get? She'd given him the address of the place where they'd rented them before. Ruban Crossing was a fair-size city, but he'd had all afternoon to find one simple address.

She opened the closet. It was full of her clothing and nothing else. She looked back at the bed. That explained why he hadn't hung his up. Obviously, there was no place left for them to hang.

She turned around, eyeing the small room with distaste, then shrugged. Tomorrow, she'd go through her things and have Bea take part of them back to the main house. It was the least she could do.

A door creaked behind her. She spun and then froze. Ryder had obviously just had a bath. Steam enveloped him as he stepped out of the doorway and into the room with her, giving him the appearance of emerging from a cloud. His hair was spiky and still dripping water as he began to towel it dry.

Her thoughts tangled. Most men would appear smaller without benefit of clothing. But not him. He enveloped the space in which he moved, almost as if he took it with him as he went.

Casey frowned again, biting at the inside of her lip and wondering why she hadn't had the foresight to wait outside. How would she ever get past the memory of this much man covered with such a small, insignificant towel?

"Sorry," Ryder said, and gave his hair a last, halfhearted rub before tossing the wet towel back into the bathroom floor. "Didn't know you were here."

Casey tilted her chin, determined he not know how shaken she was.

"Obviously," she said shortly, and then pointed toward the clothes on the bed. "I gave you money to get uniforms, not all this."

Ryder's eyes narrowed, and Casey knew the moment the words were out of her mouth that she'd ticked him off. He walked to a bedside table and withdrew a handful of money, then stuffed it in her hand.

"What's this?" Casey asked.

"Your money."

"But how did you pay for all this?"

He didn't answer, and she glared. But when he spun and started toward her, she took an instinctive step backward. When he bypassed her for the dresser beyond, she caught herself breathing a small sigh of relief. Determined to get to the bottom of his behavior, she struck again, only this time with more venom.

"I asked you a question," she snapped.

Her relief was short-lived. When he turned, the anger on his face almost stopped her heart.

"Don't go there," he said quietly.

"Go where? I don't know what you mean."

"There's one thing we'd better get straight right now. I don't take orders from you, and I don't take your money. I pay my own way."

She couldn't imagine how he'd obtained the clothes. For all she knew he might have stolen the stuff. She would have been shocked to know he had a gold credit card with an unlimited line. And, if she'd known, would have been even more surprised to learn he hadn't used it in months.

"But the uniforms...why didn't you do as you were told?"

As far as Ryder was concerned, what was in his past was none of her business. Suddenly he was right in front of her. His breath was hot, his words angry.

"Because you're not my boss, you're my wife. I gave you my name, and I'll drive you and yours anywhere they please for the next twelve months, but I'm not wearing a damned monkey suit to do it."

Casey's mouth dropped. Never in her entire life had anyone had the gall to defy her in such a manner. Before she could think of a comeback, he turned away, opened the top drawer of the dresser, withdrew a brand-new pair of white cotton briefs and dropped his towel.

She bolted, taking with her the image of a long-limbed body that was hard and fit and brown all over.

A few minutes later he emerged from the bedroom in his bare feet, wearing an old and faded pair of jeans and no shirt.

The casual are-you-still-here glance he gave her made her furious.

Disgusted with herself for not standing her ground, she watched from across the room as he sauntered into the kitchen and opened the refrigerator. When he bent down to look inside, the urge to hit him was so strong it startled her. She was not the type of woman to resort to violence. Then she rescinded her own opinion of herself. At least she *hadn't* been. But that was before she'd driven into the flatlands and brought out a husband.

He set a package of raw hamburger meat on the counter then went back to the refrigerator. She didn't know what angered her most, the fact that he was being deliberately mutinous, or that she was being ignored.

Smoothing her hands down the front of her blue summer suit, she tossed back her hair and slipped into the sarcastic mode she used to keep Miles and Erica at bay.

"Are you finished?" she drawled, wanting the bathroom all to herself.

Ryder straightened, looking at her from across the open refrigerator door. He stared at her, from the top of her hair to the open toes of her sling-back pumps. A slight grin tilted the corner of his mouth as he stepped back and closed the door.

His thoughts went to the year stretching out before them, considering which one of them would be the first to break. "Finished?" he muttered. "We haven't even started."

With that, he moved toward her.

Panic came swiftly and Casey wondered if the family would be able to hear her scream from here. She held up her hand in a warning gesture.

"Don't you dare!" she said, and winced at the squeak in her voice.

She was scared! The fact surprised him. She'd walked into a bar with a roomful of strange men and offered herself up as a golden goat without batting an eye. She'd roused a doctor, a county clerk and a judge out of bed to do her bidding. She'd stared down a roomful of antagonistic relatives and kept a lawyer out of her pants who seemed to have had his own hidden agenda, and she was suddenly scared? And of him? It didn't make sense. He hadn't done anything to warrant this.

Yet when he might have eased her fears, he found himself letting them grow.

When he got within inches of her stark, white face, he realized why. This woman, who was his wife, was damned pretty. In fact, if a man didn't get picky about that little bitty mole at the left corner of her lips, she was beautiful.

Sexually, he was a starving man and this woman was legally his wife. Although he'd cut himself off from everyone he cared for, he'd been unable to cut off the emotions of a normal, red-blooded man. Keeping her slightly afraid was a safe way of keeping her at arms' length. Yet when her eyes widened fearfully and her color rose, he relented.

"Easy," he said. "All I need to know is how you like it and do you want more than one?"

She would have sworn that her heart shot straight up her throat and she had to swallow several times to work up enough spit to be able to speak. *More than one? Oh my God!* "I don't think you understand the situation here," she stuttered.

"What? Don't tell me you don't eat meat."

Her face flushed as she thought of his lean, bare body. "Eat? Meat?"

"Do you like it hot and red, slightly pink, or hard as a rock?"

Her eyes widened even more and her voice began to quiver. "I don't do things like that," she whispered, and put her hand to her throat, unconsciously stifling that scream she'd been considering.

He frowned. Things like what? All he needed to know was if she wanted... And then it dawned on him what interpretation she'd put on their conversation. He stifled a grin and pointed back to the counter.

"Are you telling me you don't do hamburgers?"

"Hamburgers?"

He went straight past her and out a small side door onto the attached deck above the driveway, opened the lid to a smoking barbecue grill, checked the coals, then let the lid drop back down with a clank.

"The charcoal is ready." He headed back toward the kitchen, pausing at the package of hamburger. "One last chance. Do you want one hamburger or two, and how do you want it cooked?''

There was a silly grin on her face as she slumped to the floor in a dead faint.

Ryder sat in the room's only chair, watching as Casey began to regain consciousness. The sofa he'd laid her on was a small, two-cushion affair, and he'd been forced to make the decision as to whether her head would be down and her feet up, or vice versa.

He'd opted to lay her head on the cushions and let her legs dangle. No sooner had he done so than one of her legs slipped from the arm of the sofa and onto the floor, leaving her in an indelicate, spread-eagled faint.

Ryder stifled a grin. Waking in such a compromising position would embarrass anyone. For Casey, a woman obviously used to nothing but the best, it would be the height of humiliation. In a considerate move, he removed her shoes, then lifted her leg back in alignment with the other. But when it slipped off again, he decided to leave it, and her, alone.

As he watched, he couldn't help but stare at the woman who was now his wife. He was still a little shocked at himself for going along with such a hare-brained scheme. The Justice men were not impulsive. They had always considered the consequences and then lived with their decisions without regrets. Until now. While it was too late to consider anything, it remained to be seen if there would be regrets.

He kept looking at her, separating her features in his mind. It wasn't just that she was pretty, though he couldn't keep his eyes off her thick black hair and those big green eyes. And her skin—it looked like silk, ivory silk.

And Ryder remembered that when she smiled, her mouth had a tendency to curl at one corner first before the other decided to follow. It gave her an impish expression, which he knew was deceiving. If this woman had an ounce of playfulness in her, he hadn't seen it. The devil maybe, but nothing so frivolous as an imp.

While he was watching, she blinked. And when she groaned and reached for the back of her head, he grimaced. It had been thumped pretty good when she'd fainted. He felt bad about that. She might be touchy as hell, and they might not agree on anything, but he didn't want her hurt.

Casey opened her eyes. The ceiling didn't look familiar, and for a moment, she wondered where she was. A whiff of charcoal smoke drifted past her nose and, all too swiftly, her memory returned.

Seconds later, she became aware of the implications of her less than ladylike sprawl. What had that man done to her while she'd been unconscious? Better yet, where was he?

She turned her head and caught him staring at her from a chair on the other side of the coffee table. When he grinned and winked, she swiveled to an upright position, grabbing at her skirt and smoothing at her hair. When she could think without the room spinning beneath her, she glared at him.

"What did you do to me?"

He arched an eyebrow. "Not nearly as much as I wanted," he replied, and knew he'd scored a hit when she doubled up her fists. He stifled a laugh. "Easy, now. I was just kidding. I've been the picture of decorum. I picked you up from the floor, laid you on the sofa, and have been waiting for you to come to."

Her southern manners forced her to thank him. "I appreciate your consideration."

His grin widened. "Honesty won't permit me to accept your compliment. I have to admit it was hunger that kept me waiting for you. I was taught that it's bad manners to eat in front of people without offering them some, too. And, you never did answer my question. How do you want your hamburger?"

If she'd had a shoe, she would have thrown it. As it was, she had to satisfy herself with a regal, albeit shaky, exit from the room, slamming the door shut between them with a solid thud.

"Does that mean you don't want one?" Ryder yelled.

She yanked the door open long enough to give him what was left of her mind.

"You're a swine. A gentleman would have covered my legs and bathed my head with a cold compress."

"If you wanted a gentleman, you shouldn't have gone shopping for a husband down in the Delta."

She glared and slammed the door again, this time louder and firmer.

"I suppose this means no to the hamburgers?"

The door opened again, but the only thing to come out was the sound of Casey's voice at its most dignified. The shriek in her tone was gone and she was enunciating each word, as if speaking to someone lacking in mental capacity.

"No, it does not. I will have a hamburger, well-done, light on the salt, heavy on the pepper."

This time when she closed the door, it was with a ladylike click. The glitter in Ryder's eyes was sharp, the grin on his face sardonic.

"So you like it hot, do you, wife? That's interesting. Very interesting indeed."

He reentered the tiny kitchen and began making patties from the hamburger meat before carrying them out to the grill. As he slapped them on the grate, smoke began to rise and the fire began to pop and sizzle as fat dripped onto the burning charcoal.

Oddly, it reminded him of Casey in the midst of her family, putting up a smoke screen to keep them from knowing how scared she was, and popping wisecracks and issuing orders before anyone could tell her what to do.

He closed the lid and sighed. He had married a total stranger for the hell of it, but he hadn't counted on the family that came with her. In fact, they reminded him of snakes, writhing and coiling and biting out at each other in some crazy sort of frenzy.

He thought of his own family, of how loud and rambunctious—of how close and loving they'd been—of how empty and scattered they now were. And how the world as he'd known it had ended because of something he'd done.

He went back inside, leaving the hamburgers and his memories behind.

"Want another one?" Ryder asked, indicating the two remaining well-done patties congealing in their own grease on a pea green plate.

Casey eyed the plate. Besides being an atrocious shade of

green, the plate was chipped. She'd never eaten from a chipped plate before. She suspected this night was the beginning of many firsts. Dabbing at the corner of her mouth with a paper towel, she shook her head.

"No, thank you, I'm quite full." Grudgingly she added, "It was very good."

Ryder nodded and continued to stare at a ketchup stain near his fork. What now? Conversation with this woman had been nearly impossible. Every time he opened his mouth to speak, she jumped. And she watched his every move with those big green eyes, as if she expected to be pounced upon at any moment. Hell, she was beginning to make him antsy, too.

He glanced at his watch. "It's almost nine."

She paled.

He sighed.

"Easy now, lady."

"Casey," she said. "My name is Casey."

His expression darkened. "Yes, and my name is Ryder. Unfortunately, that's all we know about each other." When she looked away, his frustration rose.

"Casey, look at me."

She did, but with trepidation.

"There's something I think needs to be said. This is going to be a long haul for both of us. I suppose we each had an agenda for even considering this situation, but it's done, and for your sake, it has to work, right?"

She thought of Miles and Erica, and then of Lash. "Yes."

"Okay, then there's something I think you should know about me."

Her head jerked up and she was suddenly staring at him in a still, waiting manner. Oh dear, what was he about to reveal?

Again, he sensed her fear. "Dammit, don't look at me like that. I am not a dangerous man. I do not taunt women. I do not hurt women. I do not force women to do anything they do not want, and that includes the issue of sex."

Startled by his bluntness, Casey blushed. "I've been meaning to talk to you about that," she said.

"I'm listening."

"There won't be any."

Her announcement came as no surprise, but Ryder was unprepared for the sense of disappointment he felt. He chalked it up to several months of denial and let it go at that.

He shrugged. "I will abide by whatever rules you feel comfortable in setting, but I have a couple of my own. I am not your servant. I don't take orders...but I will listen to suggestions."

He watched her swallow a couple of times, but she remained silent.

"Well, do you have any?"

Casey blinked. "Any what?"

"Suggestions."

"Uh...no, I don't suppose so."

"Okay, then that's settled. Why don't you start the dishes? I want to make sure the fire is out in the grill."

He got up before he had time to see her panic again.

"Ryder?"

He turned.

She waved helplessly over the table and the dirty dishes. "I've never done dishes before."

"You've never...!" Then he muttered beneath his breath. "Good grief."

"What's wrong?"

"You've never done dishes."

She hated him for that dumbfounded look he was wearing.

"That's what I said. I also don't do windows," she snapped.

"And I don't suppose you can cook, either."

She had the grace to flush. "No."

He groaned.

Casey was surprised at her feelings of inadequacy. She hired and fired with the best of them, bought and sold corporations without batting an eye. How dare he consider her lacking in capabilities?

"It's not my fault," she argued.

"Then whose is it?"

She had no answer.

"If you ask me, it's high time you learned. Soap is under the sink, the dishcloth is in it. You're a smart lady. Figure the rest out for yourself."

"Where are you going?" Casey asked, as he started out the door.

"To put out a fire then take a shower."

"But you already had a shower," she said, remembering the steam…and the towel…and the bare-naked body.

"Yeah, so maybe I have more than one fire that needs quenching, okay?"

It took exactly five seconds for the implication of what he'd suggested to sink in, and another few for her to be able to move. After that, she was glad to have something to do besides think about what he'd said…and why he'd said it.

The air was thick and muggy from the lingering heat of the day. It was that time of the evening just before dusk and right after the sun has passed beyond the horizon. A family of martens swooped grass-high in daring flight then soared heavenward, constantly feeding on the mosquitos in the air.

Graystone, the home that had been in the Marlow family since before the War of Northern Aggression, loomed large upon the landscape. It was a three-story monolith which had seen better days. Its regal structure and the land upon which it sat was sadly in need of repair, yet at a distance, the charm of the pillared edifice was still imposing.

Lash reclined in an old wicker chair on the veranda of his family home, nursing his third bourbon and water and surveying all that was his. This was his favorite time of the day. It wasn't because the workday was over and he was taking a well-earned rest. It was because Graystone looked better at half-light.

He tossed back the last of his drink, trying to pinpoint exactly where his plans for glory had gone wrong. The liquor burned and he silently cursed the fact that he could no longer afford the best. He was drinking cheap bourbon, living in the servant's wing while the rest of the mansion was closed off, and down to doing for himself. He didn't even have the funds to hire a housekeeper and made only enough at his law practice to keep the taxes paid on his home and himself afloat.

His belly growled. Without conscious thought, he pushed himself up from the chair and entered the house, taking care to lock the door behind him. Just for a moment, he stood in the great hall, staring up at the spiral staircase gracing the entryway, remembering another time when the house had been alive with laughter and people.

Something moved in the far corner of the hall. He winced as the sound of scurrying feet scratched on the marble flooring, then disappeared behind a breakfront. It wasn't the first rodent of that size he'd seen inside these walls, but tonight, it would be one too many.

He started to shake, first with rage, then from despair. It was over! There would be no more dreams of bringing Graystone back to her former beauty, or of returning dignity to the Marlow name. And it was all because of Casey.

A red haze blurred his vision. He drew back and threw his glass toward the place where he'd last seen the rat. It shattered against the wall, splintering into minute crystal shards. Only afterward did he remember that it had been part of a set, but regret swiftly faded. What did it matter? His only guests wore long tails and came on four feet...in the dark...in the middle of the night.

Startled by the sound of breaking glass, the rat that had taken refuge behind the breakfront made a run down the hallway for the deeper shadows beyond. As it did, something inside of Lash snapped. He grabbed at his grandfather's ivory-handled walking stick that had been standing in the hall tree for more than forty years, and ran, catching the rat just as it neared safety. He swung down with deadly force and the sound shattered the silence within the old walls as well as what was left of Lash's reason. Glass splintered on the wall behind him as he drew back the cane, but he didn't notice.

Even after the rat was dead, Lash continued to hail it with a barrage of blows until gore began to splatter on his shoes and the cuffs of his pants.

But in his mind, the rat had been dispatched from the first blow he'd struck. He was oblivious to the overkill, or that he might have lost more than his control. He kept venting his rage on a woman who'd dashed his dreams. And it wasn't the rodent who was coming apart on the cool marble floor. It was the beautiful and complacent surface of Casey Ruban's face.

When he finally stopped, his body was shaking from exertion and the muscles in his arm were burning from the energy he'd spent. He stared in disbelief at what he'd done, then tossed the cane down on the floor, disgusted by its condition.

Weary in both body and spirit, he turned and then stared at the wall in disbelief. The mirror! The glass in the ornate, gold-rimmed mirror that had hung in this hall for as long as he could remember, was shattered. His heart began to pound as he looked at the broken and refracted image of himself—a true reflection of his life.

He stepped back in horror and reached for the rabbit's foot in the pocket of his pants. All he could think as he backed away was, Seven long years of bad luck.

Chapter 4

Casey roused from a restless sleep. Disoriented by unfamiliar surroundings, it took a few moments for reality to return. Someone moaned. Her first thought was that Ryder could be sick. Quietly, she crawled out of bed and tiptoed to the door, aware that he'd made his bed in the middle of the living room floor. The moan came again, only this time, louder.

When she'd seen him last, he'd been unfolding a sleeping bag. But this was frightening. She didn't know what to make of it. What if he was hurt, or sick?

Just as she turned the doorknob, something crashed to the floor. An image of intruders made her hesitate, but only for a moment.

The door opened inward on well-oiled hinges. She peered into the living room, searching the shadows to make certain she and Ryder were still alone. The outer door was shut, as were the windows. As she listened, the hum of the central air-conditioning unit kicked on, changing the texture of the night. She took a step forward, then another, then another until she was behind the sofa and peering over it.

Ryder was stretched out in his sleeping bag there on the floor. Lying half in and half out of the faint glow from the security lights outside, he seemed more shadow than substance.

And while she was watching, he jerked and then moaned, throwing one arm over his eyes, as if warding off some unseen blow.

This explained the sounds that had wakened her. Ryder appeared to be dreaming. She moved closer, leaning over the sofa for a better view. And as she did, accidentally scooted it with the force of her body. The wooden legs screeched across the vinyl flooring like chalk on a blackboard. The sound was enough to wake the dead...and Ryder.

He came up and out of his sleeping bag and before Casey could react, he had grabbed her by the throat, and pinned her to the wall. His face and body were in darkness, but there was enough light for her to know to be afraid. The look in his eyes was grim, and the grip he had around her throat was all but deadly. She grabbed at his wrists before his grip tightened further.

"Ryder...Ryder, it's me."

"Oh, my God!" He jerked, moving his hand from her throat to the side of her face in a quick gesture of assurance. "Dammit, Casey, I'm sorry, but you startled me."

Casey closed her eyes as her legs went weak.

She rubbed at the tightness in her throat where his fingers had been. "It's okay. It was partly my fault for sneaking up on you like that."

Remorse shafted through him as he saw her fingering her throat. Dammit, he'd hurt her. He caught her hand, and then the moment they touched, wished that he'd kept his hands to himself. She was too close and too tempting.

Her focus suddenly shifted from her throat to him. They were face-to-face—body to body, and only inches from each other's lips.

Breath caught. Hearts stopped. First hers, then his.

She swallowed. "You were having a bad dream."

He inhaled slowly then spoke. "I'm sorry I frightened you."

Once again, she was struck by the size of him, of the breadth of his shoulders blocking out the light coming through the windows behind him.

"It's okay. It was partly my fault," she said.

She moved her hand and accidentally brushed the surface of his chest. His skin felt combustible. Muscles tensed beneath her fingertips and she jerked back her hand.

When he took a deep breath, she looked up. His eyes were glittering and there was a faint sheen of perspiration on his body. At that moment, she remembered what she was wearing, and realized what he was not.

He slept in the buff.

Her gown was short and sheer.

Seduction had been the last thing on her mind when she'd bought it, but from the way Ryder was staring at her now, it wasn't far from his. She could almost hear what he was thinking. He *was* her husband. This *was* their first night alone. But from her standpoint, what he was so obviously thinking could not—must not—happen.

Ryder was in shock. To wake up from the horror of reliving the crash that had killed his father to find a beautiful, half-dressed woman within reach made him want. He wanted to make love. He wanted to feel the softness of a woman's body—a woman's lips. To get lost in that certain rapture. To celebrate life because he couldn't forget death. That's what he wanted. But it wasn't going to happen, and because he knew it, his voice was harsh and angry.

"Go back to bed."

She tried to explain. "Look, I didn't mean to—"

He pinned her against the wall with a hand on either side of her head and leaned down, so close to her that his whisper was as loud as a shout.

"Either get the hell out of my sight or take off your clothes."

Casey bolted for the bedroom, slamming the door behind her and then leaning against it, as if the weight of her body might add strength to the flimsy barrier that stood between them.

For several interminable seconds she stood without moving, listening for the sound of footsteps. When all she heard were a few muffled curses and then the sound of a slamming door, she relaxed and then panicked. What if he was leaving for good?

She opened the door with a jerk, but when she realized all of his things were still inside, she shut it again. She crawled into bed and pulled up the covers, again, erecting another puny barrier between them.

In spite of the cool air circulating throughout the room, it seemed stifling. And while she waited anxiously for him to return, she considered their temporary bonds.

Ryder Justice had promised to love and honor her, to take care of her in sickness and in health. She didn't know about the loving, but some part of her trusted that he wouldn't lie. He'd said he would stay the year and she believed him. It was that fact alone that gave her ease enough to go back to sleep.

When she woke again, the alarm on the bedside table was going off, and water was running in the shower.

Casey's first impulse was fear. He'd come into her room and she'd never known. Her second was picturing what he was doing. Remembering the condition in which he'd emerged last night, she jumped out of bed, grabbing for her robe and slippers as she ran a hasty brush through the tangles in her hair. This time when he came out of the shower, she had no intention of being anywhere in sight.

When she exited the apartment, she stood for a moment on the landing, savoring the Mississippi morning. It was going to be another hot one, she could tell. The thought of freshly brewed coffee and some of Tilly's hot biscuits and jelly drew her down the stairs with haste, across the courtyard, in the back door of the mansion, and into the kitchen.

"Something smells good," she said.

The woman standing at the stove turned in quick surprise. There was a faint flush from the heat of the oven staining her face and a warning in her eyes.

"Casey Dee, you scared me half to death."

"I'm sorry," Casey said, and went for her good-morning hug.

Tilly smoothed and fussed at the long hair hanging down Casey's back, then hugged her tightly to soften the accusation in her words. "Well now, girl, what are you doing over here without your man?"

She sighed. If only things were as simple now as they'd been back when she was a child.

"He's in the shower." Casey slumped in a chair with a pout. "Oh, Tilly, Delaney has made such a mess out of my life."

"No, ma'am. Delaney didn't do it, you did. He just went and made some silly rule, and as always, you're still running along behind him, trying to make everything right."

Casey was speechless. This wasn't the sympathy she'd been wanting. She tried to glare, but it just wasn't possible. Not at Tilly. And then she sighed. Tilly always gave her sympathy, but where Casey wanted it or not, it also came with the truth.

"So, he started it," Casey said, and managed to grin.

"And you sure did finish it, didn't you, girl? The very idea! Going down to the flatlands to find yourself a man."

Casey's eyebrows rose. "How did you know?"

Tilly snorted delicately and returned to stirring the eggs she'd been cooking. "I know, 'cause you're my baby," she said softly. "I know 'cause I make it my business to know."

The air in Casey's throat became too thick to breathe. She stood and slipped her arms around Tilly's waist, then laid her cheek in the middle of her back, relishing the familiarity of freshly ironed fabric and a steady heartbeat.

"And I thank God that you care," Casey said softly. "You and Joshua are all the family I have left."

Tilly set the skillet off the fire and turned until she and Casey were eye to eye. "No, girl, you're wrong. You've got yourself a husband now."

Casey's laugh was brittle. "I don't have a husband. I have a stranger for a year."

Tilly took her by the shoulders and shook her. "What you have is a chance. Now make the most of it." Before Casey could argue further, Tilly waved her away. "Go tell your man my biscuits are about ready to come out of the oven. By the time you two get back, bacon and eggs will be ready, too."

"But I don't know if he likes..."

Tilly's stare never wavered. "Then don't you think it's about time you found out?"

Casey exited the kitchen with as much grace as she could muster. After her and Ryder's encounter last night, she was almost afraid to face him. The tail of her robe was dragging as she walked up the stairs. When she stumbled and came close to falling, she picked it up and walked the rest of the way with the hem held above her ankles.

Ryder met her at the door. She knew that she was staring, but she hadn't been prepared for the change in his appearance. Clean-shaven, smelling like soap and something light and musky, he seemed taller than ever. She tried not to gawk, but the new blue jeans he was wearing suited him all too well, and he'd left the top three buttons on his long-sleeved white shirt undone, revealing far too much of that broad, brown chest for her peace of mind. The only thing she recognized from before were his old black boots, and even they were shining. Still damp from his shower, his hair gleamed black in the early morning sunshine.

"Mornin'," he said softly, and stepped aside to let her in. "Someone from the house just called. Said they wanted a ride into the city."

Casey blinked, telling herself to concentrate on what he was saying instead of how he looked, but it was difficult. Today, those grey eyes of his almost looked blue.

"It isn't even eight o'clock," she muttered. "You haven't had breakfast, and they can wait."

A slight grin cornered one edge of his mouth and then slid out of sight. "I don't know what we'll eat. Yesterday I forgot to buy milk."

"It doesn't matter. This morning we're having breakfast in the kitchen with Tilly. She said to hurry."

"Who's Tilly?"

"The woman who raised me after Mother and Father were killed. She's Joshua's wife. You remember him from yesterday?"

He nodded, then reached for the broad-brimmed, black Stetson hanging by the door. "Someone else's cooking sounds good to me." When Casey moved toward their bedroom, he paused. "Aren't you coming, or don't you eat with the hired help?"

She spun, and there was no mistaking the anger in her voice.

"Don't *ever,* and I mean, *ever,* refer to Tilly or Joshua as servants again. Do you understand?"

Surprised by her vehemence, his estimation of her went up a notch. ''Yes, ma'am, I believe that I do.''

Again, Casey realized she'd overreacted. He must be as off-center as she felt. ''Sorry. I didn't mean…''

''Easy now.''

Her stomach tied itself into a little knot. If only he'd quit saying those words in those tones.

''I am easy,'' she said, and then groaned beneath her breath as a grin spread across his face. ''Don't say it,'' she muttered. ''You know what I meant.''

''Casey.''

A little nervous about what he would say next, she couldn't have been more surprised by what came out.

''Don't ever apologize for having a good heart.''

After witnessing the dangerous side of him last night, his gentleness was the last thing she would have expected.

''Was that a compliment?'' she asked.

He ignored her. ''Hurry up and get dressed. I'm starving.''

''Feel free to go on ahead. Tilly will be glad to…''

''No.''

''No?''

''I'll wait for you,'' he said.

She inhaled sharply, and then shut the bedroom door behind her as she went inside. Her hands were shaking as she sorted through the closet for something to wear.

I'll wait for you.

His promise was echoing inside her head as she brushed and zipped and buttoned. Putting on makeup was even more difficult because she found herself looking through tears, but she refused to let them fall. She wasn't going to let that man get to her, not in any way.

Erica sauntered into the downstairs kitchen just as Tilly was dishing up the eggs.

''What's taking so long this morning?'' Erica grumbled, picking a strip of hot, crisp bacon from the platter and crunching it between her teeth.

''Get on out of my kitchen,'' Tilly said. ''Everything is right on time and you know it.''

Erica hated this woman's uppity manner, and at the same time, respected her authority just enough not to argue.

"It's not your kitchen," Erica grumbled, taking one last piece of bacon with her as she started out of the room.

"It's not yours, either," Tilly said sharply, and banged a spoon on the side of the pan to punctuate her remark.

Erica glared. And then the back door opened and she forgot what she'd been about to say. She forgot she was chewing, or that she was holding her next bite in her hand. All she could do was stare—right past her sister to the man behind her. Almost choking, she managed to swallow, then dropped the other piece of bacon back onto the platter.

Casey didn't see Erica. Her focus was on the woman at the stove. Until Matilda Bass passed judgment on what she'd done, she wouldn't feel right.

"Tilly, this is my, uh…this is Ryder Justice. Ryder, this is Matilda Bass. I consider her my second mother, as well as the best cook in the whole state of Mississippi."

Upon entering the kitchen, he'd taken off his hat. He extended his hand in a gesture of friendship, which Tilly accepted with obvious reticence. But Ryder behaved as if he'd known her all of his life.

"Mrs. Bass, it's a pleasure. If everything tastes as good as it smells, I'd warrant Casey is right."

Tilly's gaze wavered. She hadn't been prepared for someone like him, and he *was* someone, that she could tell. She frowned slightly. This man didn't look like any drifter out of the flatlands. He didn't sound like one, either. His words were sweet, his appearance sweeter. All she could think was, He'd better be good to my girl.

She nodded regally, accepting the praise as just. "Call me Tilly, and I'm pleased to meet you, sir. You aren't from these parts, are you?"

He grinned. "I don't answer to anything but Ryder, and no, ma'am, I'm not."

Tilly nodded in satisfaction. "I knew as much. I'd be guessing you're from Oklahoma…or Texas. Am I right?"

Startled by her perception, he didn't have it in him to lie.

"Yes, ma'am… Texas."

Casey felt strange. Here she was married to the man and

she'd been so caught up in her own agenda, she hadn't had enough curiosity about him to wonder where he was from, or how he'd gotten from there to here.

"Then sit," Tilly said. "Food's ready."

Only after they'd taken their seats did Casey realize Erica was in the room. She looked up at her and smiled, but when her sister sauntered over to Ryder and ran her fingertips lightly across his back, measuring their breadth from shoulder to shoulder, the urge to slap her away from him was almost overwhelming.

There was a cold, mirthless smile on Erica's face as she finally glanced in Casey's direction.

"Well, well, princess. Even when you fall, you land on your feet, don't you?"

Casey's hackles rose even further. "Let it go, Erica."

Erica's expression was bland, but her eyes glittered with envy. "Oh my, I guess that didn't come out quite right, did it?"

The antagonism between the two sisters was palpable. Ryder suspected it probably had more to do with old wounds than with his arrival into their midst. Nevertheless, whatever its roots, he seemed to be the latest weed to cause dissent. He took it upon himself to change the subject.

"Someone called me earlier for a ride into town. Do you know who it was?"

Erica's smile broadened. "It wasn't me, but that's not such a bad idea. I'll bet you give really good rides."

Ryder's expression blanked, and if Erica had been as astute as she believed herself to be, she would have backed off then, before it was too late. But she didn't.

"I'm even better at giving a hard time to people who tick me off," he said.

Erica's expression froze. A slap in the face couldn't have stunned her more.

If Casey had been the impulsive type, she would have thrown her arms around his neck and hugged him. But she wasn't, and the moment passed.

"Tell whoever it is that Ryder is unavailable until we've finished our breakfast," she said. "This morning, my husband

and I just want a little peace and quiet and a meal to ourselves.''

Ryder's eyebrows rose. Husband! Now she was admitting he was her husband?

Suddenly Ryder's mouth was only inches from Casey's ear. She could feel his breath—almost hear the laughter in his voice as he whispered.

"I thought we weren't using *that* word."

Casey glared.

Erica was left with nowhere to go but out. She walked away, leaving Ryder with a contemplative stare that Casey chose to ignore.

"I guess if a person is observant, they can learn something new every day," he muttered.

Casey looked up. "Like what?"

"Never knew there were any barracudas in Mississippi."

"Excuse me?"

"Nothing," Ryder said. "I was just thinking out loud."

Tilly's back was to the pair, but her smile was wide as she added the finishing touch to her eggs before setting them on the table. She wasn't the type of woman to make snap judgments, but after the way Ryder had cut Erica Dunn off at the mouth, she was pretty sure he was going to do just fine.

She set the plates before them. "Now eat up before my eggs get cold." She set a full pan of steaming hot biscuits in front of them as well. "Fresh out of the oven, Casey Dee, just the way you like them."

Casey rolled her eyes in appreciation of the golden brown tops and reached for one to butter.

"Since you're a married lady now and have your own place, I guess you'll be needing to learn how to make these," Tilly said. "When you get time, I'll be needing to teach you."

Casey looked stunned. Ryder hid his grin behind a bite of scrambled eggs. Poor Casey. It would seem that her life had taken more changes than she was ready to accept.

"Making biscuits seems a bit of a leap for a woman who can't boil water," Ryder said.

Ignoring Casey's gasp, he scooped a spoonful of strawberry preserves onto his biscuit and then bit into the hot bread, chewing with relish.

"Well, I never," she muttered.

Ryder swallowed, took a slow sip of coffee, then fixed Casey with a sultry gaze. "I know that, wife. But one of these days you will."

The implications of what he'd just said were impossible to misinterpret. He hadn't been talking about biscuits, and they both knew it. Furious that he kept catching her off guard, she stabbed at the food on her plate with undue force, scraping the tines of the fork across the china and earning her a cool I-taught-you-better-than-that look from Tilly.

The rest of the meal passed in relative silence, broken only by the coming and going of Tilly and Joshua as they carried food into the breakfast room for the family who would now be living off the fruit of Casey's labors. It was Ryder who finally broke the silence.

"That does it for me," he said. "I guess I'd better go earn my keep." He winked at Casey, taking small delight in the fact that she didn't welcome it, and tweaked her ear for the hell of it as he passed.

"Do you know where you're going?" Casey asked, as he sauntered out of the room.

He paused, then turned, and once again, she was struck by the fact that his answer had nothing to do with the question she'd asked.

"No. But then it hasn't really mattered for months now. Why should today be any different?"

When he disappeared, she was forced to accept the fact that not only had she married a stranger, but it would seem one with more secrets than he cared to tell.

She took a last gulp of her coffee and tossed down her napkin. If he had her troubles, he'd have something to complain about. She glanced at her watch. It was a quarter to nine. Past time for the boss to be at work. But, since she *was* the boss, she was going to finish her coffee.

Meanwhile, Ryder was making his way through the maze of rooms and getting a firsthand impression of the atmosphere in which Casey had grown up.

The mansion itself was grand—with three stories of granite blocks that came far too close to resembling a castle rather than a home. The only thing Ryder felt was missing was a moat. The snakes and crocodiles were already in place, but they walked on two legs, rather than four, and hid their sharp teeth behind fake smiles.

His footsteps echoed on the cold marble floors as he made his way toward the muted sound of voices coming from a room up the hallway and to the right. The breakfast room, he presumed.

As he entered the doorway, he paused, staring at the bright morning sun beaming in through spotless windows, through which an arbor of hot pink bougainvillea could be seen.

The crystal on the table was elegant. The china was a plain, classic white with a delicate gold rim, and the silverware gleamed with a high, polished gloss as the people in residence lifted it to their mouths. Flowers were everywhere. Cut and in vases. Growing from pots. In one-dimensional form, painted on canvas and framed, then hung at just the right level for the eye to see.

In spite of the heat of the day, Ryder shuddered. Such elegance. Such cold, cold, elegance. He thought of the woman who'd come storming into that bar with her long hair down and windblown, wearing that bit of a black dress, and tried to picture her being raised in a place like this. For some reason, the little he knew of Casey didn't jibe with these surroundings. How could a woman with so much passion survive in a house with no joy—no life?

And Casey Ruban Justice had passion, of that he had no doubt. Most of the time she seemed to keep it channeled toward the business end of her world, but every so often her guard slipped, and had she known it, in those moments, Ryder saw more of her soul than she would have liked.

He settled his Stetson a little tighter on his head, as if bracing himself for a gale wind, and sauntered into the breakfast room as if he owned the place.

"Who wanted the ride?"

Three sets of equally startled expressions turned in his direction. Erica was still seething from his earlier put-down and chose to ignore him.

Miles stared, holding his cup of coffee suspended halfway between table and lips, trying to picture this clean-cut, larger-than-life cowboy as the same ragged derelict who'd come trailing in behind Casey yesterday morning.

Eudora gasped and set her cup down in its saucer with a sharp, unladylike clink.

"Why, it was me," she said. "But I'm not quite ready."

Ryder smiled. "I've got all day. Don't hurry on my account."

"For future reference, you need not come into the family area," Miles drawled. "Simply wait out front."

Ryder shifted his stance. It wasn't much. Only an inch or so. But to Miles, it seemed to make the man that much taller. And it made Miles distinctly uncomfortable looking up at so much man.

"Look," Ryder growled. "Let's get one thing straight. Like it or not, and I can't say that I care much for it myself, for the time being, I *am* part of your family. Therefore, do not expect me to scuttle around outside the back door like some damned stray dog looking for a handout. Do I make myself clear?"

Miles face turned a bloody shade of red. All he could do was splutter and look toward Erica, who was usually the more verbal of the pair, for support. Unaware that Ryder had already put her in her place, he was unprepared for his sister's silence. He tried again.

"But Casey said…"

"Casey can say whatever she chooses," Ryder said. "However, you might want to remember that she's my wife, not my boss. And, you might also want to remember that while I mind my own business, I expect others to do the same." Then he touched the brim of his hat and winked at Eudora. "I'll be outside when you're ready."

He walked out.

When he was halfway down the hall, the breakfast room seemed to erupt into a cacophony of sound. Three separate voices, all talking at once in various tones of disbelief. Unable to remember the last time he'd felt this alive, he grinned all the way out the door.

Chapter 5

"Stop there!" Eudora ordered, pointing toward a boutique on the upcoming street corner.

Ryder aimed the gleaming white Lincoln toward a horizontal parking space and slid into it with nothing to spare. Before Eudora could object to the fact that he'd parked several doors down and she was going to have to walk, he had opened the door and was reaching in to help her out.

Smoothing at her hair and clothes, she began to issue her standard orders. "I don't know how long I'll be, but…"

"No problem," he said. "I'm coming with you," he said, and offered her his arm.

Ignoring the shocked expression on her face, he escorted her up the street and into the store. Eudora was so stunned by his actions that she let herself be led into The Pink Boutique.

The saleslady all but fawned as she met her at the door. "Mrs. Deathridge, please accept our condolences on your recent loss. Delaney Ruban will be missed."

"Yes, well, I thank you on behalf of the family," Eudora muttered, casting a sidelong glance at Ryder who was still standing at her side. He was too big to ignore and seemed too determined to dissuade from accompanying her. She waved toward an overstuffed chair near the alcove where the dressing rooms were situated. "You may wait over there."

Ryder took his seat without comment. Eudora watched as he carefully lifted the Stetson from his head. Placing it crown-side down in his lap, he seemed to settle.

After that she relaxed, but only slightly. There was something about that man that unnerved her. Even though he was now across the room from her and sitting still, his presence was overpowering. Frowning, she turned away and began sorting through the garments on the racks, still conscious of his eyes boring into her back. He took up space. That's what he did. He took up entirely too much space.

Half an hour came and went, along with the saleslady's patience. Eudora had picked through and complained about everything the store carried in her size. It made no difference to her that Gladys was nearly in tears, or that the manager had made several pointed trips through the room, each time giving Gladys a sharp, condemning look for not being able to placate a customer, especially one from Ruban Crossing's foremost family.

Eudora was so caught up with the seriousness of her shopping spree that she'd completely forgotten Ryder's existence, so when he spoke, he had Eudora's...and the saleslady's...immediate and undivided attention.

"Take the blue one."

Eudora spun, still holding the dress in question. "Were you speaking to me?"

Ryder tilted his head. "It matches your eyes. Always did like blue-eyed women."

Having said his piece, he stretched, giving himself permission to take up even more of the floor space by unfolding his long legs out before him. While she watched, he locked his hands across his belly as if he didn't have a care in the world.

Eudora wasn't accustomed to having anyone, especially a chauffeur, give her advice on her choices of clothing, yet this man's entrance into their world had already changed their lives. She heard herself repeating his suggestion as if it had true merit and wondered if she was finally losing her mind.

"The blue?"

He nodded, then shrugged. "Yes, ma'am, but it was just a suggestion. My father always said it never paid to rush a woman."

"Oh, do quit calling me ma'am," Eudora said. "It sounds too elderly."

Ryder looked up and almost grinned. "Well, now, Dora, didn't anyone ever tell you that age is in the mind of the beholder?"

Eudora's mouth dropped. This man was positively impossible. Of course he should have known she meant for him to call her Mrs. Deathridge, not Dora! The very idea, shortening her name like that.

But the deed had already been done, and the name rang in her ears. Dora. That was what her husband, Henry, had called her, and Henry had been dead for all these many years. She gave Ryder a sidelong glance and disappeared into the dressing room with the blue dress in her hand. Dora. Dora. What would Erica and Miles have to say about this?

She shut the door behind her then looked up. Her reflection looked back. For a moment, she almost didn't recognize herself. Her eyes were bright—from shock, of course. But the glimmer did give life to her expression. Dora. She held the blue dress up beneath her chin. He was right. It brought out the true color of her eyes. She smiled. Maybe he wasn't so bad after all.

Only after he was alone did Ryder realize what he'd said. He'd actually thought of his father without coming unglued. In fact, just for a moment, it had felt damned good to remember him at all.

He jammed his Stetson on his head then pulled the brim down low across his forehead and closed his eyes. Ah God, but he missed that old man. So much that it hurt.

Lash stood on the veranda, staring at the brake lights on the plumber's van as it slowed to take a corner. A soft, early morning breeze lifted the hair from his forehead, cooling the sweat that had beaded minutes earlier when the plumber had handed him his bill.

Despair settled a little closer upon his shoulders.

Impulsively, he walked down the steps and out into the yard, heading for the gazebo. As a child, it had been his favorite place. As an adult, it was where he went to hide.

Ivy clung to the latticed walls, crocheted by nature into heavy loops of variegated green. Inside, the air rarely moved and only the most persistent rays of sunshine were able to pick and poke their way through the dense growth.

He dropped onto the bench in a slump, then wadded the bill and tossed it into the gathering pile on the floor. Why bother to keep track if they couldn't be paid?

Minutes passed. He looked down at his watch. It was past time to open the office. With a sigh, he shoved himself off the bench, giving the pile of unpaid bills a final glance. Poor Graystone. She was so sick—in need of too many repairs for his meager pocket to accommodate.

His eyes misted as he walked across the yard. As he entered the house in search of his suit coat and briefcase, a continuing thought kept running through his mind.

It was Casey's fault. Casey had ruined it all. Beautiful, willful Casey who had so much, while he had nothing at all. He yanked his coat from a hook, thinking of the parties that would be given in her honor, coveting the priceless wedding gifts she would certainly be receiving as her due.

Despair fed anger. Anger fed hate. And something fell to the floor behind him with a clank. He spun in time to see a long, hairless tail disappearing beneath the cupboard. A rat. Another damned rat.

He grabbed a can of corn from the cabinet, firing it toward the place where he'd seen it last. "What the hell are you still doing here? I thought rats abandoned sinking ships."

Several items had fallen off a low shelf and onto the floor as the door to the cupboard flew open. The sight of spilled salt sent Lash to his knees. Scrambling to regain his sense of balance in his superstitious world, he grabbed a pinch of the salt and tossed it over his shoulder. Even though one part of his brain told him that spilled salt did not bad luck make, he was too much a product of his upbringing to ignore it all now.

Still down on his knees, he set to retrieving the few family heirlooms he hadn't sold. It wasn't until he was setting his grandfather's sorghum pewter pitcher back on the shelf that he noticed a small, flat box at the back of the cupboard. Frowning, he pulled it out. When he opened the lid, his eyes widened and a delighted smile lit up his somber expression. Grandfather's letter opener! He'd completely forgotten its existence.

He ran a tentative finger down the thin, double-edged blade, remembering the hours he'd spent in Aaron Marlow's lap, remembering the first time his grandfather had let him use it without help. For all its beauty, it was still a small and deadly thing.

A brown shadow moved to the right of Lash's hand. He reacted without thinking. Seconds later, he rocked back on his heels in shock, staring at the carcass of the rat and the small silver dagger embedded in its body.

Bile rose, burning his throat and choking him as he scrambled to his feet and ran for the sink just in time to keep from puking on himself. When he was able to look back without gagging, all he could see was his family honor embedded in the belly of the rat.

In Lash's mind, it was the last and ultimate disgrace. Wild-eyed and looking for someone else to blame, he stared at the salt. Bad luck. Bad luck. It was all a matter of bad luck.

In a daze, he yanked the dagger out of the rat, wiping off the bloody blade on the kitchen curtain. His hands were shaking as he laid it back in the box. So, he'd come to this, and thanks to Casey Justice, this is where he would stay.

He shuddered then sighed as he closed the lid to the box. Casey. He'd lost everything because of her. The box felt warm in his hands as he slipped it into his pocket before picking up his briefcase.

A muscle jerked in his jaw as he walked out of the house. Once again, he glanced at his watch. There was something he needed to do before he went to the office. He didn't know where his manners had gone. He should have thought of it before.

Casey tossed her pen down on the desk and swiveled her chair to face the window overlooking the business district of

Ruban Crossing. As she did, a flash of white caught her eye and she stood abruptly, searching for a glimpse of the family's white Lincoln.

Was that Ryder? She looked until her eyes began to burn and the muscles in the backs of her legs began to knot. Disgusted with herself, she turned away from the window to return to her chair.

The high gloss on her desk was obliterated by a mountain of paperwork to her left, which was only increments smaller than the mountain of paperwork to her right. She closed her eyes and tried to relax, playing her favorite what-if game. The one that went...what if she walked out of the office and never came back? In her mind, she was halfway out of town when her secretary, Nola Sue, buzzed.

"Mrs. Justice, you have a delivery."

The mention of her name change alone was enough to yank Casey back to reality.

"Just sign for it. I'll pick it up later."

"I'm sorry, Mrs. Justice, but the man insists on your signature only."

Casey sighed. "Then send him in."

Moments later, the door opened and a uniformed messenger came into the room. Brief and to the point, he handed her a clipboard and a pen.

"Sign here, please."

Casey did as she was told, casually eyeing the flat, oblong package the man laid on her desk.

"Good day, Mrs. Justice."

And then he was gone.

My, how word does get around in this town, Casey thought, as she slipped a letter opener between the folds of paper. A glimmer of color began to emerge from beneath the plain, brown wrapping. The second layer of paper was a thick, pure white embossed with silver doves. An obvious allusion to the wedding that hardly was. Curious now, she abandoned the letter opener for her fingers and tore through that layer to a flat black box.

It was a little over a foot in length and no more than three or four inches in width. The lid was hinged by two delicate foil butterflies. Casey gasped at the contents as a card fell out and into her lap.

Inside lay a miniature rapier on thick, black velvet. She lifted it from the case, hefting it lightly. It felt heavy, even warm in her hand, and she knew before she turned it over to view the silversmith's mark that it was probably solid silver. It was the most elaborate letter opener she'd ever seen.

Curious, she laid it aside and picked up the card, all the while wondering who would send her such a thing. She read, "Casey, On your nuptials: You deserve this...and so much more. Lash."

She frowned at the oddity of the phrasing, then laid the card aside and picked the small rapier up again, eyeing the double-edged blade with caution. Something near the tip caught her eye. At first, she thought it was rust, and that the letter opener must not be silver after all, because silver did not rust. Even after she ran the tip of her finger across the spot, it didn't come off. But when she lifted it for a closer look, she suddenly shifted in her seat, making room for the unexpected sense of foreboding that swept over her.

She swiveled her chair toward the window and full light, tilting the blade for a closer look still, then tested the spot with the tip of a fingernail. It came away on her nail. Startled, she grabbed for a tissue and wiped at her finger, unprepared for the small, red stain that suddenly appeared against stark white.

She couldn't quit staring. The spot wasn't rust, it was blood—dried blood. But in such a small amount that it might have gone unnoticed.

Now her delight in such a gift was replaced with dismay. It seemed a travesty of something pure to receive a wedding gift with blood on it. The urge to put it out of sight was strong. She laid it back in the box, closing the lid with care, but the words on the card had now taken on a sinister meaning.

You deserve this...and so much more.

Deserve what? What did she deserve? The silver...the knife...or the blood?

The phone rang. It was the private line that only family ever used. She grabbed for it like a lifeline.

"Hello."

"Casey, darling, it's Erica. Have you seen Grandmother?"

For once, she was almost thankful for the whine in her half sister's voice. It gave her something else on which to focus besides Lash's gift.

"No, I'm sorry, but I haven't."

Erica sighed. "It's nearly one o'clock. She was going to meet me for lunch, and she's thirty minutes late. She's never late, you know."

Casey frowned. That much was true. Gran had a thing about being tardy.

"It's probably all his fault," Erica said.

"All whose fault?" Casey asked.

"Your husband...the family chauffeur...however you choose to define him. He took Grandmother shopping hours ago and no one's seen a sign of them since." The tone of Erica's voice rose an octave. "We don't know a thing about him. I can't believe you actually brought a stranger into this household, shoved him down our throats and then expected us to accept his presence as status quo."

Casey stifled a sigh. This was all she needed.

"Look, Erica. Nothing has happened to Gran. If it had, Ryder would have called. He is not a fiend. Besides, why didn't you call her instead of me? There's a phone in the Lincoln."

"I know that," Erica snapped. "But no one's answering."

Casey looked at the stacks of files on her desk and wondered how her grandfather had gone so wrong. She was beating her head against a thousand brick walls and all Erica had to worry about was a late luncheon date.

"I don't know what to tell you," Casey said. "I'm sure she's fine. I'm sorry she's late."

The connection between them was broken when Erica slammed the receiver back into the cradle. For a few wonderful moments, all Casey could hear were muffled voices from the outer office. With a dogged determination of which Delaney Ruban would have been proud, Casey dropped the gift into a drawer and buzzed Nola Sue.

"Cancel my lunch with Rosewell and Associates. Reschedule for sometime next week."

"Yes, ma'am," Nola Sue said, making notations as she listened to Casey's orders. "Do you want me to order you something to eat?"

"I suppose," she said. "And call home. Tell them I'll be working late and not to hold dinner."

Within seconds, she'd forgotten about Lash Marlow's present and Erica's phone call. Her entire focus was on the figures before her and the study she would need before she could make an offer for the acquisition of the Harmon Canneries near Tupelo.

A short while later, Nola Sue set a small, plastic tub of chicken salad, a cold roll, and a melting cup of iced tea on the corner of Casey's desk and tiptoed out without uttering a word.

It was sometime later before Casey even noticed that lunch had been served.

"Want some ketchup on those fries?" Ryder asked. Eudora poked the lingering end of a fast-food French fry into her mouth and then shook her head. Seconds later, Ryder handed her a fistful of paper napkins.

"Thank you," she said.

When she was certain Ryder's attention was otherwise occupied, she licked the salt from her fingers before drying them on the paper napkins he'd tossed in her lap, then leaned back against the seat, sighing with satisfaction.

She couldn't remember the last time food had tasted this good. Stifling a small belch, she lifted her cup to her lips and latched onto the straw poking through the plastic lid, sucking with all her might. A couple of swallows later, she began to suck air.

"How about another cherry limeade?"

"No, but thank you," Eudora said, and tossed a used napkin on the floor next to the wrapper that had been around her cheeseburger.

The food had been delicious. She wasn't going to think about the fact that it had all been served in recycled paper. There was something about reusing paper—in any form or fashion—that smacked of poverty. Eudora Deathridge had not suffered a day of want in her entire life, and had no intentions of starting now. She belched again, then sighed. This had been worth her impending heartburn.

Ryder hid a grin. He'd given her hell this morning and knew it. From the time they'd entered the first store, to the last one they'd exited just before lunch, he'd been on her heels at every turn.

He had been nothing but respectful. It wasn't in him to be anything else. But he figured the 'family' needed to know right off that while he didn't mind driving them all over kingdom come, he was going to do it his way. And if that meant making himself a slight nuisance, then so be it. He was the best when it came to being a pain in the ass. If they didn't believe him, then they could just ask his...

Oh, God. He'd done it again. Micah's name kept hovering at the edge of his mind, popping out when least expected. He hated being weak, but guilt was eating him alive. No longer hungry, he began stuffing his leftovers back into the sack they'd come in.

"Here you go, Dora." He handed the half-filled sack over the seat.

Surprised by the gesture, she took it before she thought, letting it dangle between her fingers like something foul.

"What am I to do with this?"

"Trash. Put your trash in it."

She stared at the papers she'd tossed on the floorboard in disbelief. He was asking her to pick up trash? This time he'd overstepped his bounds.

"Now see here," she complained. "I don't think you..."

Ryder turned. Their gazes met. His eyes were dark and filled with a pain she hadn't expected.

"Need some help?"

"I don't believe so," she said quietly. "But thank you just the same."

She opened the sack and leaned down. A few moments later, she handed it back, watching as he tossed it in a barrel on the way out of the parking lot.

"Ryder."

He glanced up. Again, their gazes met briefly, this time in the rearview mirror.

"Yes, ma'am?"

"I'm ready to go home now."

He took the next turn, wishing he could say the same.

It was after eight o'clock. Ryder paced the small apartment like a caged bear—back and forth, from window to chair, unable to concentrate on the story on television, or eat the food congealing on his plate. Stifled by the presence of walls, he refused to admit that he was worried about Casey's absence.

Another half hour passed. By this time, he was steaming. He knew for a fact that Miles had packed up and left for a three-day trip to New Orleans to play. Erica and her grandmother had had a fight and Erica was sulking in her room because Dora had refused to grovel for forgetting their lunch date. Even Joshua and Tilly had finished up for the night and gone home. But Casey was still on the job. Something about that just didn't sit right with him, and his patience was gone.

He grabbed his hat on the way out the door. In a shorter time than one might have imagined, he had parked outside the Ruban Building and was on his way inside. A guard stopped him at the door.

"Sorry sir, but the offices are closed for the night."

Ryder shocked himself by announcing, "I'm here to pick up my wife."

"And who might that be?" the guard asked.

"Her name is—was—Casey Ruban."

The man took a quick step back, eyeing Ryder with new attention.

"You'd be the fellow Miss Ruban married."

Ryder nodded.

"Well, now, I might need to see some identification…just for the first time, you understand."

Ryder opened his wallet.

"Justice…yep, that would be you, all right," the guard said. "We heard Miss Ruban had married a man named Justice." He reached for the phone. "Just a minute, sir, and I'll let her know you're here."

"No," Ryder said, and then softened the tone of his voice with a halfhearted grin. "I was sort of planning to surprise her."

The guard smiled. "Yes, sir. I understand. Take the elevator to the top floor. Her office is the first one on your right."

"Thanks," Ryder said.

"You're welcome, sir," the guard said. "And congratulations on your marriage. Miss Ruban is a fine lady."

Ryder nodded. Even though she was a little hardheaded, he was beginning to have the same opinion of her himself.

By the time he got to her office, his sense of injustice was in high form. He walked inside and past the empty secretary's desk without pausing; his gaze fixed on the thin line of light showing from beneath the door on the far side of the room.

Casey's head hurt, her shoulders ached, and she was so far past hungry it didn't count. What was worse, she didn't even know it. Realization of her condition came only after the door to her office swung open and Ryder stalked into the room.

Startled, she stood too swiftly. The room began to tilt.

Ryder saw her sway and grabbed her arm before she staggered.

All she could think to say was, "What are you doing here?" before he took the pen from her hand, and turned out the desk lamp.

"I came to take you home. Your day is over. It's night. It's time to rest. It's time to slow the hell down. Do you understand me?"

He was mad. That was what surprised her most. Why should he be angry? It took a bit to realize that he wasn't angry at her. He was angry on her behalf. At that point, lack of food and exhaustion kicked in. Damn him, he wasn't supposed to be nice...at least, not like this.

She shrugged out of his grasp and reached for her purse. "I don't need you telling me what to do."

He stood between her and the doorway and once again, Casey caught a glimpse of the same man who'd come out of the shadows of Sonny's Place and taken a dare no other man had had the guts to take.

"Then consider it a suggestion," he said quietly, and reached for her arm.

This time she didn't pull away. They walked all the way to

the elevator without talking, then past the night guard who
grinned and winked. Silence was maintained all the way out
to the car. It was only after Casey felt the seat at the back of
her legs that she began to relax.

Ryder slid behind the wheel, then looked at her. It didn't
take him long to make the decision. "Buckle up. You choose,
but you're not going home until you eat."

Casey wrinkled her nose. "The car smells like French
fries."

"Dora spilled a few. I'll clean it out tomorrow."

It took Casey a moment for the answer to connect. Dora?
French fries? In the car? She turned where she sat, staring at
Ryder in sudden confusion.

"Who's Dora?"

"You are bad off," he said, as he put the car in gear and
backed out of the parking space. "She's your grandmother,
isn't she?"

"You called her Dora?"

He shrugged as he pulled into traffic. "Said she didn't want
me calling her ma'am."

"Why was Dora...I mean Gran...eating French fries in the
car?"

"Because they went with her cheeseburger and cherry limeade."

Casey's mouth dropped. "She ate fast food?"

He grinned. "Ate it real fast, too. Never saw a woman so
hungry."

Casey still didn't believe she was getting the story straight.
"She ate her meal in the back seat of a car?"

Ryder gave her a sidelong glance. "Are you still faint?"

She covered her face with her hands and groaned. "My
God, why did you take Gran to a fast-food restaurant?"

"Because she was hungry, that's why."

"But..."

He took the corner in a delicate skid, the likes of which the
Lincoln had never seen. "You know what?"

Casey clutched at her seat belt, almost afraid to ask.
"What?"

"You people are too uptight. You need to loosen up a little.
If you did, you might find out you like it. Better yet, you might

even live long enough to spend all that money you're so dead set on making.''

There wasn't a civil thought in her head as Ryder turned off the highway and into another parking lot. But when he opened the door to help her out, the odor of charbroiled meat made her forget her anger. A few moments later, she realized where he'd brought her, and if she hadn't been so hungry, she would have laughed.

As he led her in the restaurant, she would have been willing to bet the last dollar she had in her pocket that, by tomorrow, it would be all over Ruban Crossing that Eudora Deathridge had eaten French fries in the back seat of a car. What was going to ice this piece of gossip was the fact that Casey and her honky-tonk husband had also shared a late-night dinner at Smoky Joe's. As restaurants go, it wasn't bad. It was Smoky Joe's sideline that gave him, and his restaurant, such a bad reputation.

Casey lifted her chin as they walked inside. She could tell by the sounds coming from the back room that the floor show was in full swing.

''Wonder what's going on back there?'' Ryder asked, as he guided Casey to an empty booth.

''Mud wrestling,'' she said. One eyebrow arched as she waited for his reaction.

His interest sparked, he had to ask. ''Women or 'gators?''

''Women,'' she replied.

She watched as the light in his eyes faded. She sighed. She should have known it would take more than naked women in a hot tub's worth of red clay to get him excited.

''I think he saves the 'gators for Saturday nights.''

He handed her a menu. ''Good. It'll give us a reason to come back.''

Chapter 6

"**I**'m coming out. Are you decent?" Ryder yelled.

Casey pulled the sheet up past her breasts and tried to look relaxed as the bathroom door opened. He emerged, but she'd closed her eyes too late. My God! Doesn't he own a bathrobe? she wondered.

"I'll be through in a second," he said.

Casey could hear drawers opening and closing and clenched her eyelids even tighter. That damp towel around his waist was far too brief for her piece of mind.

Footsteps moved toward the doorway.

She opened her eyes. Too soon. She'd looked too soon. He was still there, standing in the doorway in a pair of white briefs. Lamplight spilled into the bedroom from behind him.

This time, his presence did more than unnerve her. Even though his face was in shadow, she knew he was watching her.

She held her breath.

He didn't speak.

In the bathroom next door, water dripped from the showerhead and into the tub. Then dripped again. Then again. Then again.

He started toward her, one slow step at a time. Casey stifled a moan, clutching at the sheet until her fingers went numb. Once she started to speak, and couldn't remember enough words to string together in one sentence. She went from panic to dismay to a calm she didn't expect. But when he walked past her and into the bathroom without saying a word, her calm moved to disbelief.

This time when he emerged, he didn't look back. The door swung shut between them with a firm thud and Casey was left with nothing but the sound of a racing heart. The drip no longer dripped. The man was no longer a threat. She was safe and sound and alone in her bed—and she didn't remember ever feeling as lonely as she did right now.

"What's wrong with me?"

She rolled onto her stomach, punching her pillow and yanking at her nightgown until she heard ribbons tearing. Finally, she closed her eyes, willing herself to sleep, and blamed her restless spirit on the barbecue she'd eaten at Smoky Joe's.

A chair scooted in the other room. He was obviously making his bed out on the floor. The comfort of hers as opposed to the one he was about to take made her feel guilty. She thumped her pillow and shifted her position. She just couldn't help it. He'd known from the start this wasn't going to be a normal marriage.

But no one told him he'd be sleeping on the floor for the next twelve months.

The long, unmistakable rasp of a large metal zipper being undone plucked at her conscience. The sleeping bag.

She rolled over on her back and opened her eyes. Although the king-size bed took up a lot of space in the bedroom, there was still ample room in which to move about. Their sleeping arrangements could do with an overhaul. Maybe if she traded the king-size bed for two twin-size ones—

Her nerves shifted into higher gear. That would be fair, but it would also increase the intimacy of their sleeping arrangements. She trusted herself to cope with it, but could she trust the man who was now her husband to stay in his own bed and on his own side of the room?

Well, why not? They were adults. Hopefully, two responsible adults. Nothing was going to happen. Having satisfied herself with what seemed a plausible solution, she sighed with exhaustion.

Lord, but it felt good to lie down. At the same time, she realized that she was here in bed, fed, bathed and resting because Ryder Justice had seen to it. She rolled back over on her stomach and burrowed her nose a little deeper into her pillow, savoring the knowledge that someone cared enough about her to make a scene. What she couldn't do was make a big deal out of it. Ryder Justice was simply passing through her life, not becoming a part of it.

Ryder couldn't sleep. The floor was hard. The covers hot. He kicked them back, leaving his body bare to the night, and still the cool flow of air blowing across his arms and legs could not ease the tension coiling within him.

Images kept popping into his mind. Casey alone at her desk. Casey in the other room, alone in that bed. He sat up with a jerk and reached for his jeans. Get out. Get out now before you make a mistake you can't fix.

Ryder didn't hesitate. He didn't need to know whether it was conscience or gut instinct warning him off. All he knew was he had to put some distance between himself and the woman who was his wife.

Grabbing his boots, he exited the apartment, then sat down at the top of the landing to put them on. The air outside felt thick, almost too warm and too stifling to breathe. Perspiration instantly broke the surface of his skin. He stood, then started down the stairs with no goal in mind other than to move.

Security lights dotted the grounds of the vast estate, highlighting the driveways, the doors to the house, and the area just inside the rim of trees circling the lawns. Down on the highway outside the city, he heard an eighteen-wheeler shifting gears as the driver maneuvered around a curve in the road.

Crickets rasped. A night bird called. A stringy cloud floated past the surface of a pale half-moon. Ryder lifted his head, inhaling the scents, absorbing the sounds. Ordinary sounds. But there was nothing ordinary about his situation, and there hadn't been since he'd walked out on his life six months earlier.

For lack of a better destination, he aimed for the trees at the far edge of the estate. It felt good to move, to be doing something besides lying in the dark and wishing for something he couldn't have. He glanced up at the mansion as he passed, trying to imagine what it would be like to grow up in such an austere environment. He'd had wide open spaces and brothers. Horses to ride and endless days of childhood where nothing ever changed and the status quo was your security blanket with which to sleep each night.

Music drifted to him from somewhere out beyond the ring of lights, probably from a passing car. It reminded him of the nights at home when he and Roman and Royal had been kids; of watching his mother and father dancing cheek to cheek out on the front porch while an old portable radio played nearby. He wiped a shaky hand across his face, remembering the night Barbara Justice had died leaving Micah to raise their three young sons alone.

Ryder paused, blindly reaching for the nearest tree as his composure crumpled.

You were the strong one, Daddy. You survived everything...except what I did to you.

Long, silent moments passed while Ryder stood in judgment of himself. Moments in which his heart broke and bled countless times over. And finally, it was the sound of laughter from another passing car that brought him to his senses.

Laughter. Proof that life does go on.

Angry that he was still part of that life, he moved deeper into the trees and away from temptation, unaware that he was being watched from the upper windows of the family home.

When Ryder moved out of sight, Erica stepped away from the window and flopped down on her bed, but the intensity of her conversation with Miles was still going strong. Although it was not necessary, she caught herself whispering into the phone.

"I said, I don't know what he's doing, but he's not sleeping in our dear sister's bed, that's for sure."

New Orleans at midnight was lively. More than once, Miles had given serious thought to never going home. He downed the last of the bourbon in his glass and then waved to a passing waitress for a refill before shifting his cell phone to his other ear.

"Look, sister darling, I already told you. It doesn't matter if he and Casey never get it on. The terms of the will have been met. She got married. She's living under his roof—under his protection. If it lasts a year, she's done her part."

Erica pouted. "It isn't fair."

Miles lifted his glass in a silent toast to a woman across the room before answering. "Who ever said life was fair?"

Erica kicked off her slippers and stretched out on her bed, absently admiring the color of polish on her fingers and toes. Practicing a pout she hadn't used in years, Erica's voice rose an octave.

"I can certainly vouch for the fact that life around here is deadly dull. When are you coming home?"

The woman in the bar lifted her own glass in a long-distance toast to Miles and smiled. His pulse reacted by skipping an anticipatory beat.

"Soon. Maybe tomorrow. The day after for sure."

Erica frowned. "Well, all I can say is you'd better hurry. Grandmother is beginning to waffle. In fact, if I didn't know better, I'd think she was quite smitten with Casey's honkytonk man."

That wasn't something Miles wanted to hear. "You're kidding!"

"No, I'm not. She missed a lunch date with me and has been closemouthed about the reason why. All I know is, she scolded me for a comment I made about the chauffeur and then took herself off to her room."

The woman across the room was smiling openly now. Miles knew an invitation when it was being sent, and listening to his sister whine about an old woman's bad attitude was ruining the moment.

"Look, Sis, I've got to go. When I know my flight, I'll call. Someone will have to pick me up at the airport."

He disconnected in Erica's ear. She tossed her phone aside and picked up the television remote, but there was nothing on the tube that was as interesting as the man who was wandering through their woods. Curiosity won out over caution as she rolled out of bed in search of her shoes. She wouldn't go far. Certainly no farther than the back lawn. Definitely not into the trees. But she was going. She couldn't stand the suspense any longer.

Ryder walked until the darkness lifted from his spirit. When he came to himself enough to stop, he realized he could no longer see the house. In fact, he wasn't even sure which way it was and right now he didn't much care. Out here there were no walls to hold him back. He could run as far and as fast as his legs would take him, just as he'd been doing before he'd walked into that bar down in the flatlands. Casey had changed everything. And he'd let her.

Now his running days were over. Maybe he had no purpose on which to focus, but she certainly did. He'd never seen a woman so driven, so determined to succeed at all costs. He'd given her his word—and the Justice men did not go back on their word.

In the distance, a hound bayed and another answered. He recognized the sounds. They had keyed on a prey. At that moment, in the dark, alone in the woods, he could almost empathize with whatever creature was on the run. He knew what it felt like to be lost with nowhere to go. To run and run and then wind up at a dead end and facing destruction. That's where he'd been going when Casey Ruban walked into his life. In a way, he'd come to look upon her as his anchor, because without her, he had nowhere to go.

He turned back the way he'd come. A short while later he emerged from the woods to find himself within yards of the place at which he'd entered. Instinct and the need to get back to her had led him home.

He started across the lawn when a shadow moved between him and the bush to his right. Instinctively he doubled his fists, preparing to do battle when Erica stepped into the light.

"Sorry," she said. "Did I frighten you?"

He combed a shaky hand through his hair as adrenaline began to subside.

"No."

She giggled nervously and took a step closer, then another,

then another, until she could feel the heat emanating from his body. Her eyes widened as a single bead of sweat pooled at the base of his neck, then spilled over onto the broad surface of his chest. When the sweat split the middle of Ryder's belly, she moved another step closer, tilting her chin until their gazes met. The invitation was in her eyes…in her voice…in the thrust of her breasts beneath pale yellow silk.

"Ummm, I didn't know little sister liked them this rough-cut. Poor Lash. He never stood a chance against a stud like you."

Like a moth drawn to a flame, she reached out, her intentions painfully clear, and found her arm suddenly locked in a painful grip.

Their gazes met. His dark and wary, warning her away; hers wild and frightened by what she perceived as an imminent threat.

"Let me go!" she gasped.

"Then back off," Ryder said, his voice just above a whisper.

She gasped, stung by the outrage of such an obvious refusal of her company, and yanked herself free.

"How dare you?" she said.

"No, sister dear, how dare you?"

Heat suffused her face. "I don't know what you mean," she cried.

His voice lowered, his words wrapping around her conscience, burning deeper and deeper with each angry syllable.

"Like hell. Don't tell me you only came out here to see if your sister's new husband would play hide-and-seek."

A sense of shame she didn't expect kept her momentarily silent. He was right, and she hated him for that and so much more. Unfortunately, Erica had never learned the wisdom of silence.

"I came out here because I thought I saw a prowler."

Ryder raked her with a gaze that left her feeling as if she'd been stripped and branded. If she hadn't been so afraid to turn her back on him, she would have dashed into the house.

"The only thing on the prowl out here is you," he said, and then walked away.

Her fear subsided as the distance between them grew, but

it was obvious to Erica that Ryder wasn't afraid of the dark—or of anything else on this earth.

Erica clenched her fists and thought about screaming—actually thought about tearing her own nightgown, scratching her own face and arms and crying rape just to get the son of a bitch in trouble. But she was too vain to deal with marring her skin and too angry to fake being scared.

"Damn you," she muttered, and spun on one heel before stalking back into the house. "Damn you and that stupid wife of yours all to hell!"

She slammed the door shut behind her, her breasts heaving, her face flushed with a rage she hadn't felt in years, and suddenly found herself standing in a wash of white light.

She shrieked. "Tilly! My God! You scared me to death! What do you mean by sneaking around down here in the middle of the night?"

Tilly loomed over her like a dark, avenging angel. "Well, now, Miss Erica, I was just about to ask you the same thing."

At a loss for words, Erica pushed past her. She didn't have to explain herself to the help. She was halfway down the hallway when Tilly spoke, and her voice carried all too clearly in the quiet of the house.

"I saw what you did."

Erica stumbled, then picked up the tail of her gown, and started running toward the stairs. When she reached the safety of her room, she turned the lock and then threw herself on the bed and burst into tears. Somehow, she was going to have to find a way to make this right. It wouldn't do to make her baby sister angry. Not now. Not when she controlled the purse strings and everything else that mattered in Erica's world.

Ryder shut the door behind him, then stood in the darkness, listening. Casey was asleep. Even though the bedroom door was closed, he imagined he could hear the soft, even sounds of her breathing. The air-conditioning unit kicked on and the hum quickly drowned out all but the angry thunder of his own heart.

He looked down at himself, at the sweat running down his body, at the grass stains on the legs of his jeans, and took off his boots. He dropped his jeans by the bedroom door and kept on walking. Careful not to wake Casey, he closed the door to the bathroom before turning on the light.

Completely nude, he stepped beneath the showerhead before turning on the water, uncaring that the first surge came out fast and cold. He reached for the soap and began to scrub himself clean. This time when he was through, he knew he'd be able to sleep. His mind was as weary as his body.

He wrapped another towel around his waist before turning off the light, then opened the door, standing for a moment and letting his eyes adjust to the shadows. When he could see without stumbling, he started across the room.

Later, he would tell himself if he hadn't looked down...if he hadn't seen all that long dark hair strewn across her pillow and thought about what it would feel like to sleep wrapped up in its length, he might have made it out of the room.

But, he had looked, and the thought had crossed his mind, and now he stood without moving at the foot of her bed, studying the face of the woman to whom he'd given his name.

She slept on her back with one arm flung over her head and the other resting on her belly. His first impression of her hadn't changed. She was truly a beautiful woman. But he'd learned since that first meeting in Sonny's Bar that the essence of Casey Ruban Justice did not lie in the strength of her features, but in the strength of the woman who wore them.

There in the quiet intimacy of a bedroom they had yet to share, Ryder realized he might not know the woman who was his wife, but he respected the hell out of what she stood for, and for tonight, that was enough on which to sleep.

He walked out, taking great care not to let the door bang shut behind him. The sleeping bag was right where he'd left it. He dropped his towel and crawled into it as bare as the day he'd been born, then closed his eyes, waiting for sleep to overtake his weary mind.

In the room next door and in the bathroom beyond, water dripped from the showerhead at a slow, methodic rate. And they slept, and finally, morning came back to start a new day.

Erica was playing it cool. In her mind, the incident with Casey's husband had never happened. She strode down the hall with purpose, heading for the kitchen, fully aware that was where Ryder would be eating his meal.

"There you are," she said, as if he'd been in hiding. "Miles called. You need to go to the airport and pick him up."

Tilly set a stack of dishes in the sink and wiped her hands on her apron as Ryder stood up from the table. "Oh, set yourself down and finish your food," she told him. "That boy won't be here any earlier than noon. He doesn't like to get up in the morning, so I dare say he won't be on any of the morning flights."

Erica refused to rise to Tilly's bait. "Here's his flight number and the time of his arrival. Don't be late. Miles doesn't like to be kept waiting."

Ryder slipped the note in his pocket without comment.

Erica pivoted, her duty done, and got all the way to the hallway before she got the guts to turn and ask, "Has anyone seen Casey this morning? I needed to talk to her about something."

"Board of directors meeting this morning. Been gone since seven," Ryder replied.

"Pooh," Erica said. "Business, always business."

"And that business keeps you off the streets, missy," Tilly told her sharply, banging a lid on a pan for good measure.

"And you in the kitchen where you belong," Erica retorted, and walked out, wishing she'd made a more ladylike exit by keeping her mouth shut. It seemed so common to argue with the help. Next time she wouldn't give the old biddy the satisfaction of a response.

"That woman makes my teeth ache," Tilly muttered.

Ryder kept silent, but he knew what she meant. A woman who would willingly seduce her sister's man wasn't the kind of woman who could be ever be trusted. He took a long sip of coffee. Even if the sister wasn't sleeping with the man herself, it was still crossing a line no family member should ever cross.

Tilly topped off Ryder's coffee, then did something she'd promised herself years ago never to do. She meddled in family business.

"You watch out for that woman," Tilly warned.

Ryder glanced up, more than a little surprised.

"I know more than you think I know," she said softly. "I saw what she tried to do the other night."

Ryder's eyes narrowed as he braced himself for a retribution that never came.

"And I heard what you said."

He shifted uncomfortably in his chair and busied himself with adding sugar to coffee he didn't want.

Tilly put her hand on Ryder's shoulder and kept it there until he looked up.

"I have my notions about things," she told him.

"I'll just bet that you do."

Tilly refused to be swayed by the engaging grin he gave her.

"First time I laid eyes on you, I knew you were a good man. After what I saw the other night, I know you're going to be good for my Casey, too."

This time, Ryder was more than uncomfortable.

"Look, what's between Casey and me is strictly business," he said. "She asked for help. I offered. It's as simple as that."

Tilly lifted her chin and turned away, refusing to listen to what he had to say. "You're wrong, you know. Nothing is ever simple between a man and a woman."

Ryder set his cup down with a thump, sloshing the freshly sweetened brew out onto the white-tiled tabletop.

"I better be going," he stated. "The Lincoln needs gas, and I've got to find out where the airport is before noon."

Tilly turned. "You go on and get your gas. You find that airport and do your job and bring Mr. Miles on home. But you just remember this. It doesn't matter how long and how hard you work during the day, come nighttime, you and Casey Dee are going to be all alone."

Ryder reached for his hat. He damn sure didn't need anyone reminding him of that.

"Find yourselves some common ground," Tilly called out as he left the room. "You hear me? You have to start somewhere. Forget the gap and look for the bridge."

He was still thinking about that bridge Tilly had been talking about when he took the highway exit leading to the airport.

A small, twin-engine Cessna lifted off directly in front of his view and he found himself stopping in the middle of the road to watch its ascent.

Even though the plane was a good half mile away and already several hundred feet in the air, his toes curled in his boots and he caught himself holding his breath until the plane leveled off. He lost sight of it when it turned toward the sun.

A car honked behind him, and he slipped his foot off the brake and drove on. But the damage had already been done. The hunger to fly was mixed up in his mind with the fear of repeating a deadly mistake all over again.

Get it in gear, he reminded himself, and began looking for a place to park. He didn't have to fly. He was only here to give a man a ride home. No big deal. But his hands were shaking when he got out of the car, and the closer he got to the terminal, the slower his stride became. It was all he could do to make himself walk inside, but he did it.

Cool air hit him in the face, and he inhaled deeply, welcoming the change in temperature as his nerves began to settle. He paused while he got his bearings, then started toward the arrival gate of the flight on which Miles Dunn would arrive.

His nerves were strung so tight, he caught himself holding his breath. Twice he had to remind himself to ease up. And he should have known this would happen. Just because he wasn't piloting the planes didn't make this experience any easier.

He settled the Stetson firmly upon his head and gave the announcement boards a closer look. Being here brought back too many bad memories. That was all. Just too many memories. And no man ever died from memories.

"Flight 1272 from Atlanta and New Orleans is now arriving at Gate Three."

Buoyed by the announcement, Ryder took his bearings then started walking. Erica had claimed that Miles didn't like to be kept waiting and God knows he didn't have any desire to linger in the place himself.

Miles was hung over. His head throbbed and his belly kept lurching from one side of his rib cage to the other as he filed out of the plane along with the other passengers. Bile rose as he stared at the drooping diaper of the toddler in front of him. An all too pungent odor drifted upward, adding to the nausea he already had. That kid was carrying a load and badly in need of a change. When a sickly sweat broke out on his upper lip, he mumbled an excuse and shoved his way past them, desperately searching the waiting crowd for Erica.

He saw the Stetson first, then the man beneath it and groaned. Damn her, why didn't she come herself?

"Here are my claim stubs," he said shortly, slapping them into Ryder's hand. "I'll meet you in baggage."

Ryder took the stubs without comment and waited beside the men's room until Miles came out.

"I thought I told you I'd meet you in baggage," Miles muttered.

Ryder gave him a pointed look. "Wasn't sure you'd make it that far."

Miles's face turned red.

"Lead the way," Ryder said, and Miles did.

Luggage was just beginning to come through the roundabout as Miles dropped onto a nearby bench.

"Rough flight?" Ryder asked.

Miles looked up from where he was sitting and belched.

Ryder cocked an eyebrow and stifled a grin. "Tell me which ones are yours," he said, pointing toward the varied assortment of circling suitcases.

"Four pieces. Brown-and-green alligator. Can't miss them."

Ryder nodded and a short while later, pulled the last one from the rack. Miles watched with a bleary eye, unwilling to move until he had to.

"That's it," Ryder announced, and lifted a bag in each hand. "I'll get these. You bring the rest," and started toward the exit without looking back.

Miles sat with his mouth agape while blood thundered wildly through every minuscule vein in his head. He stared at the remaining two bags in disbelief. The nerve of the man! Expecting him to carry his own luggage!

Miles staggered to his feet and hefted a bag in each hand before following Ryder's retreat.

"This just figures," he mumbled, as he staggered out of the

door. "You can't get good help these days no matter how hard you try."

When they started home, Miles began to relax, reveling in the cool, quiet ambience of the Lincoln's spacious back seat. But that was before the car phone rang. After that, Miles's homecoming took an unexpected turn.

Chapter 7

The car phone rang as Ryder was leaving the airport and turning onto the highway. He answered on the second ring.

"This is Ryder."

When that slow, deep voice settled in her ear, Casey breathed a sigh of relief.

"Ryder, where are you?"

He frowned. "Casey, is that you?"

She turned away from the noise behind her, trying to block out the paramedics' voices, as well as the police officer on the scene. "Yes, it's me."

"I already picked him up. Just a minute and I'll hand him the phone."

"Picked up who?" she asked.

"Your brother, Miles."

"I don't want to talk to Miles. I want to talk to you."

Ryder's frown deepened as her voice suddenly shattered.

"I have a problem. Can you come help me?"

Before he could answer her, the ambulance that had been parked behind her took off for the hospital with sirens running. Startled by the unexpected noises in the background of their conversation, it began to dawn on him that there was more behind her request for help than the obvious.

"Casey, what's wrong?"

He heard her inhale, and then she spoke, and her voice was so soft he had to strain to hear her answer.

"I had a wreck."

The car swerved beneath him and Miles began to curse from the back seat. Even though it was broad daylight and Ryder was driving down the highway leading into Ruban Crossing, in his mind, he saw light flash across a dark, storm-filled sky, heard the sharp crack of lightning as it struck the fuselage of his plane, and smelled smoke, even though the air inside the car was cool and clean.

His fingers curled around the steering wheel in reflex, and it took him several seconds to realize what he was experiencing was a flashback, and that everything was safe and under control. He took a deep breath and started over, asking what mattered most.

"Are you hurt?"

"No...at least not much."

An odd tension settled inside his belly. Her voice was shaking. If she wasn't hurt, then she'd at least scared herself to death.

"Are you at the hospital?"

He thought he heard a sob in her voice as she answered. "No, I'm still at the scene."

"Easy, honey. Just tell me where you are and how to get there."

She told him, and only afterward realized what he'd called her, but by then it didn't matter. He was already sliding to a stop at the intersection where the accident had occurred, and it would seem from the way the back door was flung open, he'd stopped just in time.

Miles leaned out and threw up on the right rear tire as Ryder jumped out of the front seat. After that, Casey didn't see anything but the look on her husband's face. She took a deep breath and started toward him.

Ryder felt sick. He could see a bump on her forehead that was already turning blue, and there was a small trickle of blood at the edge of her lip.

Wrecks. Damn, damn, damn, but he hated the sight of spilled fuel and crumpled metal. It reminded him of things he'd spent months trying to forget.

"Come here," he said softly, and pulled her close against his chest while he surveyed what was left of her car. The front half had been shifted all the way to the right, compliments of a one-ton truck that had run a red light. "Thank God for air bags," he said, eyeing the one that had inflated inside her car.

Her voice was shaking as she reached up, tentatively testing the size of the bump on her forehead. "It wasn't my fault."

Ryder caught her fingers, then lifted them to his lips in a quiet, easy gesture before cupping her face with his hand.

"It wouldn't matter if it was. What matters is getting you to a doctor. Why didn't they send an ambulance for you?"

"I told them I wanted to wait for you. Besides, I didn't think I needed..."

He missed whatever it was she said next. He kept hearing her say she'd been waiting for him. That did it. Whatever hesitation he'd had about holding her close was gone. He tilted her chin, carefully surveying the burgeoning bruises and angry red scrapes on the tender surface of her skin.

"I don't care what you think. You're going and that's that."

Casey rested her forehead against his chest. How long had it been since she'd had someone upon whom she could lean? When his grip around her firmed, for the first time in as long as she could remember, she felt safe...really safe. As she ran her tongue along the lower edge of her lip, tears began to well in her eyes.

She looked up at him for confirmation. "My lip is bleeding, isn't it?"

He wanted to kiss away the shock and the pain and the stunned expression in her eyes. He thought better of the urge and hugged her instead.

"Easy now. Let's get you in out of this sun. You can wait in the car with Miles while I tell that officer where I'm taking you."

"It's probably okay for me to leave," Casey said. "He already took my statement."

But she did as she was told, grateful for the fact that someone was taking over. It seemed her good sense and practicality was lost somewhere in the wreckage of her car and she couldn't think what to do next.

When she got inside, Miles was ominously silent. Casey glanced over her shoulder, wincing slightly as a strained muscle rejected the motion.

His condition would have been funny if it hadn't been too painful to laugh. He lay stretched out in the back seat with his arm thrown over his eyes, shielding them from the sun. He looked worse than she felt.

"Rough flight?"

He groaned and mumbled something she didn't understand. She turned around and closed her eyes, wishing that the world would stop spinning so she could get off.

Seconds later Ryder slid behind the wheel. He leaned over and fastened Casey's seat belt without giving her a chance to respond, then glanced in the back seat at his other passenger.

"Buckle up."

A brief, quick click broke the silence. It would seem that Ryder had made a believer out of Miles.

The trip to the emergency room was faultless, and it didn't take the doctor long to address Casey's bumps and bruises. They were minor. The injury that would take the longest to heal was to her peace of mind.

"While you're at it, you may as well give this one a going over," Ryder said, pointing at Miles who was slumped in a chair near the emergency room door.

Doctor Hitchcock frowned. "Was he in the accident, too?"

Ryder shook his head. "No. I had just picked him up at the airport when Casey called. He's a little the worse for wear. Guess his stomach's had a longer ride than it could tolerate."

Hitchcock gave Miles a judgmental look. He'd been doctoring the Ruban family for years, and it wasn't the first time he'd seen this one in a condition of his own making.

"Looks to me like he just needs a little of the hair of the dog that bit him."

It was the word *hair* that did it. Miles's stomach was too queasy for anything, including metaphors. He bolted for the bathroom seconds ahead of another surge.

Hitchcock snorted beneath his breath, but his eyes were twinkling as he glanced at Ryder.

"Casey will be ready to go by the time you bring the car around. Meanwhile, I suppose I can give the party animal something to help his nausea."

Casey tried a smile, but her lip was too swollen to do much about it, and her head was beginning to throb. "Thank you, Doctor Joe."

He patted her on the arm. "Don't thank me. Thank the good Lord for sparing you worse injury."

"Amen to that," Ryder said quietly, and went to get the car.

The doctor stared after him, then turned, giving Casey a long, intent look. "So, that's the new husband, is it?"

She sighed. "You heard."

He shook his head. "Lord, honey, who hasn't? Your sudden marriage has set the biggest piece of gossip in motion that Ruban Crossing has ever known. I don't know what Delaney was thinking when he pulled that stunt, but I can guarantee it wasn't these results."

Casey's eyes darkened in frustration. "I know what he wanted. He'd been after me for years to...let's see, how did he put it...marry well."

Hitchcock frowned. He'd known Delaney Ruban all of his life. In fact, they'd grown up together, and while Delaney had acquired more money in his lifetime than a man had a right to expect, he'd been obsessed about overcoming his upbringing as the son of a flatlands sharecropper.

"By that, I suppose you're referring to a socially acceptable marriage, such as to a fellow like Lash Marlow?"

Her shoulders slumped. "I couldn't do it, Doctor Joe. I couldn't marry a man I didn't love."

An odd smile broke the wrinkles in the old doctor's face. He looked toward the cowboy who was pulling that big white car to a stop outside the door.

"So, it must have been love at first sight for you two, then."

Casey looked startled. "Oh no! It was nothing like that. Ryder is a good man...at least I think he is. But we have an understanding. I'm just fulfilling the terms of Delaney's will. Nothing less. Nothing more. In a year, this will all be over."

Unaware that he'd been the topic of their conversation, Ryder came up the hallway, shook the doctor's hand, and all but carried Casey out to the waiting car.

Hitchcock had his own ideas about understandings. *That's what you say now, Casey Dee, but a year is a long, long time.*

As Miles Dunn staggered out of the bathroom with a wet paper towel pressed to his forehead, Hitchcock reminded himself of the vows he'd taken to administer to *all* who were sick or in need of healing and took him by the arm.

"Come with me, boy."

Miles looked out the door toward the car. He could see Casey was already seated inside. "But they're about to—"

"They'll wait," Hitchcock said. "Besides, this will make you feel better."

The doctor had said the magic words. Miles followed without further comment.

"Lord have mercy!"

If Tilly had said it once, she'd said it a dozen times since Ryder's arrival at the Ruban estate. And she was saying it again as Joshua passed through the kitchen on his way upstairs with an ice bag for Miles's head. The soup bubbling on the stove was for Casey. The tears running down her face were those of relief after she'd seen for herself that her girl was all right.

The house phone rang just as Ryder came in the back door.

Startled by the sound, Tilly jumped and the soup she was stirring sloshed over the side of the pot and splattered with a hiss onto the hot cooktop.

"Lord have mercy!" she muttered again.

"I'll get it," Ryder offered, and answered the phone before Tilly burst into a fresh set of tears.

Well aware that the call had to be from someone in the family, Ryder's answer was less than formal.

"This is Ryder, what's up?"

Erica's complaint was left hanging on the edge of her tongue. Somehow she didn't have the guts to say what she'd intended to say, at least not in the same tone of voice.

"Umm...I was wondering if someone was bringing up the ice bag for Miles's poor head."

Miles's poor head be damned, Ryder thought, but kept his opinion to himself. He glanced at Tilly.

"Erica wants to know about some ice bag."

"Tell her it's on the way up."

"It's on the way—"

"I heard her," Erica said. "Thank you."

"No problem," Ryder said, and started to hang up.

"Wait!" Erica shouted.

Ryder waited. It was her call. Her question. Her move.

"Is Casey all right? I mean, Miles said she'd had an accident."

"Come see for yourself," he offered. "She's at the apartment lying down, and I think she'd appreciate her sister's presence."

The thought of being in close proximity with Ryder gave Erica a chill. "Oh, I couldn't possibly leave Miles on his own. Grandmother isn't here and when she comes in, she's going to be beside herself that all of this happened while she was having her hair done."

A quiet anger he'd been trying to stifle suddenly bubbled over. "There's not a damned thing wrong with Miles. He's hung over, not hurt. Casey is the one who could have died today." He slammed the phone sharply onto the cradle and hoped that the disconnect popped in her ear.

Tilly hid her reaction, but she was secretly pleased. It was comforting to see someone else willing to champion her girl, especially a man who wasn't afraid to speak his mind.

Ryder turned, anger still evident in his voice. "Did Casey grow up in the same house with Miles and Erica?"

Tilly nodded.

"Then tell me something—how in blazes did she turn out so right and them so wrong? That pair must have been raised on ice water, not milk."

"They had each other," Tilly said. "After Casey's parents died, she didn't have much of anyone to baby her. Delaney loved her, but his intentions were focused on giving her the skills to run his empire, and truth be told, Mrs. Deathridge played favorites with the twins."

"Casey had you," Ryder said.

Tilly nodded. "Yes, that she did." She handed him a pot

filled with the soup she'd just made. "It's vegetable beef, her favorite."

Ryder accepted the offering. "Thanks. Considering the blow Casey took to her mouth, that's about all she's going to feel like eating."

Tilly let him out the door, then watched as he crossed the courtyard, went up the stairs and into the garage apartment, carrying the hot pot of soup as if it were the crown jewels. When he was safely inside, she stepped back and closed the door. For the first time in weeks, she felt confident that things in this household were about to change for the better.

Not only did Ryder seem to respect Casey, but it looked as if he were willing to become her protector. However, just to be on the safe side, she might concoct a little potion. It wouldn't amount to much. Just a few herbs for good luck that she could sprinkle on their doorstep. Not a real spell.

Reclining in a nest of pillows, Casey winced as she reached for the phone, then had to shift the stack of papers in her lap to allow room for the smaller pillows beneath each of her elbows. Even though the accident had caused her to miss a stockholder's luncheon, it hadn't taken her long to regroup and bring the business to her.

At her request, her secretary had sent files on the most pressing issues and left the others that were pending back at the office. With a bowl of Tilly's soup for sustenance and the knowledge that Ryder was no farther away than the sound of her voice, she set up office in the middle of her bed and began going over the reports in question.

She read until the pain between her eyebrows grew too sharp to ignore and changed her tactics to returning the phone calls that had come to her office during her absence. It wasn't any easier. By late afternoon, it felt as if her lip was swollen to twice its normal size and the left side of her jaw was becoming increasingly sore. The last time she'd gotten up to go to the bathroom, she'd groaned at the sight of her face. The abrasion on her cheek was starting to scab, and by tomorrow, she was going to have one heck of a black eye.

Twice during this time, Ryder had appeared in the doorway.

Once he'd frowned at the stack of work in her lap before disappearing without comment. The second time he'd come, the glare on his face was impossible to ignore, yet he'd still maintained a stoic silence about her behavior.

But the shock of the wreck was beginning to take its toll. Casey was near tears and wishing she could sweep everything off her bed, curl up in a ball beneath the covers and maybe cry herself to sleep. She heard footsteps coming up the outside stairs, then again inside the apartment. It was Ryder. She recognized the rhythm with which he walked.

He entered her bedroom without knocking just as the phone rang near her elbow. Before she could answer, he had it in his hands.

"Ruban Enterprises. No, I'm sorry, she is out for the rest of the day. Call 555-4000 and make an appointment with her secretary."

He tossed the portable phone completely out of her reach.

Casey frowned. "Hey! I wasn't through...."

"Yes, you are. Besides, I brought you a surprise."

Casey sputtered in useless dismay as Ryder swept aside the files on which she'd been working. When he held out his hand, she sighed and took what he offered, using his strength to lever herself to an upright position on the side of the bed, then groaned when her muscles protested.

"Oh! I feel like I've been run over by a truck."

"That's not funny," Ryder said, and scooped her into his arms before she had time to argue. "Besides, if you think you hurt now, just wait until tomorrow."

If it hadn't been so painful, she might have smiled. "Thank you for such inspiring words of wisdom," she said, and slid her arm around his neck for balance as he carried her into the living room.

When he settled her down on the couch, she put her feet up on the footstool and eased herself into a comfortable position.

"Trust me, I know what I'm talking about," he said. "By morning, every muscle you have is going to protest. At any rate, you should have been in bed hours ago."

"I was in bed," Casey argued.

"I meant, alone. Not with a half-ton of papers and that

damned phone. If you'd wanted company, you should have let me know. I would have been glad to oblige.''

When she blushed, Ryder knew he'd gotten his point across.

Refusing to give him the benefit of seeing how much his words had bothered her, she folded her hands in her lap and looked around the room.

"So, where's my surprise?"

He went to the kitchen, returning moments later with a handful of paper towels and a box he'd taken out of the freezer.

"What's this?" Casey asked, as he plopped it in her lap.

"Popsicles. Assorted flavors. Pick which one you want and I'll put the others back for later."

Her delight was only slightly more than her surprise. "Popsicles? You brought me Popsicles?"

"They won't hurt your mouth, I swear. In fact, it's going to feel pretty darn good on that swollen lip." He took the box out of her lap and tore open the top like an impatient child who couldn't wait for permission. "Which one do you want first? The red ones are cherry. The green ones are lime. The orange ones speak for themselves."

"I like grape. Are there any grape ones?"

"Grape it is," Ryder said, as he peeled the paper from a length of frozen purple ice.

Casey wrapped a paper towel around the wooden stick and took a lick, then another, then carefully eased her mouth around the end of the Popsicle and sucked gently. Cold, grape-flavored juice ran over her lips, into her mouth and onto her tongue. She closed her eyes, savoring the uniqueness of a childhood treat she hadn't had in years.

"Ummm, you were right. It tastes wonderful and doesn't hurt a bit."

Ryder caught himself holding his breath and squeezing the box of Popsicles until one broke inside the box under pressure. If someone had ever tried to tell him that women with black eyes and fat lips were sexy, he would have laughed in their face.

Unaware of the war waging inside her husband's conscience, Casey looked up. "Aren't you having any?"

Ryder shuddered then blinked. "I've had more than enough

already,'' he muttered, and when someone knocked on the door, was saved from having to explain. ''I'll get it. Sit still and eat your Popsicle before it melts.''

Surprised by the unexpectedness of company, whoever it might be, Casey lifted a hand to her face. ''I look so terrible.''

Ryder's expression went flat. ''I think your priorities got a little confused. Be glad you're alive to tell the tale.''

The chill in his voice was only less intimidating than the look he was wearing. At that moment, Casey realized how little she really knew about the man who'd given her his name.

The knock sounded again and Ryder turned with the Popsicles still in hand and strode to the door, yanking it open with an abrupt, angry motion.

Outside heat swept inside, causing moisture to condense on the outside of the Popsicle box. Ryder was speechless. It was Eudora and she was clutching at the tail of her skirt with one hand and holding down her freshly done hair with the other as a hot, hasty wind blasted against the wall of the building.

''Are you going to ask me in, or am I to blow away?'' Eudora asked.

He quickly regained his manners and stepped aside. ''Sorry.''

Eudora stepped over the threshold and into the apartment as if it were an everyday occurrence for her to be visiting the servants' quarters, when in actuality, she was quite curious as to the accommodations in which Casey had chosen to live.

The furnishings inside the garage apartment were simple compared to the elegance of the mansion, but to her surprise, the small rooms seemed comfortable...even homey. In fact it reminded her a bit of the first place she and Henry had shared.

Casey waved from where she was sitting. ''Gran! Come in! I'm so glad you...''

Eudora gasped and clutched a hand to her throat as she walked toward Casey in disbelief.

''Oh my! Erica said you'd had an accident, but she led me to believe it wasn't...''

Eudora stopped talking, aware that whatever else she said was going to make Erica out to be thoughtless and uncaring. And while she silently acknowledged that fact from time to time, she wasn't willing to admit it aloud. Tears welled as she reached out to touch the side of Casey's cheek.

"Sweetheart, your face. Your poor little face. I'm so sorry. Is there anything I can do?"

Casey shook her head and then winced at the motion. "I'm fine, Gran. Actually, I look worse than I feel."

"I doubt that," Ryder said, and then extended the box toward Eudora. "What's your pleasure? We have orange, cherry or lime. We're saving the grape ones for Casey. They're her favorite."

Casey tried not to grin, but the shock on her grandmother's face was impossible to miss.

"Excuse me?" Eudora asked, eyeing the box Ryder had thrust beneath her nose.

"Popsicles. Want one?"

Casey held hers up to demonstrate, then realized it was melting and stuck it back in her mouth and sucked, rescuing the juice that would have dripped into the paper around the stick.

"Well, I don't think..."

Ryder dangled it under her nose. "Oh, come on, Dora. Have one."

When she almost grinned, Ryder knew she was hooked. "You're real fond of cherry limeade, so I'll bet you'd like a cherry one, wouldn't you?"

Without waiting for her to answer, he took one out of the box, unwrapped it as he'd done for Casey, and handed it to her with a paper towel around the stick to catch the drips.

"If anyone wants seconds, they'll be in the freezer."

Eudora stared at the icy treat he'd thrust in her hands and then straightened her shoulders, as if bracing herself for the worst. But when she lifted it to her mouth, the taste brought back sweet memories that made her heart ache. By the time she'd regained her sense of self, Ryder had made himself scarce.

"Well, now," Eudora said, and leaned back against the sofa cushions. "He's something, isn't he?"

There wasn't much she could add to what Gran had already said. "Yes, I suppose that he is."

"The question then remains, what are you going to do with

him for the next twelve months? Somehow, I can't see him playing chauffeur forever.''

Eudora ran the Popsicle in her mouth like a straw and sucked up what was melting with a delicate slurp while Casey thought about what Gran had said. What *was* Ryder going to do for the next twelve months? Even more important, what did she want him to do?

The clock on the bedside table stared back at Casey with an unblinking response. No matter how many times she looked, it seemed that time was standing still. It was midnight, and she'd been in bed for over two hours and had yet to relax enough to sleep. But it wasn't because she wasn't tired. She was. In fact, so tired that her bones ached.

She couldn't rest because every time she closed her eyes she kept seeing that truck coming out of nowhere—feeling the jarring impact of metal against metal—hearing her own scream cut off by the air bag that inflated in her face.

She rolled over on her side, then out of frustration, kept scooting until she was out of bed. If she could just get her mind into another channel, maybe she would be able to relax.

The bedroom door was slightly ajar, and she eased into the narrow opening like a shadow moving through space. Her body felt like one giant bruise, and every step she took was a lesson in endurance. As she started toward the kitchen, the room was suddenly bathed in light. She stifled a sigh. I should have known, she thought.

''What's wrong?''

She turned and then stammered on the apology she'd been about to make. Legs. He had the longest, strongest looking legs she'd ever seen on a man, and they were moving toward her. Casey made herself focus on his face.

''Uh...I couldn't sleep.''

His touch was gentle on her forehead as he felt for a rising temperature.

''You don't have a fever,'' he said, and cupped her face, peering intently into her eyes and checking for dilated pupils or anything else that would alert him to complications from her head injury.

But that could change at any minute, Casey told herself, and took a step back.

"I thought I'd get a drink of water," she said.

"I'll get it for you." He moved past her and into the small kitchen, sucking up the space and what was left of Casey's breath.

Moments later, he thrust a glass into her hands. Ice clinked against the sides as she lifted it to her lips and drank.

"Better?" he asked, as she handed it back.

She nodded and turned away. Ryder set the glass down and followed her awkward movements through the room with a thoughtful gaze. This was about more than a restless night. The tension in her posture and on her face was impossible to miss.

"You're afraid, aren't you?"

Startled by his perception, Casey turned and then couldn't hold the intensity of his gaze.

"It's okay," Ryder said. "Anyone would feel the same."

"How do you know so much about what I feel?" she asked.

"Let's just say, I've been there."

"You mean you've been in a—"

He interrupted, and Casey got the impression that it was because he didn't want to talk about it.

"Want me to sit with you for a while?" When she hesitated, he felt obligated to add, "No strings attached. Just one friend to another, okay?"

Her legs ached, her head was throbbing, and her eyelids were burning from lack of sleep. Maybe some company *would* help her to relax.

"Are you sure you don't mind?" she asked.

His eyes darkened and his mouth quirked, just enough to make her wonder what he was really thinking.

"No, ma'am, I don't mind a bit."

"Then, yes, I would like some company. But just for a while, okay?"

He nodded. "Okay." He followed her into the bedroom, leaving the door wide open between the two rooms.

A muscle pulled at the side of her neck and she winced as she started to crawl into bed.

"Easy," he said, as he helped her slide into a more comfortable position. "Want me to rub something on those stiff muscles? It might help you relax."

"Yes, please," Casey answered.

He disappeared into the bathroom and came out moments later with a tube of ointment. Casey's eyes widened as the bed gave beneath his weight and she rolled over on her side, her heart racing as she bared her shoulder at his request.

She was stiff and nervous and he felt her resistance to his touch as if he'd invaded her space.

"Easy…just take it easy," he coaxed, and laid his palm on the curve of her arm.

Casey flinched, and then when he began to move, she closed her eyes and let herself go. Gentle. His touch was so gentle. The ointment was a lubricant between his skin and hers, smoothing the way for the pressure of his fingers as he began to knead at the offending muscle.

"Oooh, that feels good," she said with a sigh, settling into the rhythm of his touch.

Ryder clinched his jaw and tried not to think of what else could be good between them.

The room became quiet and there was nothing to hear but the slide of skin against skin and the uneven breathing of strangers who just happened to be husband and wife. Several minutes passed and Casey had been lulled into letting down her guard when Ryder spoke.

"Casey."

Her pulse jerked, a little startled by the sound of his voice. "What?"

His fingers curled around her shoulder, his thumb resting at the base of her neck beneath her hair.

"I'm very glad you're okay."

Breath caught at the back of her throat and she squeezed her eyes shut as tears suddenly seeped out from beneath her lashes.

"Thank you, Ryder. So am I."

"Does your shoulder feel better?"

Her voice was just above a whisper. "Yes."

She heard him putting the lid back on the tube of ointment and felt the bed giving beneath the movement of his body. And then she thought of the loneliness of the night and the fear that kept coming when she closed her eyes, and asked the unforgivable.

"Ryder?"

Half on and half off of the bed, he paused. "What?"

"Would you mind—" She never finished the question.

"Would I mind what?" he finally asked.

"Would you mind staying with me? Just until I fall asleep?"

She couldn't see it, but a small smile tilted the corner of his mouth as he turned to her in the dark.

"No, honey, I wouldn't mind at all."

Casey held her breath as the mattress yielded to the greater pressure of his body.

"Easy does it," he whispered, and lightly rubbed her arm to let her know that he was there.

She closed her eyes and so did he, but not for the same reason. Ryder didn't want to think about the slender indentation of her waist so near his hand, or the gentle flare of hip just below it. He didn't want to remember the silky feel of her skin beneath his touch, or the way she sounded when she sighed. She had suffered much this day, and didn't deserve what he was thinking. But as time wore on, he couldn't get past wishing they were lying in bed for something other than rest.

Chapter 8

Sometime during the night it started to rain. It was a slow, heavy downpour that rolled like thick molasses off of the roof above where Casey and Ryder were sleeping, encompassing them within a dark, wet cocoon of sound.

Ryder woke with a start, the dream in which he'd been lost still so fresh in his mind that he came close to believing it was real. He looked down at Casey who lay sleeping with her head upon his chest and her hand splayed across the beat of his heart. Any man would consider himself fortunate to be in Ryder's place. The only problem was, she wasn't as awake and willing as she'd been in his dream.

The air felt close. The room seemed smaller. He ached. He wanted. He couldn't have. He moved, but only enough to brush the thick length of her hair that had fallen across her face. Her eyelashes fluttered against his chest. Her breasts had flattened against his side and she'd thrown her leg across the lower half of his body, pinning him in place. He swallowed a groan and made himself lie still when all he wanted was to be so far inside her warmth that nothing else mattered.

But lying still didn't help his misery, and finally, he slipped out of her arms and rolled out of bed, then stood in the dark looking down at her as she slept.

She trusts you.

Rain hammered against the roof as need hammered through him.

She's been hurt.

Hard. Constant. Insistent.

Justice men do not use women.

He turned and walked out of the room, grabbing his jeans from a chair as he headed for the door. He needed some air.

Some distance. Something else on which to focus besides the thrust of her breast and the juncture of her thighs. He kept telling himself that this overwhelming feeling was nothing more than a result of proximity, that reason would return with daylight and distance, but his heart wasn't listening. He'd spent time with plenty of other women in his life and had been able to separate fact from fiction.

When he opened the door and stepped out on the landing, all he could see was a sheet of black rain falling directly before him. The security light was off. He reached back inside and flipped the light switch, clicking it on then off again. The power was out.

The porch was damp beneath his bare feet, but it felt good to be concentrating on something besides sex. He combed his fingers through his hair and took a deep breath. The lack of electricity explained the sultry temperature inside the apartment, but it didn't excuse the sluggish flow of blood through his veins. That blame lay with the woman who'd interfered in his dream.

A soft mist blowing off the rain drifted into his face. He looked up. The small overhang under which he was standing offered little shelter, yet it was enough for him to get by. Right now, he couldn't have walked back in the apartment and minded his own business if his life depended on it. The dream was too real. She'd been too willing and so soft and he'd been halfway inside her and going for broke when something...call it conscience, call it reality, had yanked him rudely awake. Now he was left with nothing but a sexual hangover, an ache with no way of release. The muscles in his belly knotted and he drew a deep breath.

"Ryder?"

He groaned. She was right behind him.

"What's wrong?" she asked. "Is something wrong?"

"Go back to bed," he said harshly, unwilling to turn around.

A hand crossed the bare surface of his back on its way to his shoulder. He pivoted, and she was right before him.

Humidity draped the fabric of her gown to every plane, angle and curve, delineating a fullness of breasts and a slim, flat belly. Sticking to places on her body it had no business, taunting Ryder by the reminder of what lay beneath.

His fingers curled into fists and he took a deep breath as he reminded himself that she was bruised and battered and didn't deserve this from him. "Are you all right?"

"I just woke up and you were gone and I thought..." Her voice trailed off into nothing as she waited for an explanation that didn't come.

Silence grew and the rain continued to fall.

Casey sensed his uneasiness but did not immediately attribute it to herself. They were still strangers. There was so much they didn't know about each other. This mood he seemed to be in could have come from a number of reasons. And then suddenly the security light on the pole beyond the apartment came on. Although it was instantly diffused by the downpour, it was more than enough by which to see.

Dear God. It was all she could think as she shrank from the wild, hungry need on his face.

The moment she moved, he knew that he'd given himself away. Because he couldn't go forward, he took a reluctant step back and walked out into the rain before one of them made a mistake that couldn't be fixed.

Shocked by his sudden departure, Casey cried out, but it was too late. He was already gone—lost in the downpour, beyond the sound of her voice.

Ryder didn't remember getting down the stairs. It was the rain that brought back his reason and calmed a wild, racing heart. Warm and heavy, it enveloped him—falling on his face, on his chest, down his body.

He began to walk, his bare feet sometimes ankle-deep in the runoff. He walked until a tree appeared in his path, then another, then another, and he realized he'd walked into the forest at the back of the estate. He paused at the edge, aware that he could go no farther in the state he was in, and found himself a place beneath the outspread limbs of an old magnolia.

Rain sounded like bullets as it peppered down on the large, waxy leaves above his head. But the longer he stood, the more the sound reminded him of hail. He drew a deep, shuddering breath and then cursed. It had hailed on them the night of the crash.

He closed his eyes, remembering the dead weight of holding his father's lifeless body in his arms. Someone moaned and as he went to his knees, he knew it was himself that he had heard. Pain shafted through him, leaving him smothered beneath a familiar cover of guilt.

"Ah, God, make this stop," he cried and then buried his face in his hands.

Back at the apartment, Casey stood on the landing, staring out at the night, anxiously watching for Ryder's return. The urge to go after him was strong, yet she stayed her ground, well aware that it was her presence that had driven him away.

Mist dampened her hair and her gown, plastering both to her face and her body and still she waited. Finally, she bowed her head and closed her eyes. "Dear Lord, help me find a way to make this right."

And the rain continued to fall.

Some time later, it stopped as suddenly as it had started—turned off at the tap with nothing but a leak now and then from a low-hanging cloud.

Ryder came up the stairs in a bone-weary daze, weary from lack of sleep and from wrestling with the demons inside himself. His bare feet split the puddle at the top of the landing and he walked inside without care for the fact that he would be dripping every inch of the way to the bath.

When he closed the door behind him, the cool waft of air that encircled his face told him the air-conditioning was back on inside. That was good. He'd had enough of close quarters to last him a lifetime and the night wasn't even over.

He walked quietly, so as not to disturb Casey's slumber in the other room, and was halfway across the floor when her voice stopped him in his tracks.

"I'm sorry," Casey said quietly. "Very, very sorry. I asked too much of you and you were too much the gentleman to tell me so." He heard her shudder on a breath. "I humbly beg your forgiveness."

A puddle was forming where he stood and yet the despair in her voice kept him pinned to the spot.

"There's nothing to forgive."

"Only me. I was selfish…thoughtless. I promise it won't happen again."

Why did that not make him happy? "Just let it go."

"I laid out some fresh towels. The bed is turned back. From this night on, we'll take turns sleeping in the bed."

The thought of her, bruised and aching and waiting up for him to come back from trying to outrun his devils made him angry, more with himself than with her; however, she caught the force of his guilt.

"Like hell. Go to bed and close your eyes. I didn't get mowed down by a truck. I don't have a busted lip or a black eye, and if I hurt, it's of my own making, not yours."

"But this arrangement isn't fair to you."

He almost laughed. "Hell, honey, there hasn't been two minutes of fair in my life in so long I wouldn't know it if it stood up and slapped my face." His voice softened. "Go to bed…please."

It was the please that did it. She stood, moving past him in the dark like a pale ghost. Only after she was safe in bed with the sheets up to her chin did she sense him coming through the room. He paused at the bathroom door.

"If I'm gone when you wake up, call Tilly. She'll bring you some breakfast."

"I'll need a ride to work," she reminded him.

"No, you won't. I think you need another day of rest. Tomorrow is Friday. That will give you a long weekend to recuperate."

She totally ignored the fact that he'd just told her what to do, but at this point, it made no sense to argue with a sensible suggestion. "Where will you be?" Casey asked.

"Checking on your car that was towed. Contacting your insurance company." This time he managed a chuckle. "You know, doing stuff."

"Thank you," she said.

"For what?"

"For doing my *stuff.*"

This time, he really did laugh, and the sound carried Casey off into a deep, dreamless sleep.

Miles fought the covers beneath which he was sleeping as his dreams jumped from one crazy scenario to another. One minute he was flying high above the ground without a plane, flapping his arms like a gut-shot crow and trying to find a safe place to land, and the next moment he was standing in the middle of the intersection where Casey had had her wreck, watching in mute horror as her black sports car and the one-ton truck with which she had collided kept coming at him over and over from different angles. Each time he would escape being crushed between their vehicles, the scene would rewind and replay. On a nearby street corner, his grandmother kept pointing her finger and shouting, "I told you so! I told you so!"

He awoke bathed in sweat, only then aware that it was pouring down rain and the electricity was off. He cursed the bad taste in his mouth and got up with a thump just as the power returned. He could tell because his digital clock started blinking and the security lights outside came on all at once, returning a familiar pale glow to the curtains at his window.

He shoved them aside, looking down through the rain to the lawn below, and knew that the weather tomorrow would be miserable. The air would feel like a sauna and the bar ditches would be filled and overflowing.

"What the hell?"

There, through the rain, he thought he saw movement! He watched, staring harder, trying to focus on the shape. Just as he was about to reach for the phone to call the police, the figure moved within a pale ring of a security light and Miles froze, his hand in midair.

"Him." He stepped forward, all but pressing his nose

against the glass for a better look. There was no mistaking who it was below. It was Ryder, half-dressed and moving at what seemed a desperate pace. He watched until the man disappeared from view before settling back down in his bed, his drink of water forgotten.

Long after it had stopped raining and he was back in bed, he kept wondering what would drive a man out of his bed and into a night like this? Had he and Casey fought? A twinge of guilt pushed at the edge of his conscience. She had gone through some hell of her own today. Tomorrow he'd send her some flowers. Having settled that, he turned over and quickly fell back asleep. It didn't occur to Miles that Casey would ultimately wind up paying for her own flowers, and if it had, he wouldn't have cared. To Miles, it was the thought that would count.

Lash awoke with a curse. Water was dripping from the ceiling and onto his left cheek. He got up to push his bed to a new location and stubbed his toe in the dark. The roof leaked. What else was new? The real problem lay in the fact that he was sleeping on the ground floor and it was still coming in through the ceiling. He didn't even want to think how the upper two stories of Graystone would be suffering tonight. Cursing his wet bed and sore toe, he crawled back between the sheets, turned his damp pillow to the other side, and lay down.

Only sleep wouldn't come. No matter how hard he tried, his mind refused to relax. He thought of the phone call he'd had this afternoon from the police. Just for a moment before they'd completely explained, he'd thought they'd been calling to inform him of Casey's death, and then he realized that because he was the family lawyer, they'd called to tell him where they'd towed her car.

What bothered him most about the incident was the lack of emotion he'd felt at the news. He loved her. At least he thought he had. Wasn't a man supposed to cry at such a loss?

He closed his eyes, trying to imagine Casey dead, picturing the hordes of people that would come to her funeral, of the eulogy he would have delivered expounding her life. He saw her lying in the casket, beautiful even in death, and felt guilt that he was letting himself play so lightly with something as serious as her life.

He rolled over, taking the sheets with him as turned on his side, still haunted by the sight of her face. As he tried to sleep, his thoughts began to unfurl like jumbled up scenes in an unedited movie.

In one scene, she stared at him, cool and patient, and he realized that he was remembering the way she'd looked the day of the reading of the will. He tossed, rolling himself and the covers to the other side of the bed where Casey lay in wait for his arrival. There she stood again, her face a study in shock that slowly turned to a cold, white rage. He remembered that well. It was the way she'd looked when he'd announced the terms of Delaney Ruban's will.

He groaned. He could have talked Delaney out of the foolishness. *Oh God, if only I had.* But it was too late. Lash had presumed too much and he knew it. Who could have known? The Casey he thought he knew would never have gone into the flatlands and come out married to some hitchhiker, to some stranger she found in a bar.

And therein lay part of Lash's dilemma. He'd bet his life and the restoration of his family's honor on a woman who had never existed outside the realm of his imagination. In other words, he'd bet the farm on a woman who didn't exist.

"Casey."

The sound of her name on his lips made him crazy. He rolled onto his back, staring up at the ceiling. If things had gone the way they should have, she would be here, right now, in bed beside him. He closed his eyes and saw her smile, imagined he could feel the touch of her hand on his face, the breath of her laughter against his neck. He reached out, tracing the shape of her body with his fingertips, watching her eyes as they grew heavy with passion. He grew hot, then hard and aching, and when there was no one around to take care of the need, he reached down and dealt with it on his own, calling her name aloud as his body betrayed him.

"More flowers for little sister," Joshua announced, carrying another vase of cut flowers into the library and setting them on a table just out of the sunlight.

Casey smiled, more at the use of her childhood name than for the flowers he carried into the room. She started to get up when he waved her back.

"You stay where you're put," he ordered. "I'll be bringin' those cards to you."

Casey laughed. "You sure are bossy today."

Joshua lifted the card from the flowers and dropped it in her lap.

"No more than usual, I'd say."

He straightened the edge of the blue afghan covering her legs then patted her knee as he'd done so often when she was a child. His dark eyes searched the marks on her face. Her lip was no longer swollen, but the bruises were spreading and the scratches had scabbed over. The sights deepened the frown on his brow. He couldn't have cared for her more if she'd been born of his blood.

"You be needin' anything, you just give me a ring, you hear?"

Casey reached out and caught his hand, pulling it to her cheek.

"Thank you, Joshie...for everything."

He shook his head, embarrassed at emotion he couldn't hide. "Don't need to thank me for doing my job," he muttered, and stalked out of the room as fast as his legs would take him.

Casey glanced at the card, then back at the flowers. These were from Libertine Delacroix and they were pulling double duty: get-well sympathies and congratulations on Casey's recent wedding. She smiled. If Delaney were here he would be eating this up. Libertine was at the top of the county's social echelon. She had a summer home in Ruban Crossing and the family home on the river outside of Jackson.

The doorbell rang at the same time that the telephone pealed. Aware that Joshua couldn't be in two places at once, she picked up the phone.

"Ruban residence."

"Casey? Is that you?"

It was Lash. At that moment, she wished with all her heart that she'd let the darned thing ring.

"Yes, it's me. What can I do for you?"

She heard him clear his throat and could imagine the papers he would be shuffling as he gathered his thoughts. However, he surprised her with a quick retort.

"I heard about your accident and am so very glad that you're all right."

"Thank you."

"Yes, well… I know this may be an inconvenient time, but I was wondering if I might come by. There are some papers you need to sign."

She frowned. The last person she wanted to see was Lash and the last thing she wanted to do was think about her grandfather's death. But if there were more papers to sign regarding Delaney's will, she would have to do both.

"Well, I was just about to—"

"It won't take long."

She was honest enough to know that what she'd done by marrying Ryder had probably ended a lifetime of plans Lash must have had. Everyone knew that Lash's father had gone through the Marlow money as if it had been water and that his mother had run off with a trucker soon afterward. Everyone also knew that while Lash was a lawyer of the courts, his only ambitions leaned toward the restoration of his family name and the family home. And, if she'd married him as Delaney had planned, it could have happened. He would have had unlimited money at his disposal.

She shuddered. It was a wonder he didn't hate her guts. She thought of the wedding gift he'd sent that was still in her desk drawer at the office. In spite of his own disappointment, Lash had found it within himself to do the right thing and wish her well. She sighed. Guilty conscience won out.

"I suppose so," she said. "If it won't take long."

"Certainly not, my dear. I can promise that what I need won't take long at all."

"Then I'll be waiting."

She hung up the phone as Ryder walked in the room carrying a bright yellow, happy face balloon. The frown on her face disappeared.

"Oh, how sweet! Who sent me the balloon? I haven't had a balloon since I was little."

He leaned over and kissed the top of her head, then handed it to her.

"It's kind of pitiful compared to all these elegant flowers, but it seemed like a good idea at the time."

Although the kiss was as harmless as if it had come from a child, Casey felt her face flush. After last night, the word *harmless* did not mesh with the man who'd walked out of the apartment and into the rain.

"Is this from you?"

He stood at the end of the couch, absorbing the aftermath of yesterday's wreck on her face. Finally, he nodded, and then he grinned and Casey thought she would forever remember the way he looked, smiling down at her with the sunlight coming through the window behind him.

"With no strings attached." Then he laughed aloud when she dangled the one tied to the balloon. "Except the obvious, of course."

Casey grinned and handed him the balloon. "Will you tie it on the back of that chair for me?"

He did as she asked, then gave the balloon a final thump and set it to bobbing as he moved away. The big yellow happy face smiled down at her from across the room. Casey smiled back, then noticed that Ryder was leaving.

"Can't you sit down and talk to me?"

Ryder stopped at the doorway. When he turned, there was an odd, almost childlike hurt on his face.

"You don't need to pretend with me, Casey."

Suddenly, last night was out in the open. All the tension that had sent him out in the rain was back between them and there was nothing to say that would change what had happened.

Angry, she threw off the afghan and stood, unwilling to say this lying down. "The last time I played pretend, I was six years old. I pretended my mother and father weren't dead. When it didn't come true, I never tried again."

Ryder absorbed her anger as well as the passion with which she spoke, letting it flow over and then around him. Just when he thought she was finished, she came at him again. It would seem she wasn't through.

"There are things that need to be said between us. I would think that saying them in the bright light of day would be a hell of a lot smarter than waiting for dark. The world closes in when the sun goes down. Even with the absence of light, I've found it a difficult place in which to hide."

Stunned by the truth in her words, he couldn't find it in himself to walk away.

"So…is this our first fight?" he asked, and was rewarded by the red flush he saw staining her cheeks.

"Can't you be serious?" she muttered.

"Well, yes, ma'am, I can be serious as hell. However, I don't think you're one bit ready for that."

Casey paled. Just when she told herself he was a comfortable man to be around, that stranger came back.

"I thought you'd like to know that carpenters will be arriving tomorrow. I'm adding on a room to the garage apartment. Since we won't be sharing a… I mean we can't… We aren't going to…" She took a deep breath and started over, ignoring the heat on her face and neck. "You won't have to sleep on the floor much longer."

He thought about waking to find her wrapped in his arms. "That's real thoughtful of you, Casey."

"It is only fair."

His voice softened. "And you're always fair, aren't you, girl?"

Before she could answer, Joshua entered the room with Lash Marlow at his heels.

"Mr. Marlow is here. Says he has an appointment."

Willing herself not to flinch at what she perceived as accusation in Lash Marlow's expression, Casey eased herself back to the couch.

"Lash, it's good to see you. Ryder and I were just about to have coffee. Won't you join us?"

Lash pivoted, surprised that he and Casey would not be alone.

"That's all right," Ryder said. "I'll just leave you two alone to—"

"No!" Casey took a deep breath and made herself relax

when she really wanted to scream. "There's no need," she said, softening her words with a smile. "It's nothing confidential. Only some papers to sign."

"She's right. Please don't leave on my account," Lash said and then smiled, and the sight made Casey shudder. It was the least happy expression she'd ever seen on anyone's face.

"Besides, I believe there should be no secrets between a man and his wife," he added.

Casey couldn't look Ryder in the face, and Ryder refused to sit down. Even after Joshua returned with the tray of coffee and Ryder had accepted his cup, the words kept ringing in his ears. *No secrets. No secrets.* Hell, there hadn't been more than ten minutes of honesty between them since he'd said "I do."

She thought he was a footloose drifter who'd wasted his life on the road. He didn't have it in him to tell her the truth because he was still trying to come to terms with some truths of his own.

There was a little matter of being responsible for his father's death and still finding the courage to live with it.

Every breath Ryder took was a reminder to him that Micah could no longer do the same. Every sunset he saw, every morning that came, came with the knowledge that, for his father, those simple pleasures had ceased. He carried his guilt with the ease of a man who's lived long with the shroud. Close to his heart. Selfish with the pain that shoved at him day after day.

Casey handed back the last of the papers. Lash took them from her, letting his fingertips accidentally brush the palm of her hand.

When she flinched, he had an urge to lean over and slap her face. How dare she have judged him and found him lacking? His family could trace their lineage back to the *Mayflower*.

Then he glanced at Ryder, careful to hide his thoughts. He would bet a lot—if he had it to bet—that this one didn't have two nickels to call his own. *At least I have my education— and several generations of a fine and noble name.* In Lash's opinion, Ryder Justice was nothing more than a stray, an alley cat of a man who'd been in the right place at the right time. That's what he was. That and nothing more.

Lash slid the papers into his briefcase and stood. "I'd better be going—let you get some rest and let your husband get on with his work."

The sarcasm was there. It wasn't obvious, but that wasn't Lash Marlow's way. Casey chose to ignore the dig, and then she remembered the gift that he'd sent.

"Lash. I haven't had time to send a card, but I want to thank you in person for the lovely wedding gift you had sent to the office. It's stunning, truly stunning."

Lash turned, and there was an odd, satisfied smile on his face. "It's an heirloom, you know. It belonged to my grandfather, Aaron Marlow."

Casey looked startled. She'd had no idea. "Why, Lash, that's generous of you, but you really shouldn't have."

His gaze turned flat, almost expressionless. "Oh, it was nothing," he said. "After all, if things had been different, it would have been yours anyway. I thought you should have something to remember me by." He ventured a look at Ryder who had remained silent throughout their entire conversation. "I don't want you to think I'm treading on your territory," he said. "It's just that Casey and I have known each other for years."

Ryder set down his cup and then glanced at Casey before looking back at Lash. "I'm not worried. Casey is a woman of her word. Besides, I'm not a man who believes in boundaries."

Lash was more than mildly interested in the concept of what Ryder had to say. "So by that are you hinting at the fact that you believe in open marriages?"

Ryder took one step forward, but it was enough to back Lash up two.

"Not only no, but hell, no," Ryder said. "A man and woman stay together out of a commitment, not because there's a fence they can't climb."

Feeling slightly threatened by something he didn't quite understand, Lash started for the door. "At any rate, I hope you both get what you deserve."

Ryder thought about what the lawyer had said long after he was gone. There was something about him that didn't quite mesh.

Chapter 9

A month to the day from their wedding, the extra room over the garage was finished, and it was none too soon. There had been far too many times when Casey had seen Ryder's brown, bare body, and Ryder had spent way too many nights alone on a floor when he had a wife who slept alone in their bed. After thirty days of marriage, they were no longer strangers, but the strangeness of their situation was about to make them enemies.

"Just put the bed over here," Casey said, pointing at the wall opposite the sliding glass doors. "And the dresser here, the easy chair there.... No, there I think, nearer the corner lamp. Yes, that's perfect."

A small, birdlike woman wearing a stiff blue uniform and high-top tennis shoes scurried into the room with an armload of Ryder's clothes, bypassing the deliverymen from the furniture store.

Her graying blond hair was pulled up in a ponytail reminiscent of the sixties. Her eyebrows were thick and black with a permanent arch, compliments of a number seven jet eyebrow pencil. The look was topped off with sky blue eyeshadow and frosted pink lipstick. Bea Bonnaducci's appearance hadn't changed since 1961, the year she'd graduated high school. The way Bea had it figured, if it had worked for her then, it should work for her now.

"Where would you be wantin' me to put the mister's things?" she asked.

"Put that stuff in the dresser and hang those in the closet. At last he has plenty of space."

Bea did as Casey directed and then scooted out of the room for a second load, leaving her to deal with the last of the furniture being carried in.

And in the midst of it all, Ryder strode into the bedroom, his nostrils flaring with indignation. He glared at the men who were setting the last pieces of the furniture in place, and when they left, he exploded.

"Damn it to hell, Casey! You waited until Dora sent me on some wild-goose chase and then you set Bea to digging in my stuff. I know you want me out of your hair, but you could have waited for me to get back."

Stunned, Casey stood mute beneath his attack, unable to find a single thing to say that would calm the fire in Ryder's eyes. She watched as he paced from one side of the room to the other. When he stepped inside the brand-new bathroom, he gave it no more than ten seconds of consideration before coming back out again.

"I thought you would be glad to have your own space," she finally said.

He spun, his posture stiff, looking for a fight that just wasn't there. "I didn't say I wasn't," he muttered. "What I said was..." He sighed, then thrust his hand through his hair in a gesture of frustration. "Oh hell, forget what I said." He stomped out of the room as suddenly as he'd appeared.

Casey plopped down on the side of the bed and knew she was going to cry. It wasn't so much the fact that he had yelled at her. It was the disappointment that did her in. He'd done so much for her over the past four weeks. All she had wanted to do was return the favor.

She doubled her fists in her lap, staring intently at a pattern on the carpet and telling herself that if she concentrated enough, the tears wouldn't come. In the midst of memorizing

the number of paisley swirls in a square, a teardrop rolled
down her cheek and into her lap. She drew a shuddering breath
and closed her eyes. It didn't stop the pain or the tears. They
rolled in silent succession.

Ryder walked back into the room carrying the last of his
clothes that were on hangers and jammed them onto the rod.

"I sent Bea back to the house," he said, and then the bottom fell out of his world. Casey was crying, and it was all his
fault.

"Oh, hell, Casey, please don't cry."

"I am not crying," she said, and hiccuped on a sob.

He stood, frozen to the spot by the pain in her voice and
wondered when it had happened. When had she gotten under
his skin? And there was no mistaking the fact that she was
there. Why else did he feel as if he were about to explode?

"I am a total bastard."

It wasn't what she'd expected him to say. She looked up.

He groaned beneath his breath. Those big green eyes, the
ones he'd come to know so well, were swimming in tears.

"I am the lowest form of a heel."

She sniffed and he dug a handkerchief out of his pocket and
laid it in her hands.

"I do not deserve to see another day."

She blew her nose and then handed the handkerchief back.
"Oh, don't be so dramatic," she said. "I suspect you were
just being a man."

He stuffed the handkerchief, snot, tears, and all into his
pocket and tried not to be offended by what she said. "Exactly
what does that mean?"

Casey shrugged. "Tilly says when men don't want to show
their emotions, they either curse or yell. You did both, which
leads me to believe you were severely upset in a way I did
not expect."

He frowned. Damn, but that woman knew way too much
about men for his peace of mind. "At any rate, I am truly
sorry. I'm sorry I yelled. I'm sorry I cursed. I will try not to
let it happen again."

She tried to glare. When angry, he was a force to behold,
but when penitent, there was something about him that made
her want to throw her arms around him and...

Her face turned red as she jumped up from the bed. "Don't make promises you can't keep," she said, and stomped from the room.

Ryder groaned and followed her into the living room. She was fiddling with a stack of magazines. It made him nervous. He had a hunch she wasn't through yanking his chain, and when she spoke, he knew he'd been right.

"Ryder?"

If he was smart, he'd walk out right now before she dug in her heels, but where Casey was concerned, he wasn't smart, he was caught, and had been since that day in the bar down in the flatlands.

"What?"

"I don't understand. Why did you get so angry?"

"I wasn't really…"

"Truth."

He sighed. Damn. Delaney Ruban had done a real good job on her. When she got a notion, she stuck to it with fierce intensity, and it wasn't in him to lie.

"I don't know. I walked in the apartment. Bea was going through my stuff. Too much was changing too fast." His voice lowered and Casey had to concentrate to hear what he said. "I guess I'm uncomfortable with change."

"But nothing has changed," she said.

"No, Casey, you're wrong. We're married." He held up his hand. "And before you tie yourself into a little knot, I know it's not a *real* marriage, but dammit, I was just getting used to, to…things."

He took a deep breath. What he was about to say was going to reveal more than he wanted, but she'd asked for the truth, and truth she was going to get.

"Even if we don't share anything but a name, there is a certain rhythm to our relationship that I was learning to accept." Then he thrust a hand through his hair and lifted his chin. She didn't have to like this, but it had to be said. "Dammit, I guess I wasn't ready to lose what little of you that I had."

Casey knew she was standing on solid ground, but for the life of her she couldn't feel it. Something inside of her kept getting lighter and lighter and she wondered if she was going to pass out...or fly.

"I didn't throw you away, Ryder. I only bought you a bed."

He took the magazines out of her hands and tossed them on the table, then pulled her into his arms. His chin rested at the crown of her head. His arms locked easily across her shoulders, holding her in place.

"I'm sorry I made you cry. I like my room. I promise to like the bed."

Casey closed her eyes and tried not to think of trying it out together just to test it for bounce. "And I'm sorry I keep bulldozing my way through your life."

His fingers itched to take down her hair, lay her across that bed and show her what bulldozing was all about. Instead, he counted to ten, pasted a smile on his face, and kissed the top of her head before letting her go.

"I suppose we should celebrate tonight," he said.

"Celebrate how?"

"You know, a room-warming. Maybe I should take you back to Smoky Joe's for some more barbecue." He grinned. "It's Saturday. That means it's alligator night, remember?"

She rolled her eyes.

"Well, then, maybe we could make it a christen-the-bed party, so to speak."

Casey's voice rose an octave. "Christen the bed?"

"Yeah, I always heard it was bad luck to sleep in a bed without breaking it in."

"Breaking?" She winced. She'd never heard herself squeak before.

"Yeah, come here, honey. I'll show you."

He dragged her across the room before she could argue and all the while she was moving she kept telling herself to do something—say something—anything except follow him across the room! But she didn't. She went where she was led as if she didn't have a brain in her head. When he leaned over the bed and picked up a pillow, adrenaline shot through her body like a bullet out of a gun.

Oh God, oh God, this is happening. It's really happening.
And then the pillow hit her square in the face.

She staggered, tasting fabric and feathers and reeling from shock. "Why on earth did you—?"

He sidestepped her and the question with a grin on his face and swung again. The blow landed on her backside, sending her sprawling facedown on the mattress. She grabbed the other pillow out of reflex, but it was instinct that made her swing and roll at the same time, crowing with delight as it caught Ryder up by the side of his head.

"That's nothing," he warned. "You're no match for me." He began to circle the foot of the bed.

"I'll make you eat those words," Casey cried, and leaped up on the mattress, using it as a bridge to get to the other side and away from Ryder's intent.

She was turning around as he drew back his arm and let fly.

The pillow shot through the air like a padded cannonball and stifled the jeer she'd been about to make. Within seconds, she found herself eating more feathers. But there was an upside to his latest attack. She now had both pillows.

"Aha!" she shouted, waving a pillow in each hand. The glee on his face made her nervous. When he started toward her, she began to retreat.

"Aha? What the hell is *aha?* I've never been hit with an *aha* before. Do they hurt?"

Casey panicked, threw both pillows at once and then ran. "No fair," she screamed.

He caught her in a flying tackle in the middle of the bed, at once mashing her face into the mattress and himself onto her. The weight of him was so great that breathing was almost impossible, and then just when she thought her lungs would burst, she found herself flat on her back and gasping for air. When she could talk and breathe at the same time, she looked up. Ryder was sitting on her legs with his arms above his head in a triumphant gesture.

"I hereby declare this bed has been thoroughly christened."

Casey doubled up her fist and thumped him in the middle of his belly.

"You cheated," she said, and tried to hit him again.

"Easy," he warned, and caught her fist before it could do

any more damage. "Justice men never cheat. We just rearrange the odds."

Casey tried to stay mad, but the grin wouldn't stay off her face. "That's priceless."

"What's priceless?" he asked.

"Rearranging the odds. Delaney Ruban would have loved you."

Ryder's expression stilled. He couldn't quit looking at the woman beneath him. At the joy in her eyes. The smile on her face. Her hand on his leg.

He touched her. First her hair, then her face. And when she bit her lower lip and looked away, he heard himself asking, "What about his granddaughter? How does she feel?"

Casey felt as if all the breath had been knocked from her lungs. She was all too aware of his weight on her legs, his hand on her face, the need in his eyes.

"I..."

"Never mind," he whispered, and braced himself above her with an arm on either side of her face. "I think I'd rather find out for myself."

She knew what the shape of his mouth felt like. They'd kissed before. Once, and just before dawn, in Judge Harris's front parlor on the day of the wedding. She thought she was prepared for what was about to happen. She couldn't have been more wrong. The man she'd kissed before had been a stranger. This time it was different. She'd seen this man wearing nothing but a towel—walked into his embrace on the day of her wreck—slept in his arms—laughed with him—cried with him—fought with him. She closed her eyes and tensed as his breath swept her cheek.

The gentle brush of mouth-to-mouth contact was familiar, even comfortable, and all of that changed when Casey's arms automatically wrapped around his neck. Ryder groaned and then rolled, taking her with him until she was the one on top and he was pinned beneath. She heard him whisper her name. Felt his hands in her hair—down her back—cupping her hips. Urgency sparked between them as their lips met again, then again, and then again.

Her pulse was racing, his body was betraying him. It was all there—from the wild glitter in his eyes, to the need coiling deep in her belly. She lowered her forehead until it was touching the space just above his heart. In spite of the heat between them she started to shake.

Ryder groaned. They'd gone too fast. But, dear Lord, who could have known they would go up in flames? They'd blindsided each other with nothing more than a kiss. He was almost afraid to guess at what might happen if they ever made love.

"Easy, Casey. Easy, honey," he said softly, rubbing his hands up and down her back in a slow, soothing motion. "That just got out of hand. I didn't mean to scare you, okay?"

She rolled off him and got as far as the side of the bed before covering her face with her hands. "Oh, my God. Oh, my God."

Ryder silently cursed himself for starting something they hadn't been ready to finish. But he'd gotten his answer. Delaney Ruban's granddaughter might not love him, but she wasn't immune to him either. There was something there. He just wasn't sure what it was. He rolled over on his side and reached out, touching her back with the palm of his hand.

"Casey, look at me."

When she flinched, he got up with a curse and walked out of the room.

She couldn't think, couldn't move, couldn't speak. All she could do was remember his weight pressing her down and never wanting the connection to stop. Of feeling his mouth cover hers, of mingling breaths and racing hearts and resenting the clothing that separated her skin from his.

The phone rang, and the timing couldn't have been worse. Moments later, Ryder walked back in the room and tossed the portable phone near her leg.

"It's for you."

Casey looked up, but he was already gone. She picked up the phone with shaking hands and cleared her throat.

"Hello?"

"Mrs. Justice, this is Charles Byner, down at the bank. I just need your authorization to clear a check. It's quite a large sum above what's in the account and I need your approval to authorize the draw."

Casey swept a hand through her hair, trying to come to

terms with reality. "I'm sorry," she said, trying to focus. "What did you say?"

"No problem," he said. "I'm really sorry to bother you at home, but Mr. Ruban had specific orders with regards to these particular accounts and since you're now the one in charge, I need authorization from you to clear the check, although it is more than a thousand dollars over the balance."

Casey sat up straight, her mind immediately jumping gears as she realized what he meant.

"Which account? Miles's or Erica's?"

The clerk lowered his voice. "It's the one in Mr. Dunn's name. The check is for twenty-six hundred dollars. That's about eleven hundred dollars above the balance."

Casey stood. "What is the balance, exactly?"

His voice lowered even more. "Let me just pull that up on the screen. Yes…here it is. The balance as of today is exactly $1,400.17."

Casey gritted her teeth. "And was the usual amount of five thousand dollars deposited into that account at the first of this month?"

"Ummm, yes, ma'am, it was."

By now, Casey was livid. Delaney had set a precedent years ago that was about to come to a screeching halt. "Honor the check, Mr. Byner. I'll have enough money transferred into the account to cover it, but I'll be at the bank first thing Monday morning to make some new arrangements."

"Yes, ma'am," the clerk said, and hung up.

Casey disconnected, then immediately rang the bank back through another department and dealt with the transfer in a no-nonsense voice. When she was finished, she headed for the house phone on the kitchen wall.

"Tilly, is Miles at home?"

"He's in the pool," Tilly answered.

"Would you please ask him to meet me in the library? There's something we need to discuss."

She hung up to find Ryder watching her.

"You okay?"

Casey's nerves were just beginning to settle. She hadn't expected it, but knowing that in spite of what had just happened between them, Ryder was still able to ask about her welfare, made her feel safe.

"No," Casey said. "But I will be."

"Need any backup?"

"Are you offering?"

The smile on his face was slight. "Are you asking?"

"It might get ugly," she said.

He dropped the clothes he was carrying onto the back of a chair.

"Honey girl, the last few months of my life haven't been anything but."

Surprised by the revelation, she would have given a lot to continue this conversation. Ryder was closemouthed with regards to anything about his past, and hearing him admit even this much was a definite surprise. But the confrontation with Miles was long overdue, and this latest stunt was, for Casey, the last straw.

"Then come if you want. For better or worse, you are part of this family."

"Unless I think it matters, you won't even know I'm around."

She nodded and started down the stairs, and it wasn't until they'd entered the house and were on their way to the library that she had fully accepted the impact of Ryder's presence in her life. The problems within her world were no longer just hers. They were theirs.

She entered the room wearing an expression the board members of Ruban Enterprises would have recognized. It was her no-holds-barred-don't-mess-with-me look. Ryder had disappeared somewhere between the library and the hall, yet she sensed he wouldn't be far away. Unlike Miles, he wasn't the kind of man who went back on his word.

And Miles wasn't far behind. She could hear the splat of bare feet on marble flooring as he made his way in from the pool. The careless smile on his face was no more than she expected as he sauntered into the library with a beach towel draped across his neck and water dripping onto the floor.

"I'm here. What's up?" he asked.

Casey schooled herself to a calm she didn't feel. "I just had a call from the bank."

If she hadn't known him so well, she might have missed the nervous flicker in his eyes.

He strolled over to the bar and poured himself a drink, even taking a sip before asking, "And what does that have to do with me?"

"Everything. It seems you wrote a check you couldn't cover."

He shrugged. "Oh, that. Delaney never used to mind when—"

"Delaney is dead, remember?"

Miles blinked. It was his only reaction to the cold, even tone of his half sister's voice.

"And in the grand scheme of things, exactly what does that mean?" he drawled.

"It means your glory days are over, Miles. I don't know what the hell you're doing with your money. I don't even want to know. What I will tell you is that your world is slightly out of sync, and as your loving sister, I intend to do all that I can to bring it back in order."

He set the glass down with a thump. "What are you getting at?"

"It's more a case of what are you trying to pull? Any unemployed, thirty-year-old man should not be spending in excess of five thousand dollars a month. Therefore, I am going to do you a favor. As of Monday, you will report to Princeton Hamilton in the legal department of Ruban Enterprises. You have a law degree. You're going to put it to work."

Miles froze. An angry flush began to spread from his neck, upward. "You bitch! You can't run my life."

Casey shrugged. "You're right. But I'm running Ruban Enterprises, aren't I? I covered this hot check, but I won't do it again. Also, there will be no more instant deposits into your account, because as of the end of this month, it will be closed. No more free rides, Miles."

Miles was so angry he couldn't form a complete sentence. His hands were shaking as he yanked the towel from around his neck and started toward her.

The urge to run was overwhelming, but Casey stood her ground as he shoved his way into her space and thrust a finger up against her nose.

"Don't let your power go to your head, sister dear. Someone might just have to knock you off that pedestal for your own damned good."

The anger on Miles's face was impossible to ignore and the knowledge that their relationship had come to this made her sick to her stomach. It hurt to know she was still the outcast when it came to family love. She reached out to him.

"I'm not trying to play God, Miles. You're my brother. I care for you very much, but don't you see? You're wasting the best years of your life."

He slapped her hand away and then grabbed her by the arm, yanking her sharply until she came close to crying aloud.

"You're going to be sorry for this," he said softly. "You're going to be very, very sorry."

He turned and walked out of the room, leaving Casey reeling from the venom in his voice. But his triumphant exit ended four steps outside the library door. Ryder had him by the arm and shoved up against the wall before he had time to call out for help. Miles had seen plenty of angry men in his life, but he'd never been afraid until now.

Ryder slammed his hand in the middle of Miles's chest, pinning him in place. "You son of a bitch. If I ever hear you talk to your sister again like that, you'll wish you'd never been born."

"It's none of your business," Miles said, and felt shame that his voice was shaking.

"That's where you're wrong. Whether any of you like it or not, she's my wife. What happens to her *is* my business. And I'm telling you now, so you'll be forewarned, if anything *ever* happens to Casey, I'm coming after you first."

So great was his fear that if Ryder hadn't been holding him up, Miles would have been on the floor.

"What the hell do you mean by that?"

"Exactly what I said," Ryder replied softly. "You better hope to God she doesn't have any enemies, because from this day forward, I hold you responsible for her welfare."

Miles's eyes bulged. "I would never wish Casey any real harm. I was just mad, that's all. Hell's fire, man, she's my sister."

"Then start acting like her brother."

Miles went limp as all the anger slid out of his heart. Truth hurt. "Let me go."

Ryder didn't move—didn't speak—and didn't turn him loose.

Miles saw himself mirrored in Ryder's eyes and didn't like what he saw.

"I didn't mean what I said to her. And I suppose in a way she's right."

Ryder turned him loose, but refused to move back. "Remember what I said. She hurts—you bleed."

Miles took off down the hall as if the devil were at his heels. By the time he got back to the pool, he'd convinced himself that putting his education to work was not only going to happen, but that it could have its benefits.

Ryder watched Miles until he was out of the house, and then stepped inside the library. Casey was at the window, staring out onto the lawn overlooking the back of the estate.

"Casey?"

She spun, and Ryder wished he'd given in to the urge and punched Miles right in the face before they'd had their little talk. She looked so hurt. So lost. So alone.

"I heard some of what you said to Miles."

Ryder could tell there was something serious on her mind. He waited for her to continue.

"I don't know how I got so lucky, but I am forever grateful for your presence in my life."

He wanted to hold her. He settled for a brief smile instead. "Oh, I don't know about that," he drawled. "I'd come near saying that I'm the lucky one. Besides, we Justice men don't take kindly to anyone messing with our women."

Casey swallowed a sigh. If only she was his woman in the ways that counted. "So, are you telling me that there's more than one of you that's been turned loose on the world out there?"

The smile slid off his face and she knew she'd said the wrong thing. "I'm not who matters," he said shortly. "I don't think Miles will give you any more trouble, but if he does, you know where I'll be."

He walked out and she had the strangest sensation that he'd just walked out of her life, rather than out of the room. In fact, the thought was so strong that she actually followed him through the house, then stood in the doorway and watched until he entered their apartment.

What did I say? What was it that turned him off and sent him running?

But there were no answers for Casey, at least not today.

However, when the mailman drove away from the Justice ranch outside of Dallas, he gave Royal Justice a clue to solving a mystery that had been worrying him and his brother, Roman, for months.

"Daddy, Daddy, I bwought you da mail."

Ignoring the trail of letters and papers she was stringing as she ran, Royal Justice swung his three-year-old daughter, Madeline, up in his arms and kissed her soundly.

"You sure did, honey. You're getting to be such a big girl."

"Gwinny helped," Maddie said, pointing at the baby-sitter who was coming behind at a fast clip, picking up the pieces that Maddie had lost.

"Good for Gwinny," Royal said. Gwinneth Anderson grinned, handed Royal Justice the rest of his mail, and took Maddie by the hand. "Come on, Scooter, it's time to feed the pups."

Maddie bolted, leaving Royal with a handful of letters and a smile on his face. He dropped into the nearest chair and began going through the mail with a practiced eye, discarding the junk and setting aside the bills to be paid. Every now and then one would be addressed to his brother, Ryder, and that one was tossed into a box with an accumulating stack that threatened to overflow. It was all he knew to do. It was Roman who'd saved Ryder's business from ruin.

Roman had taken over the charter service without batting an eye, claiming he could run his private investigation service and Ryder's charter business in the same location. He hired two pilots, an accountant, and then dug in for the long haul, convinced that Ryder would be back when he was ready.

Privately, Royal was a lot less optimistic, but that was just the difference in their personalities, not a lesser belief in the brother who was missing. He loved Ryder as much as Roman did and worried daily about his whereabouts, sometimes even wondering if he was still alive. It had been so long and they hadn't had a word.

He was down to the next-to-the-last letter in the lot, and he started to toss it in Ryder's box when he looked at the return address. MasterCard. No big deal. Everyone has credit cards.

And then he realized what he was looking at and took a deep breath as he tore into the flap. When he pulled out the itemized bill, he started to shake. Someone had used Ryder's card! Over the period of three weeks, someone had charged several hundred dollars' worth of men's clothing in Ryder's name.

Royal was as scared as he'd ever been in his life. Either Ryder was alive and well and buying up a storm, or someone was using his card. The implications of how anyone might come by Ryder's belongings was more than he could handle alone. He bolted up from the chair and headed for the phone. Moments later, a familiar voice growled in his ear.

"This is Justice Air and The Justice Way. State your business and we'll get back to you as soon as possible."

Royal groaned. That damned answering machine. When it beeped, he started talking.

"Roman, this is Royal. I just got a letter from—"

"It's me," Roman said.

"Well, hell," Royal said. "Why didn't you pick up the first time?"

"Wasn't in the mood to chitchat," he said shortly.

Royal cursed beneath his breath. That was so typically Roman. "The mail just came."

Roman snorted indelicately. "Don't tell me. You just won the Publisher's Clearing House Sweepstakes."

"Oh, shut the hell up," Royal muttered. "I'm serious."

"And I'm busy," Roman said. "Unless my favorite niece has done something utterly charming that I need to know about, I don't have time to—"

"Someone charged nearly a thousand dollars on Ryder's MasterCard. The bill came today."

Sarcasm was noticeably missing as Roman snapped, "Give me the dates. The store codes, anything that—no, wait! I've got a better idea. Fax me a copy of the bill."

"Oh, hell," Royal said. "You know I'm not good at making that damned thing work."

"Then get Maddie to help. She knows how," Roman said. "And do it now. If Ryder's alive, I'll find out soon enough. If someone is using his ID, they're going to wish they'd never been born."

"It's on its way," Royal said, and hung up the phone.

He turned, staring at the fax machine on the desk near the window, facing the fact that while he knew just about everything there was to know about ranching, the age of computers had him hanging in air. It was humiliating to know that a three-year-old could do what he had yet to accomplish, but this concerned Ryder, and it was no time to get macho about a damned old machine.

He headed for the back door at a fast clip. "Hey, Maddie," he yelled. "Come help me fax something to Uncle Roman."

Chapter 10

By Labor Day, Miles had become Eudora's fair-haired boy. Somehow, the fact that he was gainfully employed had become his idea and Casey's ultimatum had never happened. She couldn't have cared less who took the credit. His streak of ambition had even rubbed off on Erica. She kept making noises about pursuing a career of her own and spent hours each day pouring over *Fortune 500* magazines in search of ideas.

At night when it was time to go to bed, Ryder no longer wandered in and out of the bedroom in various stages of undress. Casey had her bathroom all to herself and began to realize why Ryder had become so upset when she'd moved him out of her life. The routine they'd been in had become normal, even comforting, and it was over. Because of the new bedroom, whatever connection they'd made between themselves was gone. In an odd sort of way, it was like being divorced.

But the awareness between them kept growing. It was there in the way Ryder watched her when he thought she wasn't looking—and the way his hand lingered on her arm long after the need for keeping her balance had come and gone—even the brief, sibling-like kisses they left on each other's cheek before saying good-night. They were wanna-be lovers, playing at being friends. And always, in the back of their minds, was the knowledge that the marriage they shared was a farce and the lie they were living was the very wedge that kept them apart.

It was just past noon when Casey turned off the highway and accelerated up the driveway into the Ruban estate, gunning the engine of her new car and taking the curve in a near skid. She pulled up to the garage and stopped just as Ryder slid out from beneath the Lincoln. His black hair was windblown and the grin on his face was too devil-may-care to ignore. His jeans were oil-slicked, his chest brown and bare. He was wiping his hands on a rag as he headed her way.

"Where's the fire?"

She wanted to throw her arms around his neck and beg him to crawl back under that car and take her with him, but she couldn't. At least, not today.

She bolted for the stairs. "I know, I was driving a little too fast, but I'm in a hurry." She hiked up her skirt and began to run up the steps, two at a time.

"Take off those damned high heels if you're going to run like that," Ryder yelled. When she didn't oblige, he threw down the grease rag. "Hardheaded woman," he muttered, and followed her inside.

She was in the bedroom. A suitcase was open and she was yanking clothes from a hanger and tossing them on the bed with abandon. Anxiety seized him. She was packing to travel.

"What's the rush?"

"I've got to be in Chicago by morning. I have less than an hour and a half to get packed and get to the airport." She turned in a helpless circle, then dived back into the bottom of her closet, muttering as shoes came flying out behind her. "I can't find my black heels."

Ryder bent down and picked up a pair from the pile in the floor. "Like these?"

She straightened. A smile creased her face as she yanked them from his hands. "Yes! You're a magician. Thanks a bunch."

His belly was starting to turn. He kept telling himself it was going to be okay, that the only reason this was bothering him was because the news was so sudden.

"So, what's in Chicago?"

"Digidyne Industries. We've been after them for years. Once before, Delaney had the deal all but done and they backed out. I just got a call that the CEO had a heart attack and died. The heirs are going to put it on the auction block and I want first dibs."

Ryder started to pace, sidestepping her trips from the closet and back as she packed what she needed to wear. "So, it's a big deal, huh?"

"Very! I'm lucky that Delaney's old contact even thought to make the call and let me know. Otherwise, we would have been out in the cold."

"Yeah, that was lucky all right." He sat down on the edge of the bed, staring at the toes of his boots.

Casey glanced up. "You need to hurry and clean up. We're going to have to drive like mad to make my plane." Then she grinned. "However, that should pose no problem for you." It was a joke within the household that the family chauffeur drove, as Eudora had put it, "Like a bat coming out of hell with its wings on fire."

"Yeah, no problem," Ryder said, and walked out.

A few minutes later, Casey burst into his room, her face flushed with energy, her eyes alight with excitement. "I'm ready."

Ryder walked out of the bathroom, buttoning a clean shirt. He didn't stop to analyze the wisdom of what he was about to do, he just knew that if he let her get on that damned plane without a piece of his heart, he wouldn't make it until she got back.

Casey went willingly as he took her in his arms and crushed her against his chest in a smothering embrace.

"Just be careful, okay?"

She laughed. "Tell that to the pilot. I'm afraid it's out of my hands."

He groaned and threaded his fingers through her hair, crushing the curls and dragging her closer. "Don't make light of fate, Casey Dee. Sometimes when you're not looking, it'll kick you right in the teeth.''

The first thought in Casey's mind was that he wasn't kidding. Even more, he seemed panicked about the upcoming flight.

"I'll be fine," she said. "This happens to me all the time. Year before last, Delaney and I logged over seven thousand miles in the air. Of course we were in Europe three times, but that was an unusual year."

God, keep her safe, Ryder thought, then he lowered his mouth and drew her close. Casey closed her eyes, yielding, bending to his will and embrace, swept away by the unexpected demands of a kiss that left her breathless and more than a little bit stunned.

When he whispered against her cheek, she opened her eyes. His panic had become contagious.

"I want you back in one piece."

She shivered. She'd never seen him like this. It was almost as if he were in some kind of pain.

"I'll certainly do my best," she said, trying to lighten the moment. She grabbed at the undone buttons on his shirt and started buttoning them up. "I'm sorry to repeat myself, but we've got to hurry."

He tucked in his shirt and picked up her bags. His heart was pounding.

"Go get in the car," he grumbled. "I'll make sure you catch that damned plane. But when you get back, we need to talk."

Casey looked startled. An ultimatum?

She got in the car, watching as he dumped her bags in the trunk and then slid behind the wheel. Something was wrong, terribly wrong. If only they had time to talk now. She looked at her watch. They would be lucky if they made the plane, never mind finishing a conversation.

He only glanced at her once. "Buckle up."

She'd ridden with him too many times before to doubt the necessity of doing as he'd asked. She did as she was told.

Casey was the last passenger to get on. She stood in the boarding area with her ticket in hand, waiting for the attendant to give her a boarding pass. Ryder stood beside her, pale-faced and stoic, yet his eyes never left her face. She reached out and touched his hand, wishing their circumstances were different, wishing she could throw herself in his arms and tell him he meant more to her than she could say.

"I'll call as soon as we land and let you know where I'll be staying."

Ryder nodded, trying to maintain his equilibrium, but he felt sick. The high-pitched whine of the jet's engines vibrated the windows overlooking the runway. In seconds, Casey was going to be up in that sky, and he knew only too well it was a hell of a long way down. He wanted to grab her and shake her until she listened to sense. Ruban Enterprises didn't need another Fortune 500 business. It was already a gargantuan conglomerate of its own accord. Why acquire more?

But he couldn't find a way to say what was in his heart. He couldn't say, I'm afraid I'll lose you like I lost my father. He couldn't say, I'm afraid I'll lose you before we ever make love. He couldn't say, I love you—because that wasn't part of the deal.

And then waiting was no longer an option.

"Take care!" Casey shouted, and started running down the gate toward the plane.

Ryder took several steps forward when the attendant grabbed his arm. "Sorry, sir, this is as far as you can go."

He groaned. God help him, but he'd missed his chance. Just when he'd found a way to say the words without coming apart, she was gone.

He went to the observation deck, watching as the big silver plane started backing out of its slot. His fingers knotted around the rail as it rolled onto the runway. And when liftoff came, sweat was running down the middle of his back and he was praying with every breath. When the plane was no longer in sight, Ryder leaned his forehead against the vast expanse of glass, unaware of the heat against his brow. He closed his eyes, trying to picture her face.

"I love you, Casey." But when all was said and done, he was a case of too little, too late.

* * *

It was almost sundown when Ryder walked into the apartment. His heart sank as a red blinking light winked at him from across the room. He tossed the car keys on the kitchen counter and pressed the button, waiting for the sound of Casey's voice.

"Hi, there. Sorry I missed you. I'm staying at the Ritz Carlton. Here is the number." Ryder jotted it down as she spoke, then settled back to listen to the rest of the message. "The flight was fine, just a little bumpy. I'll be in meetings all day tomorrow, but I'll try to call you tomorrow night. Take care." She paused, and Ryder would have sworn he heard her take a deep breath. "Well...anyway...I'll miss you."

The machine beeped. The message was over. Casey was gone. He played it over once more just to listen to the sound of her voice, and wished to hell that Dora hadn't broken a nail. She'd had a fit the size of Dallas and nothing had satisfied her but to make an emergency run to her manicurist to get it fixed. He'd missed Casey's call because of a broken nail.

The house phone rang. "Now what?" he muttered, and shoved himself out of the chair. Tilly was on the line.

"I'm making pot roast. You come on over here and get yourself some food."

The last thing he wanted was to eat or to talk. Casey hadn't been gone four hours and already there was a hole inside of him that food couldn't fill.

"Thanks, but I think I'll just stick around here for the evening."

"If you change your mind, you know how to get here."

"Yes, ma'am, I do."

He hung up and then headed for the shower. After he cleaned up, maybe he'd watch a little TV, have an early night. After all, he had the whole place to himself. And it was the loneliest feeling he could ever remember.

By morning, it had started to rain. By the next day, and then the next, it alternated between gray skies and drizzle, with a downpour now and then in between. And as if the rain wasn't bad enough, a line of heavy thunderstorms was pushing its way into the state and today was the day that Casey was due to come home.

He sat at the window looking out at the rain, ignoring the fact that today he'd already angered Erica and caused Eudora to have to change her plans.

He didn't give a damn that Erica had a lunch date with a banker to discuss buying a business. He couldn't have cared less whether or not Dora was going to miss her bridge luncheon. Erica knew how to drive and Dora could take a cab.

Erica argued, then whined, then begged. When she realized that nothing was working, she started in with what she considered simple reasoning. If she drove herself, then there was no way she could keep from having to walk in the rain. At this point, Ryder had heard enough.

"Where are you meeting the banker for lunch?" he asked.

She sniffed. "The Tea Room."

"Take an umbrella, and use their valet parking."

Erica knew when she'd been had. She rolled her eyes and flounced out of the library, muttering beneath her breath about hardheaded men who did not know their place.

Eudora patted her hair and straightened her belt. She was certain that the rapport she'd developed with this man would bring him around.

"Ryder, dear, it's Evadine Nelson's turn to play hostess for the bridge club. She lives right at the edge of town, remember? Hers is that big white house with the portico that I so admire."

"Yes, ma'am, I remember the house," Ryder said.

Eudora beamed. "Then you won't mind just dropping me off. It won't take more than half an hour either way. If Delaney hadn't insisted on building this place out in the middle of nowhere, we wouldn't be so isolated."

Ryder shook his head. "Dora, you weren't listening to me. I'm not budging until Casey calls. Dammit, look outside. There's a storm due in within hours. Chances are, her plane will be delayed, or the pilot will wind up trying to outrun it. Either way, I want to know what the hell is going on. I'll call a cab for you, but I'm not playing chauffeur today and that's that."

She rolled her eyes. "You know, things have been upside down ever since Casey brought you into this family. You're supposed to be the chauffeur. Chauffeurs are supposed to do as they're told." She tried to glare.

"So fire me," he said, and kissed her cheek, which brought a smile to her eyes that she just couldn't hide. "Go on with you then," she spluttered. "Go sit and wait for that phone call." She walked away, mumbling beneath her breath. "Land sakes, what will Evadine say? Me coming to her door in a cab, like some commoner."

Ryder followed her out the door. "Dora, you are a fine lady, but you are not the Queen Mother. Taking a cab now and then is good for the soul."

Eudora pivoted, giving him a cool, pointed stare. "I declare," she said, about to give him a piece of her mind, but Ryder didn't wait around to listen.

He ran from the main house all the way across the courtyard, then up the stairs just ahead of a cool gust of wind. Pausing at the landing, he looked up at the sky, judging the dark, angry swirl of clouds overhead. Today was not a good day to fly.

As soon as he entered the apartment, he turned on the television and flipped to a local station he knew would be broadcasting weather bulletins all day. With the phone at his side, he sat down to wait for her call.

A half hour went by. By this time he was pacing the floor. She'd promised to call before she left. She wasn't the kind of person who'd break a promise.

"A line of severe thunderstorms is blanketing the state," the TV announcer stated.

He turned toward the television, picked up the remote and upped the volume.

"Wind velocities have been measured at fifty to sixty miles per hour with gusts up to seventy and eighty. Authorities advise staying off of the roads and avoiding low-lying areas that are prone to flooding."

He glanced toward his bedroom. A sheet of rain splattered itself against the sliding glass doors that led onto the deck. His belly tied itself in a knot and he frowned, trying once again to focus on the weather man's report.

"The line runs from…"

Ryder groaned. On the map, the line of storms was virtually

from the top to bottom of the state and moving eastward at a very fast pace. What was even more disturbing, the front extended across a large portion of the northern states, including Illinois. Maybe that's why he hadn't heard anything. Maybe her flight had been delayed and she was waiting for new information before she called.

No sooner had he thought it than the phone rang right near his hand. He jumped and then grabbed it before it had time to ring again."

"Hello?"

"Ryder! It's me! I'm in a cab on the way to the airport. Traffic is a mess, but I'll make my flight. I should get into Ruban Crossing around three. Can you pick me up?"

"What's the weather like up there?"

"Ummm, it's raining a little, but no big deal."

No big deal. "It's raining like crazy here. Why don't you just take a later flight, or better yet, take the first one out tomorrow?"

She laughed. "Now I know I've been gone too long. You are already making excuses as to why I shouldn't come back."

He got up and walked to the sliding glass doors and then jumped when a stroke of lightning tore across the sky right above his head.

"Did you hear that?" he asked, as the phone cracked in his ear. "A storm front is moving through. Today is not a good day to fly."

There was laughter in her voice. "It will be fine. You know they won't take off if there's any danger. Besides, the pilots usually just fly above the storms and land behind them."

He felt sick. Something inside kept telling him this was wrong—so wrong. "Casey, don't. I know what I'm talking about. Please, for God's sake, don't get on that plane."

The underlying fear in his voice was about to make her nervous. She decided to change the subject. "You didn't even ask me if the deal went through!"

He sighed and shifted the phone to the other ear. "Okay, I'll bite. How did the meetings go?"

She hugged herself, resisting the urge to giggle. She was pretty sure that CEOs did not giggle. "We got it!" she crowed.

"It's a done deal. I swear, Delaney is probably rolling over in his grave as we speak."

"Don't be talking about graves."

She laughed. "Just be at the airport. I can't wait to get home."

Their connection began to break up. "Remember," Casey said. "Flight 209. Three o'clock."

"Dammit, Casey, I don't want you to—"

The line was dead. Ryder hung up with a curse and sat back down, staring at the television as if it were the lifeline between himself and sanity.

Ryder heard someone groan. That's when he looked up at the airport monitor, watching as the On Time notice of Flight 209 from Chicago was changed to Delayed.

His gut hitched itself into a knot. It figured. While it wasn't raining at the moment, the sky was black and the intermittent flashes of cloud-to-ground lightning could be seen for miles. It was an all too familiar scene. One right out of his nightmares.

He stood and walked to the observation point overlooking the runway. A couple of planes were waiting to take off, another was off-loading. Except for the weather, nothing seemed out of sync.

I'm just borrowing trouble.

Fifteen minutes passed, and then Flight 209 was a half hour late and before he knew it, an hour overdue. And, the information on the monitor hadn't changed.

He'd been up and down the terminal a dozen times, walking, trying to pass the time and ease the nervous tension that kept growing within him. Now he was back at the arrival gate, standing at the windows and watching the skies.

Suddenly, the skin crawled on the back of his neck and he turned. Nearby, a child was crying. A teenager was on a cell phone. A weary traveler had given in to exhaustion and was sound asleep, his head lolling, his mouth slack as every now and then a slight snore escaped. The attendant at the check-in desk was on the phone. Nothing out of the ordinary. Nothing to warrant the gut-wrenching instinct he'd had that he was about to be attacked.

He glanced up at the monitor and sighed, then out of curiosity, back at the attendant. But when her expression suddenly froze and he saw her look up in fright, the same sensation came over him again, this time pulling a kink in the knot already present in his belly.

Easy. It doesn't mean a thing.

Down the broad walkway, a small horn honked three times in succession. "Coming through. Coming through."

His focus shifted to the electric cart coming down the terminal. It stopped in front of the attendant's desk as she ran out from behind the counter. When she handed the driver a computer printout, the other man grimaced and wiped a hand across his face. Ryder stared as they scanned the list together. When the driver lifted his head and began to scan the waiting area, Ryder knew. He didn't know how, but he knew.

He started walking—past the crying child, past the teenager on the cell phone, past the sleeping traveler. He came to a halt directly in front of the cart and didn't wait for permission to interrupt.

"What happened?"

Both men looked up at him at once. But it was the glance they shared before one of them spoke that nearly sent Ryder to his knees. He'd been right. Something was worse than wrong.

"I'm sorry, sir? Were you speaking to us?" the driver asked.

Ryder leaned forward and pointed to the readout. "Don't play games."

Before either one of them could answer, an announcement came over the loudspeaker.

"All those waiting for information regarding the arrival of Flight 209 out of Chicago, please go to the VIP lounge in the west wing."

Ryder stared into the eyes of the man behind the wheel and felt the ground coming up to hit him in the face. He leaned forward, steadying himself on the cart.

"Are you all right?" the man asked.

Ryder took a deep breath and lifted his head. "Should I be?"

The man looked away.

Ryder's voice died on a prayer. "Oh, God...no."

"Sir, you need to go to the VIP lounge in—"

"I heard," he said shortly, and walked away, following the small crowd of people who were making their way down the terminal. A few looked nervous, aware that the request was unorthodox. Some merely followed directions—like cattle on their way to a slaughter.

An official from the airline was waiting for them inside the door. And Ryder stood with the crowd, listening to the end of his world and wondering how a man was supposed to live with so damned much regret.

"We're sorry to inform you that Flight 209 has crashed in a cornfield just outside the Illinois border."

A few started to cry. Others stood, like Ryder, waiting for the miracle that would pronounce their loved ones okay.

"At this point, we don't know why this has happened, but there have been eyewitness reports that lead us to believe the plane might have been struck by lightning. We do know it was on fire when it went down."

Someone's perfume was too strong. The cloying scent drifted up Ryder's nostrils. From this day on, he would hate the smell of musk. A woman shrieked and sank to the floor while a man somewhere behind Ryder started to curse.

"On behalf of our airline, I am very sorry to have to tell you..."

Ryder tilted his chin and closed his eyes, waiting for the blow.

"...there were no survivors."

The wail that spread across the room began as a joint groan of disbelief. Ryder covered his face and then wished he'd covered his ears, instead. Maybe if he hadn't heard it, it wouldn't be true.

They were saying something about a passenger list and a verification of names, but he couldn't stand still. He knew if he didn't get out, he was going to come undone. He burst out of the lounge, even as someone was calling him back, and started the long walk back down the terminal.

One step at a time. That's how he would get out of the airport. But how would he get home? How could he face that apartment without Casey?

But as far as he walked, he knew he couldn't run away from the truth. He'd spent the last seven months trying to forget what he'd done to his father and now this? How far, he wondered, would he have to run to get away from Casey's ghost? And with every step that he took, the thing that hurt worst was knowing he'd never said, I love you.

Casey kept glancing at her watch, then out the window of the plane. Neither hastened the arrival time of her flight. She was going to be at least an hour late getting home. Poor Ryder. He would no sooner get back to the apartment and hear her message on the machine than he'd have to come right back to the airport again.

She leaned her head against the seat and closed her eyes, weary from the grueling three-day set of negotiations. But it was done! She'd proven her mettle in more ways than one. She'd been thrust into Delaney Ruban's shoes far earlier than she'd ever envisioned, and while she'd known *what* to do, it was the *doing* she'd accomplished that made her feel proud. Delaney had worked all his life to create his empire. She couldn't have lived with herself if she'd been the cause of its ruin.

Yet the glow she had expected to feel from her success was dim in comparison to the anticipation she felt in just getting home to the man who was her husband. She kept remembering their first meeting in Sonny's Bar, of how he'd come out of the shadows and into her life. Now she couldn't imagine what her life would be like without him.

Half an hour into the flight, the plane lurched, and she grabbed at her seat belt, testing the lock that was firmly in place. A few seconds later, it leveled back off and she relaxed. Ryder had been right. This wasn't a good day to fly. Intermittent turbulence had been nonstop since takeoff, and she told herself she should have seen it coming.

Right after she'd talked to Ryder, her cab had come to a complete halt on the freeway. Traffic had snarled itself into a knot that only time had been unable to unravel. She'd known then that unless a miracle occurred, she was going to miss her flight.

For Casey, the miracle did occur, but not in the way she'd envisioned. She arrived at the airport forty-five minutes late. Not only had she missed her flight, she'd missed her lunch and her mood was not getting better. Just when she thought she was going to have to spend another night in Chicago after all, an airline with a later flight into Ruban Crossing had a cancellation. At last she was on her way home.

"Ladies and gentlemen, we will be arriving in Ruban Crossing in about five minutes. Please turn off all electronic and computer devices and prepare for landing."

Casey did so with anticipation. If Ryder hadn't already received her call about the change in flights, she would call home as soon as she got to a phone. By the time she collected her luggage, he would be picking her up.

And then the plane touched down and taxied down the runway, then up to the gate to unload. It was one of the few times in her life she wasn't flying first class, but she didn't even mind having to sit toward the back of the plane, or being one of the last to get off. She was home.

Ryder moved aside out of instinct as a fresh swarm of passengers began to come out of the hallway to his right. His hands started to shake as he watched a man laugh and wave to a woman and child who were just arriving.

It isn't fair. That damned plane got here in one piece. Why not hers?

Twice he tried to move through the crowd and was unsuccessful each time, so he stood against the wall, waiting as face after smiling face moved past. Finally the flow was down to single file and he stepped away from the wall.

"Ryder!"

The hair stood up on the back of his neck and he stopped, but couldn't bring himself to turn. He had to be hearing things. Just for a moment, he thought he'd heard Casey calling his name.

He took a deep breath, clenched his teeth, and started moving again.

"Ryder! Wait!"

He groaned. God! He hadn't even been this bad after Micah was killed.

Someone grabbed his arm and he turned.

Casey dropped her briefcase and threw her arms around his neck. "I can't believe you're still here! This is fabulous luck! I thought I would have to—"

When her arms went around his neck, he started to shake. And when he felt her breath on his face, and her laughter rumble across his senses, he lifted her off her feet.

"My God...my God." It was all he could say as he buried his face against her neck, turning them both in a small, tight circle in the middle of the crowd.

His grip was almost painful, but Casey laughed as her feet dangled off the floor. This was definitely the way to be welcomed home.

"Maybe I should have stayed that extra day after all," she said. "If absence makes the—"

"You're alive."

The laugh died in her voice. "Of course I'm alive."

He set her down on the floor, then cupped her face in his hands, and the tears in his eyes were impossible to miss.

"You missed your plane, didn't you?"

She nodded. "You wouldn't believe the traffic jam my cab got in. I missed my flight, my lunch, my—"

"The plane crashed. There were no survivors. I thought you were dead."

She paled and then clutched at his arm, fixing her gaze on the shape of his mouth and the words coming out. She shook her head, finding it difficult to believe what he was telling her, but he was too distraught to ignore. Goose bumps broke out on her skin as the impact began to sink in.

"When my cab got stuck in traffic, the first thing I thought was if I missed my plane, I wouldn't get to go home, and if I didn't get home, I would have to spend another night away from you."

Ryder's heart skipped a beat. "I missed you, too," he said softly.

"No, you don't quite understand," Casey said. "I did something selfish, very selfish, as I sat in that cab. I prayed for a miracle so I could get home. When I missed my plane, I was certain my prayer had not been answered." Tears filled her eyes. "Oh Ryder, why me? Why was I spared when so many others had to die?"

He crushed her to him. "I don't know, and I don't care. All I know is, five minutes ago I was trying to find a reason to take another damned breath and now..." Unable to finish, he held her close as a shudder swept through his body.

Suddenly, Casey felt like crying. "Ryder?"

He eased up, but was unable to quit touching her and began brushing the hair from her face. "What is it, honey?"

"Will you take me home?"

He held out his hand.

Chapter 11

Casey kept trying to focus on the familiarity of the country-side through which they were driving, but all she kept seeing was the look on Ryder's face when he'd turned around at the airport and seen her. It hadn't been filled with concern, it had been torn by devastation. To her, that meant only one thing. He cared for her as much as she had learned to care for him. Oh God, please don't let me be setting myself up for a fall, she thought.

"I'm going to let you out at the big house," Ryder said. "You need to let your family know that you're safe—just in case they've heard broadcasts about the crash."

Casey couldn't quit trembling. For some reason, her life had been spared and she didn't understand why. Ryder's presence was solid, unwavering; she felt a need to stay within the sound of his voice. "Where will you be?"

Just for a second he took his eyes off the road. "Right where I've been for the last three days. Waiting for you to come home."

She looked out the window and started to cry. "Oh Ryder, why? All those people. They'll never come home."

He saw Micah's face in his mind and as he did, suddenly

realized that the pain of the last few months wasn't as sharp as it had been. Ever conscious of the woman in the seat beside him, he had to face the fact that if it hadn't been for a tragedy, he and Casey would never have met. He tried to imagine his life without her and couldn't. Something inside him clicked.

"I don't know, but I'm beginning to accept that everything that happens to us in life happens for a reason."

Her voice was shaking. "What could possibly be the reason for so many deaths?"

His voice was gruff as he turned off the highway. "Damned if I know. Maybe it was just their time to go."

Moments later, the gray slate roof of the main house appeared over the tops of the trees, and soon afterward, the house itself was visible.

"You're home," Ryder said.

Casey's gaze moved from the mansion to the small, unobtrusive apartment over the garage. "Yes, so I am."

It was the red blinking light on the answering machine that drew him into the apartment. He knew what it said, but he played it anyway, reliving his joy as he waited for the sound of Casey's voice to fill the room.

"Ryder, it's me, again. This day couldn't get much worse. I missed my flight."

He closed his eyes, listening to the rest of the message and feeling awed by the twist fate had taken on their behalf. When it was over he put her suitcase on her bed, then looked around. Some changes had taken place since he'd left to pick her up.

The apartment was clean. Bea had probably seen to that. A fresh bouquet of flowers was on her bedside table, more than likely thanks to Eudora. She was big on flowers. He walked out of the room and into the kitchen. There was a note on the refrigerator door. Thanks to Tilly, there was food inside, ready to be eaten.

He turned on the faucet and let the water run until it was cool, then filled a glass and drank it dry; filled it again, and did the same. When he put it down empty, his hand was shaking. He walked into his bedroom and sat down on the edge of the bed.

The intense quiet assailed him and for the first time since Casey had grabbed his arm in the airport and turned the light back on in his world, he let himself think of the brief period of time when he'd thought she was dead. Uppermost had been the overwhelming sense of pain and loss, but there'd also been regret. Regret that their lives had been so screwed up when they met. Regret that he'd never said aloud what he knew in his heart to be true.

A shuddering breath slid up and out of his throat. He'd been given a second chance, and he wasn't going to waste precious time again. Footsteps sounded on the stairs outside. He tensed. It was Casey. The front door opened and he heard her call out.

"Ryder?"

He stood. For him, there was no turning back.

"Oh, there you are! It was so quiet I didn't think you were here."

He paused in the doorway, staring at her and memorizing the way she looked and the way she moved. Her long, black hair was pinned up off her neck and slightly tousled from travel. Her eyes were wide and still a little shocked, her lips looked tender, almost bruised, as if she'd bitten them to keep from crying, which he supposed she had. He watched as she absently brushed at a speck on her suit. Red was a power color, she'd told him. He could definitely agree. She held a power over him he couldn't ignore.

When she stepped out of her shoes and bent down to pick them up, the hem of her skirt slid even higher up her legs, accentuating their length. His heart filled. That woman was his wife.

"Casey."

She glanced up, her shoes still in her hand.

"I need to tell you something."

That's right! He'd told her the day she left that when she got back they needed to talk. Her heart skipped a beat as she waited for him to continue. Instead, he started toward her.

"Today, when I thought I'd lost you, do you know what I regretted most?"

She shook her head, her eyes widening as he cupped her cheek.

"That I hadn't told you the truth about how I felt." His gaze bored into hers. "I know what I'm going to say wasn't part of our bargain, but dammit, sometimes things change. I am sick and tired of pretending I'm satisfied with being your husband in name only. I love you, lady. I want to lie with you, make love with you. I don't want another night to pass without holding you in my arms. If you can't handle this, then say so, because in about three seconds, it'll be too late."

Casey's eyes were full of tears as she dropped her shoes and put her arms around his neck. "Why waste three seconds when the answer is yes...a thousand times yes?"

Ryder reached behind her and locked the door, then her feet left the floor. "Your place or mine?"

"Anywhere, Ryder, as long as you're there."

He headed for his bedroom with her in his arms. When he put her down, his hands went straight to the buttons on her suit. His voice was shaking. "God give me strength," he whispered, fumbling as he tried to push buttons through holes.

"Let me," Casey said, and finished what he'd been trying to do.

She walked toward the sliding glass doors, pulling shut the drapes as she dropped the jacket of her suit on a nearby chair. On her way back to Ryder she stepped out of her skirt.

He wasn't prepared for the woman beneath the suit; not the wisp of red bra, the matching bikini panties, the long, silk stockings or the black lace garter belt holding them up. And this time, when he swept her off her feet, he wrapped her legs around his waist and sank down onto the bed with her still in his arms.

He nuzzled the curve of her neck, savoring the joy of being able to hold her, inhaling the faint but lingering scent of her perfume, testing the soft crush of her breasts against his chest, and knowing that the tight draw of his own muscles next to that wisp of red silk between her legs was becoming difficult to ignore. He held her close, savoring the joy of knowing she was still alive.

"Today I rode a roller coaster into hell and came out with an angel in my arms. I don't know why we were given a second chance, but I don't intend to waste it."

Her arms tightened around his neck as she rained brief, tiny

kisses along the side of his cheek and his chin. He grabbed
her face, gazing into her eyes and watching them fill with tears
until he thought he could see all the way to her soul.

"I feel like I'm about to make love to a ghost. I can't believe I'm holding you, feeling your breath on my cheek, your
arms around my neck. I must be the luckiest man in the
world."

Casey's breath snagged on a sob. "I'm the one who got
lucky. The day I got lost in the flatlands and found you in
Sonny's Bar was the day my life began to change. You've
stood with me. You've stood by me. I will never be able to
repay you for what you've already done in my name."

"Hell, darlin', I don't want your money. I want your love."

"Then take it, Ryder. It's yours."

He rolled until she was lying beneath him in those bits of
red-and-black lace. With an impatient snap, he undid the
clasps on her garter belt and rolled down her stockings, silken
inch at a time.

Longing to be one with this man was driving Casey to the
brink of making a fool of herself. She struggled to help as he
undid her bra. But when he hooked his thumbs in the waistband of her bikini briefs and started pulling them down, she
moaned and closed her eyes.

Ryder leaned down and kissed the valley between her
breasts.

His breath was soft against her face as he moved to her lips.
"Are you okay?"

"No," she gasped, and tunneled her fingers through his
hair. "Unless you hurry, I may never be okay again."

After that, he came out of his clothes with no regard to
order, and when he threaded his fingers through hers and
stretched out beside her, he closed his eyes and said a last
small prayer of thanksgiving that he'd been given this chance.

Then Ryder Justice made love to his wife.

Casey propped herself on one elbow, looking at Ryder as
he slept. She knew the shape of his face, the nearly square,
stubborn jaw. Her gaze moved to his hands—broad and strong
with long, supple fingers. She shivered, remembering what

they'd done to her body in the name of love. Dear Lord, but he knew the buttons to push to make a strong woman weak with longing.

His chest rose and fell with each even breath that he drew, yet a short while ago, she'd felt the thunder of his pulse as he'd lain down upon her and driven himself into her, over and over, in mindless repetition.

Her body quickened in response to the memory and she glanced down to the bulge of him covered just below the waist with a sheet. Hers. He was hers. Before, they'd traded vows and made empty promises in front of Judge Harmon Harris. Today, they'd pledged their love in a way that would endure.

She reached out, gently laying her hand in the middle of his chest just so she could feel the steady rhythm of his heart, and as she did, he sighed and shifted in his sleep. She watched the thick brush of his eyelashes fluttering as some nameless dream pulled him further away from her. From his thick, black hair to those stormy gray eyes, she knew her man well. But she knew nothing of what made him tick.

Astute businesswoman that she was, she knew that in business, the swiftest way to achieve success was to know all there was to know about an enemy…or a competitor. And while Ryder was neither of those, he still had too many secrets for her peace of mind. He wasn't the type of man one would expect to find wandering the highways and byways of the Mississippi Delta. His education was obvious, his breeding even more so. Delaney would have called him a thoroughbred. Casey had an overpowering need to know this man who called her wife. There had to be more to him than a man who knew how to love and make love with a fine-burning passion.

She laid her head down on his chest and closed her eyes, smiling to herself as he pulled her to him. Even in sleep, his claim on her was strong.

Tomorrow. She would start the wheels of an investigation rolling tomorrow. But quiet. She'd keep it low-key and quiet. And it wouldn't be like she was snooping. She had a right to know all there was to know about the man she had married. Didn't she?

* * *

Royal Justice raced his daughter, Maddie, for the phone. He lost. Her tiny fingers curled around the receiver as she lifted it to her ear, speaking fast in order to get it all out before her daddy could snatch it out of her hands.

"Hello. This is Maddie. Is this you?"

Roman Justice kicked back in his chair and propped his feet on the top of his desk, absorbing the sweet sound of his only niece's voice.

"Well, hello, little bit. Yes, it's me. Is this you?"

Maddie giggled just as Royal got to the phone.

"Let me talk! Let me talk!" she shrieked, as Royal lifted it out of her hands. "It's Unca Roman. He called to talk to me!"

Royal shushed her with a finger to his lips and then lifted the receiver to his ear. "Roman?"

Roman flipped open a folder on the desk before him. "Brother, you're gonna have to get yourself some skates. If you can't beat a three-year-old to the phone, you're already in hot water. Just think what it'll be like when she's a teenager."

"Bite your damned lip," Royal muttered as Maddie danced around his legs, begging to be put back on the phone. "I assume you have a reason for calling."

As always, Roman Justice did not waste words. "Ryder's alive."

Royal turned and sank into a nearby chair with a sigh of relief. "Thank the good Lord. What have you learned? Why hasn't he called? Is he all right?"

"Hell, you're just like Maddie. One thing at a time. Your guess is as good as mine as to why he hasn't called, but if I had to bet on a reason, I'd say he hasn't turned loose of the guilt."

"But it wasn't his fault. The FAA told him that. We told him that. Lord have mercy, even the preacher who preached Dad's funeral told him that."

"Yeah, well you know Ryder. The only person he ever listened to was Dad and he's—"

"Yeah, right," Royal said, and pulled Maddie onto his lap, whispering a promise that she could talk when he was through. "So, what's the story?"

"Hang on to your hat, brother. He's married and living in

some place in Mississippi called Ruban Crossing.''

''He's what?''

''You heard me.''

Royal shook his head. ''Married! Ryder, of all people. His wife must be something to have talked a maverick like him into settling down. Do you think we ought to give him a call? You know—to wish him well and all that?''

A fly buzzed past Roman's ear. He never moved, but his gaze followed the flight of the fly as it sailed past his nose. Somewhere between one breath and the next, he snatched the fly in midflight, holding it captive in his fist while he finished his conversation.

''Hell, no. You know better than that. Ryder is the one who ran away from home. If we call him, it would be like that time Mama came after the three of us for sneaking off to the pond to go fishing when we were supposed to be in school, remember?''

Royal laughed. ''Remember? Lord, I had nightmares for years afterward. And you're right. If Mama had just given us time, we would have been home for supper and everything would have been all right. As it was, we were dragged home with our tails between our legs. It took weeks before I could look Dad in the face without feeling shame.''

''Just be glad we know where Ryder is.''

Royal sighed. ''Right, and thanks for calling.''

''No problem.''

Maddie tugged at Royal's arm. ''Your niece needs to tell you something, okay?''

A rare smile shifted the sternness on Roman's face. ''If it's Maddie, it's always okay.''

''Unca Roman?''

''What is it, little bit?''

''You pwomised to take me to the zoo.''

''I know.''

''So when is you gonna do it?''

The smile on his face widened. ''Whenever you want.''

''Now!'' she crowed. ''I want to do it wight now.''

The fly buzzed frantically against the palm of his hand as he glanced up at the clock. ''Put your daddy back on the phone and let me ask,'' he said.

Maddie handed her father the phone. "It's for you. And you gots to say yes."

Royal pretended to frown, but it was all a big fake. He nearly always said yes to his very best girl.

"What?"

"Your daughter and I have a date with the zoo. She wants to go now."

"Fine with me," Royal said. "Just remember, she can't have everything she wants to eat, even if she begs. The last time she threw up on your boots."

"They were my boots. My problem. I'll be there within the hour." He hung up the phone and then smashed his hand flat on the top of his desk, ending the fly's last bid for freedom.

Royal hung up. At least there was one uncle left upon whom Maddie could depend. He didn't know what he thought about Ryder getting married, and truth be told, didn't have time to worry about it. Ryder was alive and well. That was all that could matter.

Not even in Lash Marlow's worst nightmares had he envisioned the day that something this degrading would happen to him. But it was here, in his hands, on plain white bond, typed all in capitals in clear, black ink. He stuck his hand in his pocket, rubbing at the rabbit's foot over and over and the words still didn't change.

Foreclosure.

He'd slept with the knowledge all night, and when he'd awakened this morning, had almost convinced himself that it was all a bad dream. Until he'd come into the kitchen to make coffee.

The letter was there where he'd left it last night. He'd picked it up again, rereading it over and over until his stomach rolled and his heart was thundering in his ears.

One powerful word and it was enough to bring what was left of his world to an end. He tossed the letter back onto the kitchen table, forgot about the coffee, and went to the breakfront to pour himself a drink. The decanter was empty—just like his life. He stared around the room, trying to find some sense of reason for drawing his next breath when something hit the front door.

That would be the morning paper.

He waited until he was certain the paperboy was gone. Even the eleven-year-old boy who delivered the papers had quit believing the check was in the mail.

The rubber band broke as he was rolling it off the paper, snapping the palm of his hand and bringing a quick set of tears to his eyes.

"Ow! Dammit, that hurt," he muttered, and tossed the paper on the kitchen table next to the letter.

He'd make that coffee after all. At least he could have coffee with the morning paper. That was a civilized thing to do.

When the coffee began to brew, he sat down and began to unroll it, but the edges kept curling back toward the way they'd been rolled and he cursed beneath his breath. It should be against the law to roll up a paper. He remembered the days when his father had insisted on having the help iron his morning paper flat before bringing it to him to read. He grinned, also remembering the occasional times when it would arrive with one of the pages scorched. Such a commotion over paper and ink.

In the middle of pouring himself a cup of freshly brewed coffee, the phone rang. Still lost in memories of grander days, he answered without thinking.

"Mr. Marlow, this is Denzel Cusper, down at the bank. I wanted to call you early, before you left for the office. We had several checks of yours come in yesterday and I'm afraid your account is a little short of funds. You know, we value your business. Your grandfather banked with us. Your father banked with us. We value the Marlow name, and that's why I knew you'd want to take care of this right away."

There was a sick smile on Lash's face, although Denzel Cusper could not see it. He bit his lip and pretended he wasn't lying through his teeth. "Why, you're right of course! I don't know how I let that oversight occur, but I'll take care of it on my way in to the office." He could hear the Denzel Cusper's sigh of relief.

"That's just fine," Denzel said. "I'll just be holding these checks until your deposit clears."

"Thank you for calling," Lash said.

"No problem. Always glad to give a valued customer a helping hand."

Lash hung up the phone and poured his coffee down the sink. He didn't need caffeine. He needed money. He'd already spent his monthly retainer from the Ruban family, and the other clients he often represented were worse off than he was.

The foreclosure letter was still on the table right where he'd left it. Now this. Checks were going to bounce. He didn't even want to know how many. He had represented people who'd written hot checks, and he couldn't remember a one who'd gotten off without serving their time. The law was swift with regards to stealing, in any form.

Shame filled him. Thank God his grandfather hadn't lived to see this day. What his father hadn't lost, Lash had wound up selling to stay afloat. And now it was gone and Lash Marlow was sinking fast. In days gone by, there would have been only one honorable way with which to deal with this shame. Lash thought of the handgun in the drawer beneath the phone. He glanced at the paper he had yet to read. He could just picture the headlines.

"Local Lawyer—DOA."

Dead on arrival. He shuddered. There would be a scandal, but he wouldn't be around to face it. And while he was contemplating the virtue of an easy way out, his gaze fell on the corner of a familiar face pictured on the front page of the paper. He pressed the page flat.

"Ruban Heir Saved by Traffic Jam"

His eyes widened and he began to read, and when he was through, he stared down at Casey's picture in disbelief. Why? Why did someone like her keep getting all the breaks while everything he did threw him further and further off course?

"You bitch."

Startled, he looked up, expecting to see someone standing in the doorway of the kitchen. When he realized it was himself that he had heard, he looked back down and started to shake.

"You selfish, worthless, little bitch. I'd give my life to find a way to make you sorry for what you've done."

Casey's face smiled back up at him from the page, taunting him in a way he could not accept. He let go of his rage, giving hate full rein, and began to consider the wisdom of what he'd just said.

He knew people who would do very dirty deeds for very little money, which was exactly what Lash Marlow had. But if his scheme worked, when he was through, he would be the one in the dough, and that sharecropper's granddaughter would be sorry she'd thumbed her nose in a Marlow's face.

"Oh, my."

Casey's quiet remark got Ryder's attention. In the act of dressing for the day, he came out of the bedroom in nothing but his blue jeans. Casey was standing by the kitchen table, her morning cup of coffee forgotten as she stared at the headlines in disbelief.

"Ruban Heir Saved by Traffic Jam"

"How do they find these things out so fast?"

Ryder put his arms around her, reading over her shoulder as he cuddled her. When he saw the headline, he sighed. Because of who she was, she would always be news.

"It doesn't matter. As long as they leave you alone, they can print your favorite recipe for toast for all I care."

She dropped the paper on the table and leaned against him. "I don't have a recipe for toast. I can't cook. Remember?"

He grinned. "Then you have nothing to worry about, right?"

She laughed and turned in his arms. "So it would seem."

His eyes darkened as he cupped her hips and pulled her close, letting her feel what was on his mind.

Her robe slipped open, revealing the clean bare lines of her body beneath. Ryder groaned and lowered his head, razing the tender skin on her neck with a series of nips and kisses that left her trembling for more than this sensual tease.

Casey shivered. "Make love to me."

With a flip of his wrist, her robe fell to the floor at his feet. He reached out, tracing the shape of her breast with the tip of his finger, then encircling her waist with his hands, holding her fast—wishing he could hold on forever.

"You are so beautiful, Casey Dee."

Her head lolled as his hands began to work their magic.

Skin tingled. Nerves tensed. Muscles coiled.

He lowered his mouth, trapping her lips and swallowing her sigh.

Heat built.

When his hand dipped between her thighs, she groaned.

Honey flowed.

She reached for his zipper, then for him, needing him—guiding him—to her—in her.

It happened fast. One minute she was standing, the next she was on the cabinet with Ryder between her legs. "Buckle up," he whispered.

Casey wrapped her arms around his neck and her legs around his waist. It felt as if everything inside of her was fighting to get out. Her heart was pounding against her chest. Her blood was racing through her veins. That sweet, sweet heat was building in her belly and she wanted the release. Clutching at him as hard as she could, she buried her face against his shoulder.

"Oh, Ryder, please now."

He began to surge against her in a hard, even rhythm. Over and over. Minute upon minute. Rocking. Hammering. Driving toward pleasure. Too close to hold back.

Casey's senses were swimming. There was nothing upon which she could focus except him inside her. And suddenly gravity shifted and she lost her sense of balance. Grabbing him tighter, she arched toward a thrust, crying aloud. "Ryder...Ryder...I'm coming undone."

Sweat ran down the middle of his back as she held him, encompassed him, pulling him deeper and deeper toward total release. He shifted his hands from her back to her hips—pulling her forward—moving faster. His voice was harsh, his words low and thick with oncoming passion.

"Then let it happen. I'm coming with you."

One cry broke the silence, then another, deeper and more prolonged, followed by soft, shaken sobs and gentle words of praise.

A short time later, Ryder picked up his wife and carried her out of the room. The newspaper that had sparked the mood lay forgotten on the floor. Had Casey seen it again, she would now have disputed the claim. The traffic jam wasn't the first thing to save her life. It was the man she'd found in the flatlands down at Sonny's Bar.

Chapter 12

"This is all I have to go on. See what you can come up with. Oh, and I want this kept confidential, understand?"

"Yes, Mrs. Justice. Of course."

Casey hung up the phone then swiveled her chair until she was gazing out the office windows. Outside, sunshine beamed down on Ruban Crossing, sweltering the inhabitants with a humidity that left everyone limp and weary. A flock of seagulls swooped past her vision, then disappeared around the corner of the building. On their way to the river—on their way to someplace cool.

She told herself what she'd done was for the best, and that no matter what her investigator found out about Ryder, she would love him just the same. But in the following weeks since they'd first made love, she sensed he was holding something back and it made her nervous. What if the revelation of his secrets brought an end to their relationship? She closed her eyes and said a small, quiet prayer. That just couldn't happen. She couldn't give him up. Not when he'd become the most important thing in her life.

The intercom buzzed. She turned back to her desk.

"Yes?"

"Libertine Delacroix on line two for you."

Casey picked up the phone. "Libby, it's been a long time!"

"Yes, darlin', way too long," Libertine said. "I would have called about this sooner, but I thought that with Delaney goin' 'an dyin' on us like he did, and then you gettin' married and all, well—I just thought I'd give everythin' time to settle."

Casey grinned. Libertine Delacroix's southern drawl was too thick to be believed, especially when Casey knew for certain that Libertine had been born and raised in Utah. The only thing south about her upbringing had been the window over her bed. However, after marrying Winston Delacroix and moving to their family home outside of Jackson, Mississippi, Libertine's speech had become as rich as southern fried chicken.

"How is that darlin' husband of yours, anyway?" Libertine asked.

An image of Ryder's face above hers as he slid into her body flashed through Casey's mind. She closed her eyes and leaned back in her chair, suddenly weak with longing.

"Why, he's just fine. Thank you for asking," Casey said.

"Good. I'm havin' a little party Saturday night. I want you two to come. You'll be the guests of honor, of course."

Casey opened her eyes and sat up straight. Libertine had never had a *little* party in her life.

"That sounds wonderful," she said. "But what do you mean by little?"

"Oh, no more than forty or fifty. It'll be fun! Come in costume of course, and be prepared to be showered with belated wedding gifts as well."

Casey rolled her eyes. Good grief. A sit-down, costume party, wedding shower dinner? Only Libertine would attempt to pull off such a stunt.

"Thank you, Libby, Ryder and I will be looking forward to it."

Libertine giggled. "I do declare. I hear he's just the handsomest thing. Leave it up to you to pull the coup of the decade. I wouldn't have had the nerve, you know—goin' down in the Delta like that and callin' Delaney's bluff. Oh well, see you Saturday night, sugar. Eightish—costumes—prepare to have fun!"

Casey winced as Libertine disconnected. Lord have mercy!

Costumes. She hadn't been able to get him in a chauffeur's uniform. What was he going to say about this?

A dragonfly darted past Casey's nose as she leaned on the fender of the Lincoln, watching while Ryder poured oil into the engine. Still in her work clothes, she was careful not to get grime on her suit. It was an original and one of her favorites.

Ryder didn't seem to have the same set of worries. He was minus a shirt, minus his hat, and as of moments ago when she'd unloaded the news about Libertine's call, minus his good humor.

"So, you're going to put me on parade. I was wondering when this might happen."

Casey winced. "That's not fair. I'm not the one hosting this party, therefore I am not the one putting you anywhere. Libertine Delacroix is famous for her parties. She was also one of my mother's closest friends—at least, that's what Tilly says."

Ryder tossed the empty oil can into the trash and wiped his hands. "Step back," he ordered, and slammed the hood shut with a resounding thump.

Casey followed him into the garage. "Her food is always fabulous. She has the best chef in the county, you know."

"Can't be better than Tilly's," he said shortly.

"They're giving us a belated wedding shower. I didn't know how to say no."

Ryder turned, and there was a light in his eyes she recognized all too well. "Oh, I don't know about that. You pretty much said a big loud no to the terms of your grandfather's will."

She glared. "That's different."

He grinned.

"We're to go in costume."

The grin slid off of his face. "Like hell."

Casey groaned. "Ryder, please. Don't be difficult about this. I love you madly. You can't blame me for wanting all of my acquaintances to meet you."

"Yeah, right, and I'm supposed to remember these people

the next time I see them when I've been introduced to them in costumes? Let's see, what would I say? Oh, I know. You were the pirate, right? And you—weren't you that Playboy Bunny?''

She grinned. ''I can heartily assure you that there will not be a single Playboy Bunny present.''

He yanked his shirt from a hook and pulled it on with a jerk. ''Well hell, you know that refusing you is impossible. However…just remember you're going to owe me, big time.''

Casey threw her arms around his neck and kissed him full on the lips. ''Thank you, thank you, thank you.''

The corner of his mouth tilted as he nuzzled the spot just below her right ear. ''You're very welcome.''

Before their play went beyond a point of no return, Tilly stepped out the back door. ''Casey, honey, telephone call for you.''

Casey waved to let Tilly know that she'd heard, then turned back to Ryder. ''So, what kind of costume do you want to wear?''

He cursed beneath his breath.

''Ryder, you promised.''

''You don't worry about what I'll wear,'' he muttered. ''I said I'd go, so I'll dress the part.''

It wasn't what she wanted to hear, but knowing Ryder, it was the best she was going to get.

''Want to go out to dinner?'' she asked.

''Want to go to Smoky Joe's?''

Casey groaned. She knew when she'd been had. ''It's not alligator night.''

He grinned. ''I don't care. I have a hankering to see someone else's tail get slapped in the mud besides mine.''

She made a face and then ran for the phone.

''Don't run in those damned heels,'' he yelled, but it was too late. She'd already done it. He frowned. One of these days she was going to break her leg pulling a stunt like that.

Casey leaned over the deck and waved at Miles and Erica as they came out of the main house. Erica's white antebellum dress floated just above the ground, billowing out around her and swaying with every step that she took. Miles looked dashing in black and quite reminiscent of a riverboat gambler. Eudora was sick with a cold and had declined the invitation with no small amount of regret. But she couldn't show up at a party with a box of tissues beneath her arm, no matter what costume she might wear. It just wasn't done.

"Hurry up!" Miles shouted, pointing toward a long white limousine pulling up in the driveway. "The limo's here."

"I'll be right down!" she called, and ran back into the apartment, closing and locking the patio door behind her.

Without Ryder, the apartment seemed too large and empty. He'd been gone for more than two hours, and although he called over an hour ago, claiming his costume had been undergoing alterations, he still wasn't back.

"Oh, Ryder, if you let me down at this late date, I'll never forgive you," she muttered, as she made a last-minute check through the apartment, making sure she had everything she'd intended to take.

She paused before the mirror then turned, glancing over her shoulder, making sure her own costume was in place, then smiling in satisfaction at the fluffy, white bunny tail right in the middle of her backside. She turned, ignoring the plunge of fabric barely covering her breasts and readjusted her long white ears. The black fishnet stockings made her legs look sexy, and her three-inch heels completed the picture. Yes, she made a darn good Playboy Bunny, even if she did think so herself.

As she started down the stairs to the waiting limo, she made a bet with herself. *By the time I get to the bottom of the stairs, Ryder will be driving up.* When her foot hit the last one she looked up. The Lincoln was nowhere in sight.

"Damn and double damn," she mumbled, and started across the courtyard. *Okay, by the time I get to the limo, he'll be home.*

When she drew even with the limousine's back bumper, she lifted her head to gaze down the long empty driveway. Her expression fell. She couldn't believe it. He'd actually let her down. What was she going to say to Libertine when they arrived?

The driver hurried around the car to where she was standing, then opened the door.

"Watch your ears—and your tail, darlin'. Wouldn't want either one of them to fall off before you got the chance to shine."

She looked up, then gasped. "Ryder!"

"Your ride awaits. Now don't tell me you're about to change your mind after I went to all this trouble."

She blinked. It was him. Resplendent in a dark, double-breasted chauffeur's uniform with more gold braid and buttons than an admiral might wear.

He tipped his cap and held the door ajar. "Ma'am?"

She threw her arms around his neck. "You are going to steal the show."

He held her close, patting at the fluff of her tail. "I'd a whole lot rather steal me a rabbit."

"Oh, for Pete's sake," Miles grumbled from inside the car. "Let's get a move on or we're going to be late."

Casey quickly took her seat, quite out of place beside a riverboat gambler and an old-fashioned southern belle.

Erica glared. Leave it up to Casey. "I swear, little sister, whatever you do tonight, don't bend over. You'll positively *spill* out of that disreputable thing you are wearing."

Miles grinned, for once taking Casey's side instead of his twin's. "Oh, I don't know about that, Erica. Even if she is our sister, she looks rather stunning."

Erica sniffed. "You would say that. After all, you're just a man."

The glass door slid open behind Casey's head. Ryder's voice drifted out into the uneasy silence. "Buckle up."

"Have mercy," Erica shrieked, and grabbed for a seat belt as the limo took off, leaving a black streak of rubber to show where it had been.

Miles needed no warning. He was already strapped and waiting for takeoff when the limo accelerated. He'd ridden with this man before.

Casey laughed aloud, then blew Ryder a kiss as he turned onto the highway. Tonight was just about perfect.

* * *

Of the guests who'd come in full costume to Libertine's party, nine were in Rebel gray. Of those nine, only Lash Marlow wore the uniform of a southern general, and he wore it with pride. His great-great-grandfather Marlow had been a general during the War of Northern Aggression. It seemed fitting that he carry out the tradition, if only for the night.

But his pride in the past died a humiliating death when the Ruban party arrived. His gaze went past Miles and Erica Dunn. They were Rubans by marriage only. In the grand scheme of things, and blood being thicker than water, it was Casey who counted. But when he saw her and then the man at her side, it was all he could do to stay quiet. How dare she flaunt what she'd done to him?

Libertine Delacroix, who for tonight had dressed as Lady Liberty, was speechless for all of twenty seconds when she saw them, and then broke into peals of laughter.

"Casey, darlin', I should have known you'd outshine us all. And just look at this man on your arm! Introduce me this instant, you hear?"

Casey grinned. "Libby, this is my husband, Ryder Justice. Ryder, my very dear friend, Libertine Delacroix."

Libertine held out her hand. Ryder took it, then lifted it to his lips. "I'm real partial to liberated women, Mrs. Delacroix. It's a pleasure to meet you."

Libertine giggled at his play of words on her costume and name. "The pleasure is all mine, I'm sure," she drawled, then slipped her hand beneath his elbow. "Come along, you two. There's a ton of people who are just dyin' to meet you."

"I'll just bet," he muttered beneath his breath.

Casey pinched his arm. He looked down and winked at her. "You promised to be nice," she warned.

"No, I didn't. I just promised to come."

She laughed at the sparkle in his eyes. Dear Lord, but she loved this man, so much that sometimes it scared her. She threaded her fingers through his, content for tonight to follow his lead.

An oblong silver tray glittered beneath the lights of the chandelier in the great hall as the wedding gifts were unwrapped before the guests. Crystal sparkled, fine china gleamed. Lash stood among the crowd, oohing and aahing along with them as each new piece was put up on display, and all the while, the idea he'd been fostering took deeper root in his mind.

Damn her—and him. He stared at the tall man in the chauffeur's uniform and resented him for not being ashamed. How can he hold his head high? By wearing that ridiculous costume, he'd all but announced to the world that he was nothing but hired help. Yet when Ryder casually tucked a wayward curl on Casey's forehead back beneath the rabbit ears she was wearing, Lash's stomach rolled. The look she gave him made gorge rise in his throat. *Damn her to hell. She never looked at me like that.* And that hurt, more than he was able to admit.

Out on the patio behind him, the band Libertine had hired was setting up to play. The thought of making small talk and pretending for another two or three hours seemed impossible to Lash, but he couldn't bring himself to leave.

Unaware of Lash's growing antagonism, Casey undid the bow on the very last gift and then lifted the box lid, pulling out a crystal-and-silver ice bucket and tongs.

"It won't hold a six-pack, but it sure is pretty," Ryder drawled.

Casey grinned at him as everyone laughed. By now, the guests had figured out that Casey Ruban's husband had been one jump ahead of them all night. Instead of trying to be something he wasn't, he dared them to dislike who he was. They had tried and failed miserably. Ryder Justice was too intriguing to dislike and too handsome to ignore.

"This has been wonderful," Casey said. "Ryder and I thank you for your kindness and generosity."

Ryder took Casey by the hand and stood. "All kidding aside, it's been a pleasure meeting my wife's friends. Maybe one day we can return the favor."

Casey was surprised at his initiative, and more than a little bit pleased. He kept coming through for her, again and again.

Libertine waved her hand above the crowd. "This way, this way, my dears. We've dined. We've showered. The evening can't end without dancing."

The crowd followed her through open French doors and out

onto a massive flagstone patio. People broke off into couples and soon the impromptu dance floor was crowded.

Inside, Casey wound her arms around Ryder's neck and leaned her head on his shoulder.

"What's the matter, Hoppy, are you tired?"

She tried not to laugh, but his jest was entirely too charming to ignore.

"Yes, but deliciously so." His hands were stroking at the small of her back, right where it ached the most. She wondered how he knew.

"Think you might have one good dance in you? I just realized I've never danced with my wife."

"If you don't mind dancing with a barefoot bunny, I'd be delighted."

He cocked an eyebrow. "It can happen. I like bare."

She ran a finger down the middle of his chest, stopping just above the spot where his belly button would be. "Yes, I know."

He waited. She kicked off her shoes. He took her in his arms just as the next song began. Drums hammered out a rollicking beat and a guitarist joined in, running his fingers up and down the frets as the strings vibrated beneath his touch.

"Oh darn," Casey said. "It's too fast."

Ryder took her hand and placed it in the center of his chest. "You're listening to the wrong rhythm," he said softly. "Feel the one in here. It's the one to follow."

He glanced down at her feet. "I'd sure hate to mash one of those poor little toes. Better hitch a ride on my boots, honey, then all you'll have to worry about is hanging on."

A lump came to Casey's throat as she stepped up on his toes. Sure enough, when Ryder started to move, she could almost hear the slow, steady beat of a loving man's heart. The ache in her feet disappeared. She laid her cheek on his shoulder and followed his lead as he circled them slowly up and down the marbled floors of Libertine Delacroix's great hall.

Out on the patio, Lash Marlow stood in the shadows, staring back into the house. The intimacy of the lady bunny standing on the chauffeur's feet was not lost on him, nor were the tender kisses he saw Ryder giving his wife.

Lash's hand slid to the long sword hanging from the belt

around his waist. It would be all too easy to draw it now while everyone was otherwise occupied and slash those stupid smiles off of both their faces, but that wouldn't get him what he deserved. No, he had other plans for Casey, and it wouldn't be long before he set them in motion.

Bunny ears hung on one corner of the bedpost, a chauffeur's cap on the other. Clothing was strewn across the floor and the chairs. In the bed, Ryder and Casey slept as bare as the day they'd been born, entwined within each other's arms.

Outside, a wind began to blow. A cool front was moving in. Something clattered against the patio door leading onto the deck. Ryder shifted in his sleep and rolled onto his back as he fell deeper and deeper into the dream playing out in his head.

Lightning flashed and the plane bucked. Seconds afterward, smoke began filling the cabin. There was a whine to the engines as the plane began to lose altitude. Ryder pulled back on the stick, fighting the pull of gravity with all of his strength.

"God help us both," Micah said.

Ryder jerked, his head tossing on the pillow from side to side. He hadn't remembered hearing his father's voice—until now.

Lightning flashed again, illuminating the horizon and the tops of a stand of trees, but Ryder was hardly aware. It was all he could do to see the instrument panel through the thick veil of smoke. Muscles in his arms began to jerk from the stress of trying to control the plane's rapid descent, and still he would not let go. Yet no matter how hard he fought, it would not respond.

"I love you, boy."

Tears seeped from beneath Ryder's lashes and out onto the surface of his cheeks.

I love you, too, Dad.

One of the windows in the cockpit shattered. Smoke dissipated at an alarming rate. Visibility cleared, and then Ryder wished it had not. There was at least half a second's worth of time to see that they were going to die.

He sat up with a jerk, gasping for air, unaware that his cheeks were wet with tears.

"Oh, God."

He rolled out of the bed and reached for his jeans. He had to get out. He had to move. He couldn't breathe.

Casey felt the bed give. Suddenly she was no longer lying on Ryder's chest. She blinked, then opened her eyes. The sight of him jerking on pants and stomping out of the room was enough to yank her rudely awake. She didn't have to turn on a light to know something was dreadfully wrong. It was there in the shadowy movements of his body as he fled from the room. Seconds later, the front door banged, and Casey knew he was gone.

She crawled out of bed on all fours, searching for something to wear as she hurried through the house. One of his T-shirts was hanging on the doorknob. She grabbed it, pulling it over her head as she ran. It hung to a point just above her knees, but when she opened the front door, the fierce wind quickly plastered it to her body, leaving her feeling naked all over again.

She stood at the top of the landing, searching the grounds for a sign of where Ryder had gone. And then she saw him moving toward the trees at the back of the estate, and she bolted down the stairs after him.

Ryder moved without thought, trying to escape the dream clinging fast to his mind. It was just like before. No matter how fast he ran, he couldn't escape the truth. Micah had died, but he hadn't.

Wind whistled through the trees just ahead. It was an eerie wail, not unlike that of a woman's shriek. Without looking to the sky, he knew a storm was brewing. He stopped, then lifted his arms out on either side of his body like a bird in flight, and faced the force of nature for what it was. Unpredictable.

Unstoppable. Uncontrollable.

The first drops of rain were beginning to fall when Casey caught him. She didn't stop to ask him why. She didn't care that she was getting wet. She just threw herself into his arms, becoming his anchor against the storm.

Ryder groaned and wrapped his arms around her, and although the wind still blew and the rain still fell, he knew a sudden sense of peace. He dug his hands through the wind-whipped tangle of her hair and shuddered as she bent to his will.

Rain was falling harder now and he couldn't find the words to explain the horror and guilt that he lived with every day.

Casey clutched at him in desperation. His gaze became fixed upon her face, and she could see his eyes. They were as wild and as stormy as the night. His fingers coiled in her hair. His body was trembling against hers. A chill began to seep into her bones, and she knew she had to get them out of the weather. The gardener's shed was nearby. She pushed out of his arms, then grabbed him by the hand and started running. To her everlasting relief, he followed.

When she slammed the door shut behind them, the sound of the rain upon the metal roof was almost deafening, but at least they were no longer standing in the midst of it all.

"Lord have mercy," she said, and shivered as she lifted her hair from her neck and twisted it. Water ran out, then down her shoulder and onto her feet. She reached for the light switch.

It didn't work. It figured. In Ruban Crossing, if the wind blew or rain fell, inevitably, the power went out.

She turned, and knew Ryder was right before her, although she could barely see his face.

"Ryder?"

His hand cupped her shoulder, then her cheek. He stepped closer until their foreheads were touching and she could hear the ragged sounds of his breath. She lifted a hand to his face, and even though they'd just come out of a storm, she had the strangest sensation that what she felt were tears, not rain.

"Sweetheart?"

His lips found hers, stifling whatever else she might have said. They were cool and wet and softened upon impact, molding themselves to her mouth with tender persistence.

Casey sighed and when his arms encircled her, she leaned into his embrace. His hands were moving up and down her arms, across her shoulders, upon her hips. When he discovered she wore nothing beneath his shirt but herself, she felt him pause. His voice came out of the silence, little more than a whisper, but what he said made her blush in the dark.

Her hesitation was brief. There was nothing he could ask that would shame her. There was nothing she wouldn't do with or for this man who called her wife. She pulled the wet T-shirt over her head and dropped it on the floor. Her hands moved to his waist, then beneath the wet denim covering the straining thrust of his manhood.

When she took him in her hands, he groaned. When she knelt, she heard him take a deep breath. And she knew for the rest of her life, the sound of rain on a roof would bring back the memory of what she had done in the dark to bring Ryder Justice to his knees.

Joshua came into the kitchen. "Found this in the gardener's shed this morning."

Casey looked up from the kitchen table. Pink tinged her cheeks, but her expression remained calm.

Ryder glanced at Casey, then looked away. Even after the onslaught of emotions they'd shared last night, he'd been unable to explain what had sent him into the storm.

"It looks like one of my T-shirts," Ryder said. "I know I left one in the garage, but *I* didn't leave one in the shed."

Casey sighed. He hadn't lied. Not really. She was the one who left the shirt. Not him.

Joshua shrugged. "I think it will clean up all right. It's not torn, just wet and muddy."

"Thanks," Ryder said, and returned to the paper he'd been reading.

Tilly stared at the couple sitting side by side at her kitchen table. Everything seemed the same—except her instincts told her it wasn't.

"Is there something you'd be wanting to talk about?" she asked.

Ryder and Casey looked up, first at her, then at each other, before shaking their heads. Casey smiled. "No, ma'am."

Tilly glared. "I didn't get to be fifty-nine years old by being a fool." She banged a pot on the stove to accentuate her claim. "I know when something's not right. Did you two have a fight? 'Cause if you did, I'm telling you now, the best way to end it is talk it all out.'' She pointed a spoon at Joshua. "Tell them Josh! Tell them I know what I'm talking about.''

Joshua rolled his eyes, thankful he was on the far side of the room from that spoon. "My Tilly knows what she's talking about. She always does. If you don't believe me, then ask her.''

Ryder grinned behind his paper as Tilly lit into Joshua for making jest of her claims. It was just as well. It changed the subject, which was fine with him.

He glanced at Casey. Worry was there on her face. He'd have to be a fool not to see it. But he'd give her credit. She hadn't asked a single question. She'd just been there, giving herself to soothe his pain.

He glanced at her face—at her mouth—at her hands. Dear Lord, but she had soothed much more than his pain. Impulsively, he leaned over, slid his hand at the back of her head and pulled her forward. Their mouths met. More than slightly surprised, she parted her lips. His were hard and unyielding, demanding that she remember what they were, what they shared.

She gave herself up to the kiss and felt more pain than passion behind the embrace. One day. One day he would talk. Until then, she would have to be satisfied with waiting for his answers—or with what she learned on her own. The private investigator she'd hired was due back on Monday with a final report. Surely she would have some sort of answer by then. Even if it didn't come from Ryder, she had a right to know.

Chapter 13

Last night's rain had washed everything clean. Lash took his morning cup of coffee out onto the veranda and gazed across the yard into the trees beyond. Although it wasn't visible from where he stood, he could hear the water rushing through the creek below. He smiled to himself and took a slow, careful sip of the hot brew, careful not to burn his lips.

It was all falling into place. The kidnapping of Delaney Ruban's heir was a brilliant plan. He knew exactly how it was going to happen—who was going to do the deed—even the amount of ransom he was going to ask for the safe return of Ryder Justice's wife.

The ideal location in which she would be hidden had all but fallen into his lap. An aging client had been admitted to a nursing home via letter and phone by a distant cousin. The law offices of Marlow Incorporated had been given power of attorney to see to her monetary needs, as well as prepare for the impending funeral that was bound to occur.

Lash had done as the family had asked. Fostoria Biggers was now residing in the second room on the right at the Natchez Home for the Aged. Fostoria's money was in the bank, but Lash Marlow's name was on the signature card of her account. Her home out in the country was to be put on the market, and it would be—as soon as he no longer had need of it, which would be right after the Rubans coughed up three million dollars for Casey's safe return.

Friday he'd closed his office and gone to Natchez. The two men he'd hired with five hundred dollars he'd borrowed from Fostoria Biggers's account had come into town last night and were in a motel waiting for his call. The five hundred dollars was just a down payment on what he'd promised them when Casey's abduction was completed.

He took another sip of his coffee as he came down from the steps. He laughed to himself, and the sound caused a pair of white egrets roosting in an overhead tree to take flight. Fifty thousand dollars. Last month he couldn't have come up with fifty dollars, and now he had promised Bernie Pike and Skeet Wilson fifty thousand. And, compared to what he would have in his pocket before the week was over, it was a pittance.

The air was rich with the scent of bougainvillea that grew wild within the skeletal arms of a long-dead oak. The grass was still wet from last night's rain and by the time he reached the ivy-covered gazebo, the hems of his slacks were damp.

He stepped inside, then set down his cup and looked around. For the first time in more years than he cared to count, he could see light at the end of his tunnel of financial woes. It wouldn't be long before he could begin the repairs on Graystone and he could hardly wait. Even the gazebo was long overdue for a face-lift. And while it would have to wait just a little bit longer, there was one thing he could do.

He began gathering up the unpaid bills he'd been tossing on the gazebo floor, making a pile of them in the middle of the yard. Since the grass was damp, he had no qualms about what he did next.

He struck a match and gave it a toss. The papers were damp as well, but finally one caught—then another—then another, and while he watched, the ugly reminders of his past went up in smoke.

The folder from Childers Investigations lay on Casey's desk unopened. The private investigator was gone—had been for over twenty minutes, and Casey hadn't been able to bring herself to read the report. Fear overlayed curiosity as she stared at the name beneath the Childers logo.

Ryder Justice—Confidential

Right now her world was just about perfect. But when she opened this up, it could reveal a Pandora's box of despair that no amount of money could buy, sell or fix.

She walked to the window overlooking the downtown area of Ruban Crossing and stared out onto the street without seeing the traffic or the flow of people coming and going into the Ruban Building itself. And because she was so lost in thought, she didn't see Ryder drive up and park, nor did she see him getting out of the Lincoln with her briefcase—the one she'd left in the kitchen chair during breakfast.

She glanced back at her desk, then walked to the far side of the room to refill her coffee cup. Another cup couldn't hurt. And it was as good an excuse as any to put off reading the report.

Her intercom buzzed, then Nola Sue's voice lisped into the silence.

"Mrs. Justice, your husband is here with your briefcase. He's on his way in."

A smile of delight broke the somberness of Casey's features as Ryder came through the doorway, dangling her briefcase from the ends of his fingers.

"Hi, darlin', sorry to interrupt, but I thought you might be needing this. I'll just lay it on your desk and get out of your hair."

Casey gasped. The report! It was on her desk! Before she could think to move, Ryder was halfway there.

Hot coffee sloshed on her fingers as she shoved the cup on the counter and made a run for the desk. "Ryder, wait!"

Startled by the urgency of her shout, the briefcase slid across the desk and then onto the floor, taking everything with it as it fell.

"Sorry about that," he said quickly, and knelt, intent on gathering up what he had spilled. But he froze in the act, unable to ignore the fact that his name was on every sheet of paper he picked up.

"It's not what you think," Casey said quickly, as she grabbed at the papers he was holding.

The look on Ryder's face had undergone a frightening transformation. The sexy smile he'd worn into the room had been replaced by a grim expression of disbelief. He stood, his words thick with anger.

"What does this mean?"

"I...uh—"

"You had me investigated?"

"You don't understand."

"So—you're telling me you *didn't* have me investigated." Casey couldn't look him in the face. "I didn't say that."

"Then...what you're trying to say is that file is not a dossier of my life story."

Because she was so afraid, she took the defensive. "What I did was—"

"What you just did was stand there and tell me a lie."

She paled. The cold, hard glitter in his eyes was scaring her to death. Dear God, what had she done?

"I did it for you," she said. "For us."

He pivoted, then picked up a cup full of pencils from her desk and flung them against the wall. They shattered and scattered like so much buckshot against a tin barn. Moments later, Casey's secretary burst into the room.

Ryder spun. "Get out."

Nola Sue gave Casey a wild, helpless glance and left at Casey's quick nod.

Ryder was so hurt, so betrayed by what she had done that he didn't trust himself to touch her. When she reached for him, he shoved her hand aside. "Well? Did you find what you were looking for?"

Panic-stricken, she wanted to throw herself into his arms and beg his forgiveness. But she couldn't weaken now, not when their future was at stake.

"I didn't read it."

The curse he flung into the air between them was short and to the point. Casey took it as her just due.

"But it's true. I was afraid to read it."

He grabbed at the scattered sheets he'd tossed on her desk and waved them in her face. "Why, Casey? Don't you know enough about me by now? Couldn't you trust that there was nothing in my past that could hurt you?" He groaned, and threw the papers on the floor. "Damn you. I would die before I let anyone hurt you—even myself."

This time she couldn't stop the tears. They spilled in silent misery.

He kicked at the papers on which he was standing, sending them scooting across the floor. "Then if you haven't read them, I'll save you the trouble. Depending on the depth of the report the investigator did, you will see that I'm the middle child of three sons born to Micah and Barbara Justice. They were ranchers. My older brother, Royal, still lives on the family ranch south of Dallas. My younger brother, Roman, is ex-military and is now a private investigator. I am a pilot. I own and run a charter service out of a private airport on the outskirts of Fort Worth. I also own a little under fourteen hundred acres of prime real estate on the outskirts of San Antonio, Texas, and unlike what you believed about me when we met, I am comfortably solvent. Before you, I had never been married, but last winter, I did something I'd never done before in my entire life."

Casey tensed.

"I ran away from home."

It wasn't what she'd expected him to say. Truth be told, she didn't know what she'd expected, but that certainly hadn't been it.

"I don't understand. What happened to make you turn your back on family and friends? Has it anything to do with the nightmares you have? The ones that drive you out of our bed? The ones you won't talk about?"

He started to shake, and Casey wished to God she'd never meddled.

"I was piloting a plane that crashed. I walked away. My father did not. He's dead because of me."

The look that passed between them was full of painful memories. For Casey, they were of the panic she'd seen on his face when he'd taken her to the airport. Of the plea in his voice not to fly in the storm. Of the desperation in his touch when he'd seen she was alive.

For Ryder, it was the death of a myth he'd been living. Of

pretending that everything between them was perfect. Of hiding behind a marriage of convenience instead of facing the truth.

"You know, wife—I don't think you should be so judgmental about the terms your grandfather put in his will. From where I'm standing, you've picked up his manipulating ways all too well."

With that, he turned and walked out of the office, ignoring the sound of her voice crying out his name—calling him back.

It was all Casey could do not to cry. "Are you sure you haven't seen him all day?"

Joshua shook his head. "No, sugar, I'm sorry. The last time I saw him he was on his way to your office with your briefcase."

She groaned, folded her arms on Tilly's kitchen table and hid her face from the truth. *Please don't let him be gone.*

Tilly sat down beside her. "I knew something was wrong between you two the other day. I told Joshua so, didn't I?"

Joshua nodded.

Casey slammed her fist down on the table. "The other day was nothing." She stood, unable to sit still any longer. "If only I could turn the clock back to that morning, none of this would have happened."

Eudora came hurrying into the kitchen. "What on earth is wrong? I could hear shouting all the way down the hall."

"Mr. Ryder is gone," Tilly said, and then started to cry.

Eudora looked startled, then glanced at Casey for confirmation. "Is this true?"

Casey threw up her hands. "I don't know. He isn't in the habit of telling me anything important in his life," and slammed the door behind her as she left.

"Well, I declare," Eudora said, and dabbed at her eyes with a tissue as Erica came into the kitchen.

"What's going on?" Erica asked.

"Ryder is missing," Eudora said.

Erica looked startled and turned as her brother, Miles, sauntered into the kitchen with his hands in his pockets, as if he didn't have a care in the world. "What's everyone doing in the kitchen?"

"Ryder ran off," Erica said.

His expression changed from one of boredom to intrigue. "Really?"

Eudora frowned. "I don't believe it. I've seen the way he looks at Casey. I suspect they've just had an argument."

Miles scratched his head, as if a thought just occurred.

"If he's gone, I wonder what that does to the terms of Delaney's will?"

It was one of the few times in his life that his grandmother chose to slap his face.

Sometime toward morning, Casey cried herself to sleep. She would have been happy to know Ryder hadn't gone too far. But she didn't know, and because of the press it would cause, she hadn't called the police. If she had, though, it wouldn't have taken them long to locate that familiar white Lincoln. It was parked at the airport in very plain sight. And it wouldn't have taken all that much longer to locate the driver. He was standing outside of the fences that separated the highway from runway, watching as planes took off and landed, trying to exorcise the demon that had driven the wedge between him and the woman he loved. It had taken hours before his conscience would let him admit that while she'd gone about it all wrong, she'd had the right to know.

As he watched, a small private plane was taxiing for takeoff, and he curled his fingers through the holes in the chain links, forcing himself to stand as the plane belied the laws of gravity. Since his arrival, over fifty planes had moved past his location, and not a one had crashed on takeoff or landing.

Then why spare me?

The question haunted him as much, if not more, than the fact that his father was dead. Weary in body and soul, he finally moved from the fence toward the car. He didn't know how, but he and Casey had to find a way to make things right. Living life without her wasn't worth the breath it would take.

But when he reached the car, it wouldn't start. The battery was so dead that jumper cables wouldn't even work, and because the battery was dead, the car phone was also inoperable.

Ryder cursed luck and fate and everything in between, knowing that all he had to do was go inside the terminal and call home, but the idea of getting Casey out at four in the morning didn't seem all that wise, especially after the fight they'd had.

Forced to wait until daybreak when a mobile repairman could be called, he crawled into the back seat of the car, locked himself inside, and lay down and went to sleep. When he awoke, sun was beaming in the window on his face and it was long past nine. He groaned. Casey would be at the office. It would be tonight before they could talk.

"So," Miles said. "You're saying if Casey doesn't fulfill the terms of Delaney's will by staying with her husband for the entire year, it could still mean default?"

Lash leaned back in his chair and nodded, while his heart skipped a beat. This was his chance. This was the opportunity he'd been waiting for. Adrenaline surged as he contemplated the call he would make. Suddenly, he wanted Miles Dunn out of his face and he wanted it now.

"Look, Miles, it's simply a matter of wait and see. All married couples argue and they usually make up. I don't advise you to put too much hope in what you're thinking."

Miles looked slightly embarrassed as he stood. "Of course you're right. And I hope you don't think I was looking to gain anything by Casey's misfortune."

"Of course not," Lash said, as he ushered him out of his office.

When Miles was finally gone, Lash told his secretary to hold all his calls, then he slipped out the back door. He intended to make certain that the call he was about to make could not be traced back to him.

Casey was trying to concentrate on a stockholders' report when the phone by her elbow suddenly rang. It was the private line that only family used. She grabbed at the receiver, answering on the first ring. It had to be Ryder. Please God, let it be him.

"Hello?"

"Is this Miz Justice? Miz Ryder Justice?"

She frowned. The voice was crude and unfamiliar. "Yes, to whom am I speaking?"

"This here is Taft Glass. There's a fellow out here by my place who done went and had hisself a bad wreck. I found him myself when I went out this mornin' to check my trot lines. Looks like he'd been there all night. He's pinned in this big white car and all, and they're workin' to get him out, but he keeps callin' out your name. I told them medics I'd come up here to the bait and tackle shop and give you a call."

All the blood drained from Casey's face. She gripped the phone in desperation. Oh my God, she thought. I lay in bed and slept last night while Ryder was alone and hurt and crying out for help. Her hand started to shake and she gripped the phone tighter. This was why he hadn't come home.

She reached for paper and pen. "Give me the directions to the scene of the accident," she demanded, and wrote at a furious pace as Taft Glass continued to speak.

She grabbed for her purse at the same time she disconnected. Her legs were shaking and she wanted to cry, but this was no time for her to be weak. Ryder's well-being was all that counted.

Halfway to the door, she thought of the wallet she'd tossed in the desk drawer this morning and raced back to get it. She reached in and grabbed, getting a handful of pens along with the small leather case. Without taking time to sift through the mess, she tossed it all in her handbag and dashed out the door.

"Nola Sue, cancel all of my appointments. I don't know when I'll be back, but I'll call. My husband has been injured in a wreck."

Nola Sue was still registering shock as the door slammed shut behind Casey's exit.

"It's got to be here somewhere," Casey muttered, glancing down again at her hastily written map, as she had more than once during the last half hour.

This part of the countryside was one she'd never been in. She was deep in the Mississippi marshlands and hadn't seen a house since she'd turn off the last gravel road.

She took the upcoming curve at a high rate of speed, skidding slightly as the road suddenly straightened. Suddenly, her nerves went on alert. A few hundred yards up ahead she could see a cluster of parked vehicles. She'd found them!

It didn't occur to her to wonder why there were no police cars in sight, and no medical units trying to get Ryder free. All she saw was the front half of a white car buried in a bayou and the back half sticking up in the air, like an awkward straw in a giant cup of thick, soupy mud.

Fear for Ryder made her miss the fact that the buried car was a '59 Ford and that it had certainly been in the water longer than overnight. Fact was, it had been there closer to a year, and it was still there because the owner had moved away soon after, leaving it stuck the same way he'd left owing rent.

But to Casey, the sight was appalling. Her heart nearly stopped. Dear Lord, the man hadn't told her the car had gone off into water. She couldn't bring herself to think about Ryder not being alive. She had to explain to him about the investigation. He had to understand that she'd done it because she loved him, not because she didn't trust him. In a panic, she braked to a skidding halt, unable to contemplate the idea of growing old without him.

A heavyset man separated himself from the cluster of vehicles and started toward her, while another man, tall and skinny with long, graying hair, watched from the tailgate of his truck. The man coming toward her was short and his T-shirted belly had a tendency to laze over the waistband of his faded blue jeans. The baseball cap he wore scrunched over his ears accentuated the fact that he was in dire need of a haircut. Unruly blond wisps stuck out from beneath the rim of the cap like greasy duck feathers.

A niggle of warning ticked off in Casey's head. This wasn't what she'd been expecting. When he leaned in the window and leered, she knew something wasn't right.

"Miz Justice?"

"Yes, I'm Casey Justice.

Bernie Pike grinned and yanked her out of the car. "Damn, lady. It took you long enough to get here."

Panic shafted through her as she struggled to pull herself free.

"Where's Ryder? Where's my husband?"

He laughed. "Now, that's probably about what he's going to be asking himself when you don't show up tonight."

"What do you mean?"

He slapped a rag on her face. It smelled of hospital corridors and science classes she thought she'd forgotten.

"Consider yourself kidnapped, honey, and hope that someone in your family thinks you're worth the price it's gonna take to get you back home."

She screamed and fought, tearing the cloth from her eyes and kicking off her shoes as she tried to run. Something sharp pierced her arm, then the world opened up and swallowed her whole.

Ryder got as far as the edge of town and knew he couldn't wait any longer to see his wife. Night was too far away. In spite of the fact that he looked as if he'd slept in his clothes, which he had, he needed to see Casey now. He parked in front of the Ruban Building and told himself they would find a way to make things right.

Nola Sue gasped as Ryder walked into the office. "Mr. Justice, thank goodness you're all right!"

Casey's secretary wasn't making much sense. "What do you mean?"

"You know. With your wreck and all, we had no way of knowing how serious your injuries might be."

He frowned. "I wasn't in any wreck."

Her hands fluttered around her throat as his words sank in. "But Mrs. Justice said you'd had a wreck. She raced out of here in a terrible state."

Suddenly there was a knot in the pit of his stomach. He didn't want to think about what this might mean. "When?"

Nola Sue glanced at the clock. "Oh, at least an hour ago, maybe longer."

A muscle jerked in Ryder's jaw. "Who told her something like that?"

She shrugged. "I don't know. I just know that someone called her on the private line. You know, the one the family uses." She blushed. "I heard it ring. The walls aren't all that thick."

Damn, this doesn't feel right. "I want to look inside her

office. Would you come with me? You'll know better than I would if something important is missing."

Nola Sue followed Ryder inside, and together they made a thorough search of the place.

"No, I'm sorry, sir, but everything looks the same."

Ryder tried a smile. "I'm sure we're just borrowing trouble. She's probably at home, cursing the fact that someone sent her on a wild-goose chase."

Nola Sue nodded. "I'll bet you're right."

Even though he suspected it was useless, Ryder continued to stand in the middle of the room. He kept thinking that they'd missed something. He could almost feel it.

When they'd started their search, her top desk drawer had been half-open, but Nola Sue had said nothing was missing. There was a pad of paper and a pen right by the phone, just like—

He froze. The pad. Maybe she'd written something on there that would give him a clue. He raced to the desk, then dug a pencil out of the drawer. Carefully, he rubbed the side of the lead on the blank piece of paper, going from side to side as he moved down the page. Inch by inch, a set of directions was slowly revealed.

Nola Sue leaned over his shoulder. "Oh my goodness. That's way out of town. In fact, if I remember correctly, that's out in the marsh."

His gut kicked, reminding him that fate was not kind. "Call the house. See if she's home."

Nola Sue did as she was told and, moments later, gave him the bad news. No one had seen her since early this morning.

Ryder looked down at the pad, afraid to consider where his thoughts were leading, and picked up the phone.

"Where are you doing?" she asked.

"Calling the police. Something's not right. Someone has played a pretty sick joke on Casey, or her life could be in danger. Either way, I'm not waiting to find out."

Casey woke up with a start. Several things became obvious to her all at once. She couldn't see. She couldn't move. Her arm was sore and there was a bitter taste in her mouth. And, she remembered why. She took a deep breath and heard herself sob.

"So, girlie, girlie, I see you're comin' around."

She froze. *Oh God, I am not alone.*

"Please, let me go."

He laughed, and Casey felt like a fool. It had been a stupid thing to ask, but she'd had to, just the same.

"Now, we can't be doin' that. Not until your people come up with the dough. We went to a lot of trouble to set this all up, you know. Don't you think we ought to be paid for our time?"

Dear God, I've been kidnapped! "They'll pay," she said, and then choked on a sob.

He laughed again. "And why the hell not? It ain't like you're short on dough, now, is it?"

Something skittered across her leg and she kicked and screamed in sudden fright.

"Hey! Ain't no need for all that screamin'. If you can't keep your mouth shut, I'll just have to gag you, too—you hear?"

Her voice was still shaking, but there was just enough indignation to get the man's attention. "Something ran across my leg."

"Probably just a lizard. They's all kinds of water critters down here. Be glad it wasn't no snake."

She shuddered and thought of Ryder. Obviously, he hadn't been in any wreck. They'd used that excuse to sucker her right into their hands. If she'd had a foot free, she would have kicked herself. And along with that knowledge, came a question she was afraid to have answered. If Ryder wasn't in a wreck, then where was he? The thought of never seeing him again, of dying and not being able to explain to him why she'd done what she'd done was devastating.

"I need to go to the bathroom."

The man cursed. "I told 'em not to leave me out here. I told 'em somethin' like this was bound to happen. But hell no, did anyone listen?"

"Please."

He yanked at the cord binding her wrists to get her attention, then untied her ankles, dragging her up from the bed and standing her on her bare feet. A few steps later, he gave her a push.

"You got a couple of minutes, no more. And don't try nothin', either." His hand cupped her breast, and Casey could feel his breath on her face. "You'll be sorry if you do."

Casey wouldn't move, wouldn't let him know how scared she was, or how repulsed she was by his touch.

"Well, what the hell are you waitin' for?" he yelled.

She held out her hands. "For you to untie me."

He cursed, but moments later, she felt the rope come loose around her wrists and heard the door slam shut between them.

"No funny business," he yelled. "And remember, I'm right outside this door."

Her hands were shaking as she tore at the rag covering her eyes. When it fell free to the floor, she staggered from the unexpected glare of light. Quick to take advantage of the privilege she'd been granted, she did what she had to do, aware that it could be hours before he might let her get up again.

As she washed her hands, she searched her surroundings for something—anything, that might help her escape. But there was nothing in sight. Not even a window in the tiny, airless room.

The only remarkable thing she could see was a varied assortment of crocheted knickknacks sitting on floors, on shelves, even hanging from the walls. It explained nothing.

"Get out here, now!" the man yelled, and Casey jumped. "And put that blindfold back on your face or you'll be sorry."

She did as she was told, although she was already as sorry as a woman could be and still be breathing. If only she could start this day over.

Her hand was on the doorknob when the man suddenly yanked it open. He grabbed her by the hand, retied her wrists and ankles, and shoved her back down on a bed.

Loath to recline in a room with a man she could not see, Casey sat with her back against the bedstead, her knees pulled toward her chin. It wasn't much, but it was as good a defensive position as she could manage. The urge to come undone was almost overwhelming, but she refused to give way. She was going to need all of her wits to survive.

Chapter 14

Just as Ryder had feared, Casey's car was found at the location she'd written on the notepad. What broke his heart was learning they'd also found her shoes. For once, she must have heeded his warning and kicked off her shoes before trying to run.

Unfortunately, it had done her no good. There wasn't a clue as to where she'd been taken.

Now, just like before when she'd gone to Chicago, Ryder sat by the phone, again waiting for word. Only this time, the phone had been tapped, and when they heard—if they heard—he knew the request wouldn't be for a ride home. If Ryder's fears were correct, it would be for money in return for his wife.

Eudora had been given a sedative and was in her room asleep.

Erica was curled in a chair in the corner with her head on her knees, trying to come to terms with the fact that a member of their family was a possible kidnap victim and trying not to let herself think that if Casey didn't ever come home, everything that had been Delaney Ruban's would then belong to her and Miles. It shamed her to realize that she'd already envisioned what she would wear to her sister's funeral. She didn't want Casey to be dead. Not really. Right now, she would be perfectly satisfied if Casey were back and being the constant source of discord in their lives.

Before Mason Gant had become a detective on the police force in Ruban Crossing, he had been a star running back on his college football team. He'd planned on a career in the NFL, not one behind a badge. But a single tackle had changed his plans and the rest of his life. Before he knew it, fifteen years had come and gone and he was now Detective Gant, and carried a notebook and pen, not a pigskin.

Because of the identity of the missing person, he knew that this could very well be one of the most important investigations of his career and was not giving an inch as to protocol. He'd interviewed all of the hired help and the immediate family, except one. Miles Dunn had been the last to come home and the last to be apprised of his sister's situation. And as Miles slumped in a chair, it was Gant's opinion that Dunn wasn't nearly as bereaved as he would have liked.

"And where were you?" Gant asked, pinning Miles in place with a casual stare.

Miles raised his eyebrows in disbelief. "Why on earth should it matter where I was at? My sister is missing. Why aren't you out trying to find her?" Taking heart in the fact that several of Ruban Crossing's finest were present, he glanced at Ryder, confident that he could say what was on his mind without coming to harm. "Better yet, why aren't you questioning her husband? We don't really know a thing about him."

"Oh, but we do, and his story checks out clean. Besides, he has nothing to gain from her demise. On the other hand, you and your sister have several hundred millions dollars at stake. Am I right?"

Erica stood up with a gasp of indignation as Miles shifted nervously in his seat. "Of course not. Casey inherited."

The detective persisted. "But what happens if she dies?"

Miles shrugged. "I wouldn't really know."

As the family lawyer, Lash was in attendance. At this point he interrupted, but seemed hesitant to do so. "That's not exactly true, Miles. You did come to my office this morning and ask what would happen if Casey defaulted on the terms of Delaney's will.''

Ryder came to his feet, and if there hadn't been a desk and a chair between them, he would have put his fist in Miles's face.

Miles spun, his face livid with anger. "You're twisting everything. You knew I was asking because we all thought Ryder had flown the coop."

Lash looked repentant. "I'm sorry, Miles, but I felt obligated to tell the truth. If anyone needs me, you know where I can be reached." He picked up his briefcase and made a quick exit.

Ryder was shaking with anger. "You son of a bitch. Do you remember what I told you? If Casey hurts—you bleed."

The low, even tone in Ryder's voice frightened Miles far more than any shout of rage could have done. He scrambled to his feet and backed toward the door, looking frantically toward the police for protection.

"Sit down!" Gant said, and then glanced at Ryder. "While I can understand your indignation, this isn't getting us anywhere. A woman is missing and all you people seem able to do is fight among yourselves."

Ryder hunched his shoulders and stalked to the windows overlooking the courtyard, looking up at the small apartment over the garage. Precious minutes passed as pain twisted within him, drawing and pulling like a dull knife. The night before last, he'd slept in Casey's arms. They'd made love with an abandon that had surprised even him. And less than thirty-six hours later, someone had lied to Casey and stolen from Ryder the thing he cared for most—his wife.

And then suddenly the phone rang, and everyone jumped as if they'd been shot.

"You answer it," Gant directed, pointing at Ryder.

Ryder said a prayer and picked up the phone. "Hello."

"This is a recording. I will not repeat myself, so pay attention. Casey Justice is with me. At the moment, she is alive. If you choose to ignore my conditions, she will not stay that way long. For her release, I want three million dollars in small, unmarked bills, none of them larger in denomination than a fifty, none of them smaller than a five. I will call you at five o'clock, day after tomorrow, and tell you where and when to make the drop."

The line went dead, with the computerized sound of an altered voice still grinding in his ear. "Did you get that?" Ryder asked.

Gant nodded. "All we can do now is wait."

Ryder slammed the phone down. "Like hell. That's three days. In three days, anything could happen to Casey. Don't you have any leads? Didn't anything turn up when forensics went over her car?"

Gant was a man who believed in telling it like it was. "Forensics is still going over her car, and you know as well as I do that we don't have any other leads. However, we will actively be pursuing the investigation."

Ryder covered his face with his hands and turned away. He felt sick to his stomach and couldn't quit shaking. He kept thinking about Casey. Of how afraid she must be. "Dear Lord. Why is this happening?"

Gant briefly touched Ryder's arm. "Because someone got greedy, Mr. Justice. Now I suggest you try to get some rest.

The next forty-eight hours will be crucial. The FBI should be here by morning." He grinned wryly. "You'll probably have to repeat everything you've told me to them. They're kind of partial to taking their own statements." His smile faded. "I think you should be prepared for the possibility that the kidnappers are going to want you, or another member of the family, to make the drop."

"I'll do whatever they ask, but I'm not very good at waiting." He exhaled slowly, as if the action pained him. "There will be time to rest after Casey gets home."

Gant looked away. He was too aware that the odds of that happening weren't all that good.

"If anyone needs me, I'll be at the apartment," Ryder said, and started down the hall when Erica caught up with him.

"Ryder."

He stopped and turned.

Looking him straight in the face was the hardest thing she'd ever done. From start to finish, she was ashamed of the way she'd behaved, but she didn't know how to say it without admitting she'd been in the wrong.

"What do you want?" he asked.

"If you don't want to be by yourself, I know Casey would want you to stay here in the main house. You could have her room."

"I don't think so, but thanks." He turned away.

"Ryder, wait, please!"

He took a deep breath and turned around again. "Yeah?"

"I'm sorry."

He didn't respond.

"I have never regretted anything as much as I have regretted the stunt I pulled with you. All I can say is, I have envied Casey her place in this family all of her life, and it's not even her fault. She was born a Ruban. Our mother became one by marriage. Miles and I have been on the outside looking in ever since the day Mother said, 'I do.'" Her chin quivered as she continued. "However, not even in my ugliest moment have I ever wished Casey to come to harm. I ask your forgiveness, and when Casey comes home, I will ask hers, too."

Ryder knew truth when he heard it, and in his opinion, it was probably the first time in her life that Erica Dunn had been completely honest, with herself, and with someone else. And because she was Casey's sister, he held out his hand.

"Truce."

She smiled. "Truce." And she accepted the offer of friendship.

"Sure I can't change your mind?"

He shook his head and then hurried out the door. Erica watched as he ran up the stairs to the apartment, and although she couldn't hear it, imagined the thud as he slammed the door shut behind him.

Ryder grabbed the phone as soon as he came in the door, then sat down with it in his lap. Within seconds, he was punching in numbers, then waiting as it began to ring. Four rings later, the answering machine kicked on.

He closed his eyes as he listened to the message. It had been so long—too long since he'd heard the sound of his brother's voice.

"This is Justice Air and The Justice Way. State your name, your business, and if you want a call back, leave your number. Wait for the beep."

It didn't register to be surprised that Roman was now in charge of his business as well. Casey was foremost on his mind.

"Roman, it's Ryder. For once, pick up the damned phone."

A distinct click sounded in Ryder's ear, and he closed his eyes with relief.

"It's about damned time," Roman growled.

"Give me grief later," Ryder said. "Right now, I need you, brother, as I have never needed you before."

Roman sat up. Ryder was thirty-three years old and to Roman's knowledge, he had never asked a soul for help before in his life. "What's wrong?"

"My wife has been kidnapped. I want her back, Roman." His voice broke. "Dammit, I need her back. If anything happens to her, I won't—"

"Where are you?"

"Ruban Crossing, Mississippi."

"Hell, I knew that," Roman muttered. "I mean physical directions to your home."

Startled, it took Ryder a moment to reconnect his thoughts. Then he sighed. He should have known. After all, his brother *was* a private investigator.

"Got a pen and paper?" he asked.

"Does a bear—"

Ryder laughed aloud, drowning out the rest of Roman's remark. It made him feel good, almost normal, to hear Roman's ever present sarcasm. Some things never change.

He gave Roman directions to the Ruban estate, and when he hung up, for the first time since this nightmare had started to unfold, he knew a small sense of relief.

In a small, unused room in a forgotten part of Delaney Ruban's house, candles were burning, on pedestals, in cups, on plates, even on the floor. Candlelight flickered upon the walls and on the bare, lithe body of Matilda Bass, giving the cafe au lait color of her skin a rich, golden glow.

Her hair was undone and hanging well below her waist and she moved as one in a trance, methodically unrolling a cloth she'd brought into the room. A handful of small, white bones fell out of the folds, arranging themselves in a crude sort of circle as they rolled to a stop.

She leaned forward, her bare breasts shifting, and she was barely aware of the thick, silken length of her hair against the skin on her back, blind to the candlelight surrounding her as she sat.

At her side lay a knife, the shaft, old and yellowed. The blade was long and thin, the kind that pierces and kills and leaves nothing behind but a tiny, red mark. The carvings on the handle were old and held a power all of their own.

When Joshua entered, Tilly sensed the air in the room stirring, and somewhere within her mind, she sifted through the change and knew that nothing threatened what she was about to do. Her focus shifted again as she went to her knees before the circle of bones, whispering in a language that she'd learned at her grandmother's knee.

Lash downshifted Fostoria Biggers's small white compact and turned into the overgrown driveway leading up to her house. It was nearly dark, and he knew that coming out here was risky, but he wanted to see for himself that the mighty Casey Ruban had been brought to her knees. Using Fostoria's car was just another way of blurring his trail.

The house was small and nearing total dilapidation. In fact, if possible, it was in worse condition than his beloved Graystone. Fostoria's porch had sagged some years ago, and was nearly rotted through from the wetlands upon which it had been built. Paint had peeled off all the siding except in a few sheltered places, and the curtains that hung at the windows were faded and limp. The grass in the yard was ankle high and Lash winced as he thought of walking through it. There was no telling what kind of reptiles were lying in wait.

He made it through the yard and onto the porch. Sidestepping the worst of the sag in the planks, he walked into the house as if he owned it. Bernie Pike spun toward the sound, his gun pointed directly at Lash's chest.

"Dammit, Marlow, you scared the hell out of me."

Lash frowned. "Point that thing somewhere else."

Bernie did as he was told.

"Where is she?" Lash asked.

Bernie pointed toward the first door on the right down the hall. "I put her in there. It was the only room that had a bed."

Lash nodded.

"When's Skeet comin' to relieve me?"

Lash frowned. "I told you two to guard her. I didn't think I would have to set up a work schedule for you as well. Call him and find out for yourself."

Bernie shivered and glanced nervously out the open door. "I'm ready to get my money and get the hell out of this swamp. There's snakes and lizards and all matter of critters out here. When is it all goin' down?"

"Day after tomorrow."

Bernie frowned and then cursed. "What's the holdup? I thought them people had plenty of money."

Lash glanced down the hall at the closed door and then grinned. "Oh, they do, but I intend to delay the inevitable as long as possible. Why put her out of her misery—until she knows what real misery is like?"

There was an expression on Lash Marlow's face that made Bernie Pike shudder. He shifted his gun to his other hand, thankful that he was working for this man, not running from him.

"So, what do you want me to do?" Bernie asked.

Lash took a deep breath, his pulse quickening as he glanced at the closed door. "Get out. Get out and don't come back inside until I tell you to."

Bernie looked startled and then a slow grin spread across his face as he did what he was told.

When the house was quiet, and Lash could hear nothing but the sound of his own heartbeat in his ears, he gave his rabbit's foot a last quick rub, and started down the hall.

Casey's hands were numb and her throat was dry. She needed a drink in the very worst way, but calling attention to herself was the last thing she wanted to do. As long as her abductor thought she was asleep, he pretty much left her alone.

Something was crawling on the floor beside the bed and she prayed it stayed there. But the scritch-scratch of toenails on hardwood flooring was impossible to ignore. She kept telling herself that as long as she couldn't see what was making the noise, then she couldn't be afraid.

And then the air shifted, and another sound blended with those in her head and she tensed. That was the door! Someone was inside the room. Casey had learned a trick from Delaney early on in her life to take control of a situation by being the first to speak. She saw no reason to change her strategy now.

"I would like a drink of water."

A low, ugly chuckle centered itself within the waiting silence and Casey gasped. That didn't sound like her abductor. Someone else had entered the picture.

"Casey, Casey, ever the prima donna, aren't you? Tied up like a sow going to market and still giving orders. Now what do you suppose it would take to bring you to your knees?"

"Lash?"

The blindfold was yanked from her face.

Casey blinked rapidly, trying to clear her vision as her eyes adjusted to the change in light. Lash leaned down and pinched the sides of her cheeks with his thumbs and fingers, squeezing and squeezing until speech was impossible and tears sprang to her eyes.

"That's it. Cry for me, honey. Show me you care."

Casey jerked, trying to free herself from his grasp, and then to her surprise, he turned her loose and shoved her, sending her sprawling. Before she could think, he had untied her ankles and straddled her legs.

Panic shafted through Casey's mind. Lash's intentions were all too plain. And when he leaned forward, pressing the palms of his hands against the swell of her breasts, she groaned and wrestled with the ties still binding her wrists. They wouldn't give.

"Lash, for God's sake, don't."

His slap ricocheted off the side of her jaw. "You don't tell me what to do. I'm the one in control. I'm the one who calls the plays, princess, and right now, I'm going to take a little of what was rightfully mine."

His fingers curled in the top of her blouse, and when he yanked, buttons flew, hitting the wall and scattering across the floor. Something scurried out from under the bed and Casey knew that one good thing had come from Lash's arrival. At least that creature was gone. If she only knew how to get rid of this one for good, she would never ask for anything again.

He laughed, and then grabbed at the hem of her skirt as adrenaline surged through him. This was power. He wished he'd thought of it sooner. At last he felt like a man.

Casey kicked and bit and screamed until her throat was hoarse. It served no purpose other than to arouse him more. His hands were at the juncture of her legs when the room began to grow dark before her eyes. A fresh sheen of perspiration broke out on Casey's skin as the sensation of fainting became imminent. Horrified at what he would do if she was unconscious and helpless, Casey thought of a prayer that didn't make it aloud. The darkness in the room was growing, and it was beginning to pull her in.

Her submission was so unexpected that Lash also paused, wondering what trick she was trying to pull. But she was far too limp and far too still for a joke. Frustrated that she would not be awake to suffer his touch, he thrust a knee between her legs, readying to shove himself in as well. And then Casey began to speak.

Surprised, he looked down. Her eyes were still closed. She was still limp—almost lifeless. And he would have sworn the voice that he heard was not her own.

Her breathing had slowed, and at first glance, she seemed to be asleep. But the words pouring out of her mouth were fluent in cadence, foreign in sound and speech, universal in intent. One brief, staccato sentence after another, she was invoking a curse of such magnitude upon Lash Marlow's head that he couldn't do anything but stare. Word after word, the curse continued, pouring upon every living person hereafter who might carry an ounce of his blood in their veins. Spoken in the old patois of French-speaking slaves, the threat became even more insidious as the promises continued.

Lash jerked his hand back from her legs as if he'd been burned. Pale and sickening, a cold sweat suddenly beaded upon his face. Lash was a true son of the south. He'd been born and bred in the ways of the past. He, too, spoke French like a native, and although he was a well-read, highly educated man, there was that part of him that had grown up believing in curses and superstitions and extremely bad luck.

"Shut up! Shut up!" His scream rent the air as he drew back and slapped her in the face.

It was after Casey tasted her own blood that she took a deep breath and opened her eyes.

Horror crawled up the back of Lash's spine. The woman looking out at him from Casey's face wasn't the green-eyed woman he'd known and coveted. This woman's eyes were black, and she was staring at him from hell.

He grabbed at his clothes, scrambling to get off of her legs and away from her body like a man gone crazy. When he was on the other side of the room, he pointed a finger toward where she lay and told himself it didn't matter. Words were just words. She couldn't stop the success of what he'd set in place. But everywhere he moved, her eyes followed him, staring— blaming—reminding him of what she'd just said.

"Say what you will, you stupid bitch," he growled. Then he laughed. But it was a nervous, jerky sort of bark. "Day after tomorrow it will all be over. I'll be rich, and you'll be dead."

And then he was gone, and while she lay on the bed, she came to an acceptance she didn't understand. Even though she was locked in this room and helpless in the face of her abductors, for a while, she had not been alone. Instead of being afraid, she took comfort in the knowledge. All she could remember was feeling sick and then falling into a deep, black hole. What had transpired after that, she could only guess, but she knew she had not been raped. And in the face of all that, it still wasn't the biggest horror of all.

Lash Marlow had purposefully let her see his face. She closed her eyes. She would never see Ryder again.

It was 3:00 a.m. when the knock sounded on Ryder's front door. Half in and half out of a weary doze, he staggered to his feet and made his way through the darkened rooms, turning on lights as he went. He grabbed the doorknob and jerked.

Roman walked inside, tossed a suitcase on the sofa and kicked the door shut behind him. Brother to brother, the two men looked at each other, judging the changes in each that the last few months had made. Finally, it was Roman who broke the silence.

"You look like hell."

Ryder walked into his brother's outstretched arms. Their embrace was brief, but it served its purpose. It was proof to Ryder that the connection he'd tried to sever with his family was still as strong as it had ever been.

"You got here fast," he said.

Roman glanced around the room. "I figured I'd better."

Ryder hadn't expected to be so overwhelmed by the sight of his brother's face. It was all he could do to speak without breaking down. "Help me, Roman. Help me find her and get her back."

Roman's grasp was strong on Ryder's arm. "That's why I came, brother. That's why I came."

Like the sleuth that he was, Roman began to move about the room, picking up things and laying them down again, feeling, judging, absorbing the world in which his brother had been living. A photograph sat on a nearby table. Roman picked it up.

"Is this her?"

Ryder nodded. It had been taken the night of Libertine Delacroix's party. It hurt to look at it and remember how happy they'd been. "Yeah, minus the ears and tail," Ryder said.

One of Roman's rare grins slid into place. "Leave it up to you to run away from home and come out smelling like a rose."

"Well, I do declare!"

Eudora's ladylike gasp that accompanied her remark was in reaction to seeing the Justice brothers coming through the front door of the main house.

From the cold, handsome faces to the dark straight hair and those square, stubborn chins, they were alike as two peas in a pod. Their blue jeans were pressed and starched and their long-sleeved white shirts were a perfect contrast to the tan of their skin. The tilt of their Stetsons rode at the same cocky slant, and their steps synchronized as they stepped off space on the pale, marble floor.

"Dora, this is my brother, Roman Justice. Roman—Casey's grandmother, Eudora Deathridge."

Roman's expression never changed as he tilted his hat. "Ma'am."

A shiver moved through her as she looked into Roman's eyes. They were dark, and the expression seemed hard and flat. And she knew if he hadn't looked so much like Ryder, she would have been afraid of this man.

Ryder touched her arm. "We're going to use the library for a while, okay?"

"Why, yes, dear. Whatever you need," she said, and then made as graceful an exit as she could manage.

"There it is," Ryder said, pointing to the computer system in the far corner of the room.

Roman headed for it with unerring intent. Within moments, he was into the system and had it on-line.

"How did you do that?" Ryder asked. "I can never make those things do what I want them to do."

Roman looked up. "You just don't use the right kind of persuasion," he replied, then moved his eyes back to the screen.

Ryder found himself a chair and sat down. This morning, Roman had asked him for a list of names of people with whom Casey most closely associated. The question had surprised him. All this time he'd been thinking in terms of faceless strangers, not a betrayal from family or friend.

He'd asked why and was still shaken by his brother's cold answer. "Because trust will betray you every time."

It hurt him to know the depth of Roman's bitterness toward the human race. But his own life was in such a mess, he couldn't argue the point. All he could do was trust the fact that Roman had been in this business long enough to know what he was doing.

"Well, now, this is interesting."

Ryder came out of his chair like a shot. They were the first words that Roman had spoken since he'd sat down at the computer over an hour ago.

"What?" Ryder asked.

Roman leaned back in his chair. "Besides being the family lawyer, what is Lash Marlow to Casey?"

Ryder frowned. "Nothing, although I think her grandfather would have wished it otherwise. Remember what I told you about the will, and how we met?"

Roman nodded.

"Casey once mentioned that when Lash Marlow read that clause in the will, he was almost gloating. You know, like an I've-got-you-now look."

Roman stared at the screen. "He's broke."

Startled, Ryder moved to look over Roman's shoulder. "You must be mistaken. His family is old money. That's what everyone says."

"He has been served with a foreclosure notice, and up until two weeks ago, his accounts were all overdrawn."

Ryder frowned. "How the hell did you get that computer to do that?"

"That's privileged info, brother."

"Did you hack into the bank's computers?"

Roman spun his chair around as one of his rare smiles slowly broke across his face. "Now, Ryder, why would I do a thing like that? It's illegal."

Ryder started to pace. "Okay, so Lash Marlow is hard up for money. I'd venture to say at least half the people in Ruban Crossing could say the same."

He paused to look out the window overlooking the grounds. His gaze fell on the gardener's shed. Despair surfaced as he thought of holding Casey in his arms, and what they'd done that night in the name of love. It was all he could do to focus on what had to be done.

"Look Roman, there's no guarantee that whoever has Casey is even a local. In the business world, the Ruban name is known worldwide. Their holdings are vast. Casey's inheritance has recently been in all the papers...twice. Once when Delaney died. Again when that plane she was supposed to be on crashed and burned with all aboard."

Roman listened without comment, but when he turned back

to the computer, his gaze was fixed, his thoughts whirling. He kept thinking of what his C.O. used to say just before they'd go out on a mission. *Never overlook the obvious. It will get you killed every time.* In Roman's opinion, Lash Marlow had an obvious axe to grind. What remained to be seen was if he was the kind of man who could betray a client...or a friend.

The family was gathering in the main salon, and while they whispered among themselves as to the possible reason Detective Gant might have for calling them all together again, Ryder's thoughts were on something else. A few moments ago, he'd glanced up at the clock. Forty-eight hours ago to the minute, he'd walked into Casey's office a happy man. Within the space of time it took to spill papers from a desk, his world had come to an end. All last night he'd kept hearing the sound of her voice as she'd begged him to come back inside her office. If only he had.

A few moments later, the doorbell chimed and they heard Joshua directing Mason Gant into the room.

"Thanks for being so prompt," Gant said, waving away Joshua's offer of coffee. He glanced around the room. "I have some news," he announced, and when Ryder took a step forward, he held up his hand. "Sorry, I phrased that wrong. It is news, but not of Casey."

The doorbell pealed again and Joshua hurried from the room. Moments later, Lash Marlow followed him back.

"Sorry I'm late," Lash said, smoothing his hand over his windblown hair. "Had to be in court first thing this morning."

Gant nodded. "I just got here myself." He looked around. "Is everyone here?"

"Everyone but Bea. Today's her day off," Tilly said.

Gant pulled out his notebook. "I have her address. I'll catch up with her later."

"Detective Gant, before you start, there's someone I want you to meet."

Gant looked up, surprised by Ryder's remark. He thought he'd met everyone when he was here before. Suddenly a man walked into his line of vision and he realized that the fellow had been standing in plain sight all along, but had been so quiet and so still that he'd completely overlooked his presence.

His first impression was that the man was military. His second was special forces. And then he focused on his face and Gant knew before he spoke that this man was Ryder's brother...if not his twin.

"I'd wager your last name is Justice," Gant said.

Roman held out his hand. "Roman Justice, private investigator out of Dallas. I won't get in your way if you don't get in mine."

Gant grinned as they shook hands. He liked a man who said what he thought.

A coffee cup shattered, breaking the brief silence as everyone turned toward the sound. Lash was against the wall. He was pale and shaking and staring down at the floor.

"It slipped out of my hands."

Joshua ran to get a broom as Tilly fussed with the splatters that dappled the edge of a soft, moss-green rug.

Ryder stared at Lash, as if seeing him for the very first time. He couldn't bring himself to believe that anyone who knew Casey would want to cause her harm. And Marlow was, as usual, every inch the gentleman—from the cut of his clothes to the style of his hair. But why was Lash so upset over a spilled cup of coffee? Ryder kept staring and staring, remembering his brother's words and trying to see past the obvious to the man beneath. Suddenly, something about Lash's appearance struck a sour note.

"Hey, Marlow."

At the sound of Ryder's voice, Lash jerked as if he'd been slapped. He looked up. "Yes?"

"What the hell happened to your hand?"

He didn't have to look down to know they were referring to the row of skinned knuckles on his right hand and the long red gash that ran from one edge of his wrist to the other. Gorge rose in his throat as he struggled with an answer they all might believe. He could hardly tell them it was the remnants of his bout with Casey.

He managed a laugh. "I locked myself out of the house last night. Graystone may be past her prime, but like the lady she is, she does not easily part with her virtue. I broke a window trying to get inside. Lucky for me I didn't cut my own wrist, right?''

The answer was plausible enough. Ryder shrugged. If the man had cut his own throat, he couldn't have cared less. If there was news that pertained to Casey, he wanted to know now.

"Look, Gant, let's get down to business. Why did you call us all together?''

Lash was counting his blessings that the subject of his wounds had been changed. But his relief was short-lived when Gant started to talk.

"Forensics came up with a print on Casey's car that doesn't match anyone else in the family.''

Ryder stiffened. Was this their first break? "Do you have an ID?''

Gant nodded. "Belongs to a low-life hood out of Natchez named Bernie Pike.''

Lash felt his legs going out from under him and slid into a chair before he made another social faux pas. By the time everyone present had assured the detective they knew nothing about the name, he had himself under control.

Although Gant's meeting with the family had been necessary, he hadn't really expected anything to come from this lead. At least, not from this quarter. He was gathering his things and readying to leave when he suddenly remembered another fact he needed to verify.

Lash Marlow was on his way out the door when Gant called him back.

"Marlow! Wait!''

Lash spun, his nerves tightening with every breath that he took. "Yes?''

"About the ransom. Will you be able to get it all together by tomorrow?''

He went weak with relief. "Yes, sir. The bank has been most helpful in this case. Some of it arrived today by armored car. The rest should be here before noon tomorrow.''

Gant nodded. "Good. I don't want any last minutes hitches. When that call comes in, I want to be ready to roll.''

Lash stifled a smile. "I couldn't agree with you more.''

Chapter 15

Now that Casey was no longer blindfolded, the thick layer of dust covering the floor in the room where she was being held was obvious. The footprints marring the gray-white surface were evidence of the degree of traffic that had come into Fostoria Biggers's home since she'd been gone. The absence of glass in two of the three windows of her temporary cell did little to offer an avenue for her to escape. They had all been boarded up from the outside. She couldn't get out and fresh air couldn't get in.

Last night when they thought she'd been sleeping, she'd dug and pulled and pushed at the boards until her fingers were raw and her nails were gone. Only after she heard one of the men stirring around had she ceased her futile bid for freedom.

Now, she thought it was some time after daybreak. The smell of morning coffee had drifted into the room. On the one hand, she felt justified in celebrating the arrival of a new day, but if Lash was to be believed, she would not celebrate another.

She stood at the door, holding her breath and desperately trying to hear what the two men in the other room were saying.

It was impossible. Their voices were too low and the door was too thick to hear anything other than an occasional murmur.

A plate lay on the floor near her feet. Remnants of the sandwich they'd given her yesterday to eat. She'd taken the food and a good look at the filth on their hands and decided she would rather go to her grave hungry.

Whatever it was that kept coming and going through a hole in the floor had made a meal of it last night. By now she didn't much care what she shared the room with, as long as it came on four feet instead of two

In deference to her constant requests for drinks of water and bathroom privileges, her feet and hands were no longer tied. And, since Lash's departure yesterday, the blindfold had also been discarded. But while she now had an odd sort of freedom within the small, boarded-up room, the implications behind it were frightening. They no longer cared if she saw their faces because she would not be alive to tell the tale.

The sound of a chair being scooted across the floor made Casey bolt for the other side of the room. Ever since the arrival of Skeet Wilson, Pike's cohort, Casey had been afraid to sleep. Bernie had threatened her, but it was Skeet Wilson whom she knew would willingly do the deed. He was tall and skinny and walked with a limp. His hair was long and gray and tied at the back of his neck with a piece of shoestring. Some sort of blanket fuzz was caught in the knot and it was Casey's opinion that the shoestring had been there for a very long time. Skeet bore more scars on his face than teeth in his head, and he carried them all with a wild sort of pride. He had a face straight out of a nightmare with the disposition to match.

She stood with her back against the wall, holding her breath and praying that it would be Bernie who came in the door. If she'd been betting on the odds of that happening, she would have lost.

Skeet Wilson stepped inside then paused, carefully eyeing the tall, slender woman with her back against the wall. Even though the blue suit she was wearing was filthy and torn and her legs and feet were bare and scratched, there was an odd sort of dignity to the way she was braced. In a way, he admired

But it didn't matter what he thought. Skeet was a man

who could be bought. And right now, Casey Justice wasn't a woman to him, she was fifty thousand dollars on the hoof.

"What?" Casey asked, as always, choosing to be the first one to speak.

Skeet grinned and smoothed his hand down the front of his fly, just to remind her who was boss. "Bed check."

Unless a miracle occurred, today was the last day of her life, but she refused to go out screaming and crying and begging for mercy they weren't capable of giving. She lifted her chin and squarely met his gaze.

"It's certainly obvious where you spent your last vacation."

It crossed his mind to be pissed, but her reference to the fact that his speech was peppered with penitentiary lingo was too good to ignore. He grinned, revealing his lack of a full set of teeth. And she was right. His world did revolve around the legal system. Just not on the side of law and order.

"Don't get too prissy, lady. You're real close to meetin' your maker."

Don't let him see your fear.

The thought came out of nowhere, and somehow Casey knew that at that moment, Ryder was with her in the only way he could be. Her hands fisted as she stared him down.

"That's what the mugger said before he snatched the old lady's purse and ran into the street."

Skeet's smirk froze on his face. Either she was losing her mind or it was already gone. He'd never known a woman with the balls to try to tell a joke to someone who was holding her captive. "That don't make much sense."

"It does if you know that, seconds later, the mugger was run over by a car. The old lady then walked into the street, lifted her purse out of the dead mugger's hands and bent over and whispered something in his ear."

Skeet knew he shouldn't ask, but he was too intrigued to let the subject lie.

"So, what did she say?"

Casey grinned. "To tell her maker hello."

Skeet cursed and slammed the door shut between them. He wasn't all that smart, but it didn't take a genius to figure out what she'd been getting at and he didn't like it.

He and Bernie had gone through a lot these last two days.

Marlow had threatened them with everything from murder to reneging on the last of their money if they so much as touched a hair on Casey Justice's head. Marlow had all but frothed at the mouth, claiming that right was to be his. Sick of his ranting, they'd finally complied. But Skeet wouldn't be sorry to see the last of her. She was too damned mouthy for her own good.

He kicked at an empty bean can in the middle of the floor and flopped back down in his chair. There wasn't any way this plan could fail. By tonight, he and Bernie would be rolling in dough. After that, he didn't give a damn what Marlow did with the bitch. Whatever it was, it was still less than she deserved.

"What are those?" Ryder asked, as Roman sorted through a small case in his lap.

"Tracking devices, something like the ones the FBI will probably put in with the ransom money."

Ryder nodded, although his opinion of the FBI left a lot to be desired. In his opinion, they asked too many questions and didn't give enough answers. They acted as if what was going on was none of his business.

"Won't the kidnappers be expecting something like that?"

Roman looked up. "That's why I've got these. The Feds can do their thing. I'm going to do mine."

"They're not going to like it," Ryder warned. "You already ticked Wyandott off yesterday."

Roman leaned back in his chair, remembering the confrontation he'd had with the special agent in charge. "No one dies from being ticked."

"You are a hard man, Roman Justice."

"Tell it to Uncle Sam. He took credit for making me this way. He can take the blame, as well."

If the situation had been anything else, Ryder could have laughed. As it was, he almost felt sorry for the man who got in his brother's way.

He glanced at the clock. It was almost noon. Where the hell was Lash Marlow with the money? He kept remembering what Roman had told him about Marlow's financial situation. It seemed to him that there was a fault in the theory that Lash should be responsible for its deliverance. It was like giving a starving man the keys to the cupboard.

The doorbell rang. Ryder jumped, then started down the hall, unwilling to wait for Joshua to let whoever it was in. Maybe there was news of Casey. But the Feds beat him to it. Lash was admitted carrying two large duffel bags.

"I've got it!" he crowed.

Two men in dark suits relieved him of the bags, leaving him standing in the hall with a jubilant smile on his face. Lash could hardly contain his joy. It was almost over.

"The armored car was late," Lash said, by way of an explanation for his tardiness.

Ryder listened without comment.

Lash smoothed a hand over his hair. "Any news?"

Ryder shook his head. "No."

What seemed to be a genuine grimace of dismay spread across his face. "You know, sometimes this all seems like a dream."

"More like a nightmare, if you ask me."

Lash nodded. "Of course, that's what I meant."

A man Ryder had never seen before came out into the hall from the main salon. Another Fed.

"Mr. Marlow, Detective Gant wants to speak with you."

Lash straightened his suit coat and followed the man into the room. Ryder was right behind.

Gant waved his hand toward the open bags. "It's all here, I presume?"

Lash nodded. "Three million dollars in unmarked bills. None of them larger in denomination than a fifty, none of them smaller than a five."

Gant nodded and turned back to the desk while Ryder struggled with a notion that wouldn't come. Something Lash had just said rang a chord of memory, but he couldn't figure out why.

Lash started toward the door. "If you have no further need of me, court awaits."

Gant paused and looked to Wyandott, who was officially in charge of the investigation. Wyandott didn't bother to look up.

Gant shrugged. "I guess not. But if something comes up, I'll know where to find you, right?"

Lash chuckled. "One can only hope."

Ryder's hands were itching. The urge to grab Lash was overwhelming. It was all he could do to stay put as Marlow left. But at this point, Ryder couldn't pinpoint what it was that was bugging him.

The front door slammed behind Lash as Roman walked in the room.

"Who was here?" Roman asked.

"Marlow. He brought the ransom money."

Ryder pointed toward the bags on the desk and the men who were working on securing tracking devices within the bags.

It was when Roman started toward the desk that the notion hovering in the back of Ryder's mind started to take shape.

"Hey, Gant."

Gant looked up. "Yeah?"

"Marlow was gone when the kidnapper called, remember?" Gant nodded.

"Then who told him how the money was to be paid?"

"I did," Gant said, then glanced at Wyandott, who had already expressed some displeasure in the way Gant had handled things thus far. "I knew it wouldn't be easy to accumulate that much money in small bills. Thought he needed as much time as possible."

But that wasn't what Ryder needed to know. "No...exactly what did you tell him?"

"I don't follow you," Gant said. "What are you getting at?"

Ryder's nerves were on edge. The more he thought about Lash, the more certain he became. "I want to know what you told him to bring."

"I said something to the effect that we needed three million dollars in small, unmarked bills by noon today."

"Did you tell him what denominations?"

"I told him no hundred dollars bills. Everything had to be smaller than one hundred dollar bills."

Oh, my God. What if Roman was right on target about Lash

Marlow's involvement all along? "Then did you or any of your men ever play that tape for Marlow?"

"What tape?" Gant asked.

"The one you made when the ransom call came in."

Gant shrugged. "I don't know. I know I didn't." He looked at Wyandott. "Did you or any of your men?" All answers were negative.

The flesh crawled on the back of Ryder's neck. "Then can any of you explain to me why Marlow just quoted the kidnapper's exact terminology of the request he made for ransom?"

Roman pivoted, already following the line of his brother's thoughts. "I wasn't in here. What did Marlow say?"

Ryder stared around the room, daring the men to disagree. "You all heard him. He said, 'Three million dollars in unmarked bills. None of them larger in denomination than a fifty, none of them smaller than a five.'"

"Son of a bitch." Gant's epitaph was echoed in more than one man's thoughts. "If memory serves, that's just about word for word."

Wyandott looked surprised, then began issuing new orders as Ryder turned and started running. Roman caught him at the door.

"You can't do what you're thinking."

Ryder yanked himself free. His words came out a cold, even tone. "You don't know what I'm thinking."

Roman tightened his hold. "That's where you're wrong. I know exactly what you're thinking, and I don't blame you one bit. But you've got to think of Casey. If Marlow is involved and he's alerted before the drop even goes down, what's going to happen to her? Better yet, how the hell would we know where to find her?"

Ryder hit the wall with the flat of his palm and then wiped a hand across his face. Every time he took a step he wanted to run, but to where? What had they done with his wife?

"My God," he said. "What the hell do you expect me to do? Wait until someone brings her back to me in a body bag?"

Roman got up in his face, and this time, he was the one on the defensive. "No, I expect you to let me do my job."

Ryder doubled his fists and refused to give an inch, even to his brother. Helpless in the face of so much logic, the urge to lash out was overwhelming.

Roman sighed. He didn't understand this kind of commitment between a man and a woman, but he'd seen enough of it to know it went beyond any blood ties. And as he gazed into his brother's face, he had a flashback of a little boy with mud in his hair and fire in his eyes. He remembered that same little boy had not only whipped the boy who'd beaten him up to take away his baseball, but he'd gotten the ball back, too. Even then, Ryder Justice had been a force with which to reckon.

"So, what's it going to be?" Roman asked.

Even though the urge to argue was overwhelming, Ryder relented, slumping against the wall. "Then do it. Just know that every step you take I'm going to be on your heels."

"Wouldn't have it any other way, brother, but that will come later. Right now, there's one little thing I need to do before the day gets any older, and I don't want help in getting it done."

It felt wrong, and it hurt like hell to watch Roman going out the door without him, but Ryder stood his ground. Roman was right. He'd asked for his help. The least he could do was give him the leeway to do it.

"Give 'em hell, Roman."

Roman looked back, just as he started out the door. "Is there any other way?"

Lash was making himself a ham and cheese sandwich. He'd even gotten out his mother's good china on which to eat it. He slathered mustard on one slice of bread and mayonnaise on the other. *And why not? It's about time things started going my way.*

The sandwich was thick with meat, cheese, and lettuce. He pushed a toothpick into an olive, then topped his sandwich by stabbing the toothpick into the bread with a flourish. Now there was only one thing left. He opened the refrigerator and took out a bottle of wine. Chilled to perfection.

He walked out of the kitchen toward the old dining hall

with china, wine and food in hand. When he stepped inside, there was a feeling of relief unlike any he'd ever known.

Spiderwebs draped the dust-covered chandelier above the table like torn and tattered lace. One of the panes was out at the top of a floor-to-ceiling window overlooking the back of the property and there was a bird's nest in the corner of the room. But Lash didn't see the ruin and decay. His jubilation was focused on former glory and future renovation.

The cork popped on the wine and he smiled to himself as he filled his glass. As he sipped, the chill of the grape and the dry, vintage taste of fine wine tingled on his tongue. He set the half-empty glass down in a patch of sunlight, admiring the way a sunbeam pierced the liquid.

He pulled the toothpick out of his food, popped the olive into his mouth, and chewed down. There was an instant awareness of an odd, unfamiliar taste as he gasped and spit the olive out into his hand.

And the moment he saw it, his flesh crawled. Somewhere within his mind, a drumbeat sounded. Then it began to hammer, faster and faster until he couldn't move—couldn't speak. He heard a cry, and then the faint, but unmistakable, sounds of a woman's soft voice. The language was French, spoken in the patois of the slaves his great-great-grandfather had once owned.

He jumped up from his chair and flung what was left of the olive onto the dust-covered table before running out of the room. The celebration and his meal were forgotten in the horror of what he'd just seen. And as the sounds of his footsteps faded away, the carcass of a small, white worm fell out of the olive and into the patch of sunlight beaming down through the wine.

Lash ran out of the house and into the woods, searching for a solace his mind couldn't find. To any other person, it would have been an unfortunate choice of an olive from a nearly full jar, but to Lash, it was the first step in a curse that had started to come true.

Decay. Everything around you will fall to decay. Flesh will fall off of your bones and be consumed by the worms.

Raised in a superstition as old as the land itself, in Lash Marlow's mind, the curse Casey invoked had begun. He thought about what would happen if he just called the whole thing off. If he could, he would have turned back the clock, stopped what he'd started before it was too late. As always, Lash's instinct for good was too little, too late.

Roman crouched beneath the low-hanging branches of a weeping willow, watching as Marlow came out of his house and ran into the woods bordering the backyard. He frowned. Whatever it was that had sent him running couldn't have come at a better time. And still he waited, ever cautious, searching the grounds around the house for signs of other life. Except for the leaves in the trees, nothing moved.

Like a shadow, he came out from hiding, heading straight toward the dark blue sedan parked in front of the house. Within seconds of reaching it, he had secured a tracking device under the frame and was on his way back when he saw something that gave him pause. The fender of a small white car was just visible through the partially opened door of a nearby shed.

He frowned. According to the information he'd pulled from the Department of Motor Vehicles, Lash Marlow owned one car—a midnight blue, four-door sedan. He swerved in midstep and bolted for the shed, constantly searching the area for signs of Marlow's arrival.

The car was a small, white compact—at least eight, maybe ten years old. He glanced in at the gauges and whistled softly beneath his breath as he saw the odometer. Less than thirty thousand miles on a ten-year-old car?

What the hell, he thought. So, maybe Marlow just bought himself a second car and the change of ownership had yet to be registered. The mileage alone would make the car worthwhile. But he couldn't let go of the notion that he was wrong. This was a little old lady's car, not the type a man like Marlow would want to be seen driving.

And then it hit him. Little old lady! As in a woman named Fostoria Biggers? Her name had come up in conjunction with Marlow's when he'd been into the bank records and he'd thought little of a lawyer being an executor of an estate. It was done every day. But what if…?

He dropped to his knees. Regardless of why it was here, it was another vehicle that would be at Lash Marlow's disposal. Without wasting any more time, he affixed a bug to this car as well, and while he was on his knees, his attention was drawn from the car itself to the condition of the tires. He crawled closer. The treads were packed with mud and grass. He picked at the grass. To his surprise, it still bent to the touch. He frowned. Someone had recently been driving this car. But where?

A door slammed. Roman's nerves went on alert. It was time to get out. He'd done what he'd come to do.

The call came in at exactly one minute to five. Every man in the room went on alert as Ryder reached for the phone.

"Ryder Justice speaking."

Like before, the voice had been altered. A mechanical whir was audible in the background.

"This is a recording. In fifteen minutes, Ryder Justice is to bring the money to the corner of Delaney and Fourth. There is a newsstand nearby. It will be closed. Set the bags inside the stand and drive away. If anyone attempts to follow the man who picks them up, Delaney Ruban's granddaughter will be meat for the 'gators. If you do as you're told, Casey Justice will be released."

The recording ended long before a trace could be made. Ryder cursed beneath his breath as he hung up the phone. He felt sick to his stomach. 'Gator meat? God help them all.

He started toward the front door. "Put the bags in the car."

"Wait!" Wyandott shouted.

Ryder turned. "Do what I said," he ordered. "Delaney and Fourth is halfway across town. I'll be lucky to get there in fifteen minutes as it is."

"I want one of my men in the back seat of your car."

Ryder grabbed him by the arm and pushed him up against a nearby desk. His voice was shaking. "I don't give a tinker's damn what you want. That's not your wife someone threatened to feed to the 'gators, it's mine. Now put the damned bags in the car or I'll do it myself."

Roman peeled Ryder's hands off of the agent's jacket "Easy, brother. He's just doing his job."

Ryder spun, his eyes blazing with anger. "Don't push me Roman. I've been hanging on the edge of reason for so damned long it hardly matters." His voice broke. "If I lose Casey—"

"Put the bags in the car," Wyandott said. "We won't be far behind."

Ryder pointed at Wyandott. "I don't know who will pick up these bags after I'm gone, but if one of your men even sneezes in his direction and my wife dies as a direct result, I will kill him...and then you for giving the order."

Wyandott's face reddened, but he stepped aside.

Within seconds, Ryder was in the car and out of the driveway, leaving a cloud of dust and a group of men running for their cars to keep up. Roman watched from the step until they had all disappeared, and then he jumped in his car and drove out of the driveway in the opposite direction. He had his own agenda to follow.

Eudora watched from an upstairs window and then returned to her bed in tears. Downstairs in the library, Miles and Erica sat in uneasy silence, now and then venturing a glance at the other without voicing their thoughts.

Out in the kitchen, Tilly sat in a chair near a window overlooking the drive. Her posture was straight, her expression fixed. Only her eyes revealed her pain. They were wide and tear-filled as she watched for someone to bring her sweet baby home.

Everyone was waiting for a miracle.

Bernie Pike opened the door to Casey's room as his partner, Skeet, entered carrying another plate of food and a can of some sort of cola.

"Last meal," Skeet said, waving the plate in Casey's direction.

The urge to cry was almost more than she could bear. If only she was somewhere else and lying in Ryder's arms. But she didn't cry, and she wasn't in Ryder's arms, and she crawled off of the bed with undue haste. She wouldn't put herself in the position of giving Bernie and Skeet any more ideas than they already had. She didn't know that Lash had threatened everything but death to them if they so much as touched a hair on her head. She didn't know he'd saved that joy for himself.

"I thought prisoners were given a choice as to what they wanted to eat."

Skeet chuckled and dropped the plate at the foot of the bed and tossed the unopened can of soda beside it.

"Sorry, sweet thing. You get beans and weiners."

Casey glanced at the plate. The only thing good about it was that the small, lunch-size can of beans and weiners was still unopened. "And I was so hoping for your head on a platter."

Skeet slapped his leg and laughed, then elbowed Bernie and laughed again. "She's a hoot, ain't she Bernie? It's a damned shame Marlow is gonna 'do' her." Before Casey could think to react, Skeet reached for her breast. "I still think I'd like a little taste of what she has to offer. What Marlow won't know won't hurt him, right?"

Casey grabbed the can of beans from the plate and bounced it off of his head.

Skeet ducked, but it was too late. He yelped in pain when the can hit the corner of his temple. Seconds later, she was flat on her back on the bed with Skeet on top of her.

"You bitch! I'll make you…"

Bernie cursed and grabbed, pulling his partner off the woman and the bed. "Get away from her, dammit. You heard Marlow. You might want to part with your dillydally, but I don't. Besides, you asked for it."

Skeet's rage was slow to subside as he considered whether or not Lash Marlow was capable of castrating anyone. Finally, he decided he didn't want to test the theory enough to try again.

"You got about two more hours to play hell on this earth, then you can die on an empty stomach," he yelled, and out of spite, took the can of beans and weiners and stomped out of the room.

Bernie looked at Casey and shrugged, as if to say it was all her fault, then shut the door behind him. The lock turned with a sharp, distinct *click* and when they were gone, Casey dropped to the floor and pulled her knees up close to her chest.

For the first time since the ordeal had begun, she was losing all hope. And the worst was in knowing Ryder would never know how sorry she was for betraying him by the investigation. They'd parted in anger and she would die with that on her conscience.

Despair shattered the last of her resolve. She slumped onto the floor, her legs drawn up against her chest in a fetal position, and she started to cry—slow, aching tears that welled and spilled in a continuous flow of pain.

Casey cried until she lost all track of time. Had it been two hours or two minutes since Skeet's warning that her time to die was close at hand? Was Lash already on his way? She remembered the wild expression on his face when last she'd seen him.

"God help me," she prayed, and then choked on a sob as she realized she was lying in a position to see directly beneath her bed.

The elongated neck and small, unblinking eyes of the creature beneath her bed were startling, but for Casey, who'd lived in imminent fear for the last three days of being eaten alive, it was a large relief.

"Well, my word," she said, and reached under the bed, pulling out a small, brown terrapin that had taken her move as threatening and disappeared into its shell. "So it was you I heard all the time."

Sympathetic to the fear that had caused it to retreat, Casey quickly set it free, and as she did, saw something else under the bed that made her heart leap. There, in the corner beneath her bed! It looked like—

She crawled to her feet and pulled the bed away from the wall just enough to reach behind. When her fingers curled around the butter soft leather, she pulled. She was right! It was her purse.

She clutched it to her chest as she crawled onto the bed, then held her breath, listening to make sure that Bernie and Skeet were not about to come in.

Three days ago seemed like a lifetime. Casey couldn't remember what she'd been carrying in her purse, or even what she'd been doing when she'd gotten the call about Ryder's wreck. Her fingers were shaking as she undid the clasp. But when she opened it up, her hopes fell. Her shoulders slumped as the dumped the meager contents onto the bed.

Her wallet was gone, as was the compact cell phone she usually carried. She should have known this would be too good to be true. There wasn't anything left but a handful of tissues, some pencils and pens, her lipstick and a small, plastic bottle of lotion.

Frustrated by the letdown, she slammed the purse down on the bed beside her and then winced when something within the purse itself hurt her hand.

"What in the…?"

She opened it back up. There was nothing inside but the black satin lining. She tilted it, then thrust in her hand, feeling within the bag itself. Something was there…but not inside…it was beneath…no, between. She pulled at the lining like turning a sock inside out, and saw the rent in the fabric near the clasp.

Curious now as to what was inside, she stuck her finger in the fragile lining and pulled. It ripped and then parted. Carefully, Casey thrust a finger inside, then another, and searched until she felt something cool and hard and sharp. And as she traced the object's length, realization dawned. Her hands were shaking as she pulled it out. She tried to think of how the letter opener Lash had given her as a gift had gotten out of her desk drawer and into her purse.

And then she remembered running back to grab her wallet on the day of the call, and of grabbing a handful of pens along with it as she dropped it inside her purse. That must have been it. She'd gotten the letter opener with everything else. And because it had been so sharp, it had gone straight through the lining and lodged in between.

She looked toward the door as her fingers curled around the miniature rapier's silver shaft. It wasn't much, but it was the first means she'd had of self-defense and she had no intention of letting it go to waste.

A laugh boomed out in a nearby room. Casey flinched, then shoved the dagger beneath her pillow. Not now, she told herself. Only when it was time. When it was time.

Chapter Sixteen

Ryder pulled up to the newsstand with less than a minute to spare. He double-parked in the street and grabbed the two bags, moving in an all-out sprint. The stand was closed, just as the kidnapper had promised, but a small, side door stood ajar, and he shouldered his way inside.

It was little more than three walls and a roof. The half wall that opened up to the public could be propped overhead like a porch, shading the counter beneath. The concrete sidewalk served as its floor, and Ryder dropped both bags on it with a thump and walked out.

All the way back to the car, he had the impression that he was being watched. He didn't know whether that came from the Feds who had followed him here, or from the kidnapper waiting for him to leave. When he slid into the driver's seat and started the car, his instincts kept telling him not to leave—not to leave Casey's welfare up to kidnappers. But he ignored the urge and drove away, and had never been this afraid in his life—not even the night his plane had crashed—not even when he'd known that Micah was dead. He left with the knowledge that he'd done all he could do. The ransom had been delivered. Hopefully, his next point of contact would be the phone call telling him where to pick up his wife.

As Ryder drove away, Wyandott and his men began to slip into place around the area. A couple of blocks away, Gant watched from his car with binoculars trained on the door through which Ryder had come and gone.

And the wait began.

Five minutes passed, then ten, then twenty. In spite of the coolness of the evening breeze blowing through his window, Gant was starting to sweat. He could just imagine what was going through Wyandott's mind. The Feds must have been made. If the kidnappers got spooked and didn't pick up the ransom, he wouldn't give a plug nickel for Casey Justice's chance of survival.

Just when he thought it was over, an old man turned the corner and headed down the street, pulling a little red wagon behind him as he made toward the stand. Gant thought nothing of his presence until the man paused at the door, opened it up and then stepped in, leaving his wagon just outside.

Gant sat straight up in the seat, adjusting his binoculars for a clearer view as the man emerged. But it wasn't the bags Ryder had put inside that he was carrying out. It was a large black garbage bag. He tossed it into the wagon and started down the street when Wyandott's men suddenly converged upon him.

Gant threw down his binoculars in disbelief and started his car. In spite of the kidnapper's instructions, Wyandott was pulling him in. God help them all if this stunt got Casey Justice killed.

"You're under arrest!" Wyandott shouted, as two of his agents wrestled the old man to the ground.

The terror on the old fellow's face seemed sincere. "What did I do? What did I do?"

An agent slapped handcuffs around his wrists while another tore into the bag. But they all stared in disbelief as a cascade of crushed aluminum cans fell onto the street.

"What the hell?" Wyandott muttered.

"They're mine, fair and square," the old man cried, as they pulled him to his feet. "Anthony gave them to me."

Wyandott turned. "Who the hell is Anthony?"

"The man who owns the newsstand. I pick them up once a week, regular as clockwork. Everyone knows. Anthony doesn't care. He saves them for me."

A knot was beginning to form in the pit of Wyandott's belly. He pivoted and pointed toward the stand. "Check it out!" Two of the agents were already running as Gant's car slid to a halt near the curb.

Gant strode toward Wyandott with murder in his eyes. "Have you lost your mind?"

Wyandott hunched his shoulders and thrust out his jaw. "Mind your own damned business."

"This is my city. That makes it my business," Gant yelled.

One of the agents came running. "Sir! You'd better come take a look."

Everyone converged on the stand, leaving the old man handcuffed and alone in the street near his cans.

The bags were gone!

"This is impossible," Wyandott muttered. "We didn't take our eyes off of this stand for a second. Not a damned second."

Gant stepped inside, and, as he did, caught his toe. He staggered, then looked down. A certainty came over him that they'd been lying in wait for nothing. Chances were that the bags had disappeared seconds after Ryder had left.

"He didn't take them out, he took them down," Gant said, pointing toward the slightly raised edge of a lid covering the opening that led down to the sewers.

Wyandott paled. "Hell." He grabbed his two-way. "Ambrewster...is that bug sending?"

The radio crackled, and then the man's voice came over the air loud and clear. "No sir. Everything is status quo."

Gant was on his knees and pulling at the lid when several of the agents followed his lead and began to help. A flashlight was produced, and even though they were yards above them, and it was black as a devil's heart down below, there was enough light to see two empty bags lying at the foot of the ladder.

And they had their answer. The signal wasn't sending because the bags were more or less right where Ryder had left them...minus the three million dollars that had been inside.

The radio crackled again. Wyandott jerked.

"Captain...this is Tucker...come in, sir."

"Go ahead."

"Sir, we've been following Marlow as you ordered. He parked his car and went into the courthouse at fourteen hundred hours. We have men stationed at every exit and he has yet to come out."

Wyandott was starting to worry. He kept thinking of the threat Justice had made to his face. This wasn't going down as he'd planned.

"I want to know if he's inside. Look for him, dammit, and don't stop until you do. He's mixed up in this somehow, I know it."

Ryder turned off of the highway without slowing down and skidded to a halt in front of the mansion. He was out of the car before the dust had time to settle.

But when Roman came around the house on the run, Ryder paused at the front door with his hand on the knob. He could tell by the look on his brother's face that something had happened.

"What?"

Roman grabbed him by the arm. "Gant just called me. The drop went sour. The kidnapper went underground into the sewers. He's got the money and all they've got left are those damned bags."

Disbelief, coupled with a pain Ryder couldn't name, nearly sent him to his knees. It was coming undone.

Roman grabbed him by the arm. "Don't give out on me now. We're going to plan B. Come with me. We don't have much time."

For the first time since Ryder had exited the car, he became aware of a loud, popping sound, but he was too focused on Roman to consider the source. "Where are we going?"

"Marlow is on the move," Roman said. "I've been tracking him, but he's moving out of range. You're going to have to help me, brother, or we're going to lose our best chance to find your wife.''

They had just cleared the corner of the house in full stride, when Ryder stopped in his tracks.

''Son of a bitch.''

Roman grabbed him by the arm, almost yelling in his face to be heard above the noise. ''It's a Bell Jet Ranger, just like the one you have at home.''

''I know what it is,'' Ryder said, staring at the helicopter's spinning rotors. ''Where the hell did you get it?''

Roman almost grinned. ''I borrowed it, so don't wreck the damned thing. I have to take it back when we're through.''

Ryder started to sweat. Wreck? Hell, that meant making it fly first.

Roman grabbed him by the shoulder and jerked. ''Are you going to stand there, or are we going to try to save your wife?''

Ryder started to run. ''If you stole this, I'll break your neck.''

''Just shut up and get in,'' Roman yelled, as he leaped into the passenger seat and grabbed at a laptop computer he'd laid on the floor.

A strange sensation swept through Ryder's body as he climbed into the seat. The sounds were familiar, even the feel of the seat at his back and the scent of fuel mixing with the dust and debris flying through the air caused by the rotor's massive pull.

Then he glanced at his brother and the moving blip on the computer screen in front of him. The tracking devices! Roman had bugged Marlow's car after all. His pulse surged. ''Is that him?''

Roman nodded. ''Yes, but I'm losing him. Take her up!''

Ryder stared. That blip kept blinking—blinking—blinking—like a pulse. Like Casey's pulse. He grabbed the seat belt. It snapped shut with a click he felt rather than heard. He took a deep breath and pushed in on the throttle and it felt as if the helicopter took a deep breath. Ryder glanced at the blip one last time and the guilt he'd been living with for the better part of a year simply disappeared.

''Roman.''

Roman glanced at his brother.

"Buckle up."

Seconds later, the chopper went straight up in the air, then flew into the setting sun like a hawk flying out of a storm.

Lash was ecstatic. It had all been too easy. Just this afternoon, he'd driven Fostoria Biggers's little car to an abandoned garage near the downtown courthouse, then taken a cab back home. A short time later, he got in his own sedan, drove to his office, picked up some legal briefs, then drove to the courthouse and parked in his usual place.

Only when he got into the elevator, he didn't go up, he went down. Down into the basement. Down through a maze of heating pipes and furnaces, past the janitor's quarters where he picked up two large bags he'd hidden earlier, as well as a pair of gloves which he immediately put on. He was smarter than Pike. He wasn't leaving traces of himself anywhere to be found.

Down he went into a shaft leading straight to the sewers beneath the city. Counting tunnels and watching for numbers written on the walls beside the ladders with something akin to delight, Lash knew when he reached number seventy-nine that he was directly beneath the newsstand.

He waited, and minutes later, he heard the echo of boots against metal as Ryder Justice walked across the sewer lid and dropped the bags full of money…his money. A smile broke the concentration on his face. So far, so good.

He knew the bags were bugged. He'd watched the Feds planting the bugs himself. So he transferred the money from their bags into the ones he'd brought, and left the original bags and their bugs right where he knew they would eventually be found.

Once again, he was using the underground sewers of Ruban Crossing as a means by which to travel. With the narrow beam of a small flashlight for guidance, he began to count tunnels and ladders again until he came to ladder number sixty-five. This time he went up, coming out in the alley just outside the abandoned garage where he'd parked Fostoria Biggers's car.

When he drove out of the city, he was three million dollars

to the good. As for the fifty thousand he was supposed to pay Bernie and Skeet, it was unfortunate, but he was going to have to renege.

It wasn't his fault Bernie had left fingerprints behind when they'd yanked Casey out of her car. Eventually the police would find Bernie Pike. And if they found Bernie, Skeet Wilson would not be far behind. Lash didn't trust them to keep quiet about his part in the crime. He couldn't leave witnesses. Not after he'd gone this far.

As he drove, he reached down and felt the outside of his pocket, reassuring himself that his gun was still there. Once or twice, as he pictured pulling the trigger and ending two men's lives, he came close to rethinking his decision. And then he would remind himself that, for three million dollars, he could live with a little bit of guilt.

All he had to do was walk in the house, pull the trigger two times and they would be out of the picture. At this point, his imagination began to wane. He kept picturing himself opening the door to the room in which Casey was being kept and pointing his gun at her as well. After that, the image faded. Would she beg? Would she cry? Would he be able to kill the woman he once thought he loved?

Fostoria Biggers's little car fishtailed in loose dirt as Lash sailed down the road toward her home. Only a few more miles.

"He's turning south," Roman said, and held on to his laptop as, moments later, the helicopter took the same turn, yielding to Ryder's skill.

Roman's gaze was completely focused on the screen before him. And the farther they flew, the more certain he was of where Lash Marlow was going.

"There's nothing out here but swamp grass and trees," Ryder muttered, as he banked the chopper sharp to the right, sometimes skimming so close to the treetops that the skids tore the leaves as they flew by.

Roman frowned, grabbing at the computer and leaning into another sharp turn. "If you were partial to driving there, you should have said so—I'd have gotten one of these things with wheels."

"Am I still on course?" Ryder asked.

Roman looked down at the screen. "Yes. We can't be more than a half a mile behind."

Half a mile. Would that be the difference between Casey's life—or Casey's death?

"I don't like this," Ryder said, glancing down at the blur of terrain beneath them. "There's nothing out here but snakes, alligators and wildcats."

"And the house where Fostoria Biggers was born and raised."

The helicopter dipped. Not much, but enough to let Roman know Ryder had been startled by what he'd said.

"Who is Fostoria Biggers?"

"One of Marlow's clients. I thought it was a little too convenient that Marlow has her car and her power of attorney. I checked land records at the courthouse. Would you believe that her house is just a little farther south...in the direction in which Marlow has been driving?"

Ryder looked startled. "How long have you known about this?"

Roman shrugged. "Bits and pieces of it since the first day. But it didn't all start falling into place until you caught Marlow repeating the kidnapper's demands, word for word. After that, we didn't exactly have time to talk. I figured you wouldn't mind if I took the initiative."

Ryder's expression was grim. "I don't care what you do. But when we get where we're going, Marlow is mine."

Roman nodded. That much he understood. He glanced back at the screen. "Read 'em and weep, brother. It looks like our runner is about to stop."

Ryder's heart skipped a beat as he looked down at the screen. For the first time since they'd gone airborne, the blip was stationary. He glanced out the windows, searching for a sign of the car and a place to set down.

It was Roman who saw it first. "There!" he shouted. "I see the top of a roof up ahead in that clearing." He leaned farther forward and pointed across Ryder's line of vision. "There's the road, just to your left."

"I see it," Ryder drawled. He gave his brother one last

glance, and there was a wealth of understanding between them in that single look. "Hang on. We're going down."

It was getting late. Casey could tell by the temperature of the bare wooden floors beneath her feet. Every nerve she had was on alert. She'd said her prayers, and such as it was, her little game plan was already in place. The contents of the bottle of lotion she'd found in her purse was in a puddle on the floor just inside her door. Her letter opener was in one hand, held fast at the hilt, and an unopened can of beans was in the other.

Oddly enough, Bernie had had a change of heart, and sneaked them back in to her when Skeet wasn't looking. From the size of his belly hanging over his belt, she supposed he didn't think a person should die on an empty stomach. And, she was as ready to die as she would ever be, but not without a fight.

Just as she was about to get herself a drink of water from the bathroom sink, she heard a shout of jubilation outside her door. Her thirst forgotten, she stifled a moan. That could only mean one thing. Lash had arrived. Bernie and Skeet were about to get paid.

Lash pulled up to the house and put the car into Park, but left it running. This trip was going to be a real hit-and-run. He had to get back into the city and pick up his car at the courthouse. It was the final stage of his plan, and one that would tie up the last loose ends.

He was halfway up the steps when Bernie Pike met him at the door. "Did you get it!?" Bernie asked.

Lash grinned and nodded as he put his hand in his pocket. "Where's Skeet?" Lash asked. "I want to pay you both at the same time."

"I'm right here," Skeet said.

"Hot damn," Bernie said. "My horoscope said this was my lucky day."

The gun was in Lash's hand before either man thought to react. Bernie went down still wearing his smile. Skeet had started to run and then stumbled and fell when Lash's second shot caught him square in the back. The echo of the gunshots beneath the roof of the old porch were still ringing in Lash's ears as he nudged each man with the toe of his shoe. Neither moved, nor would they ever again.

While Lash was staring down at their bodies, something fell on his sleeve. He looked down and then shrieked in sudden panic. Frantic, he brushed it off with the butt of the gun, then stomped it flat. What was left of a caterpillar lay squashed on the floor of the porch.

Another worm. A rapid staccato of drumbeats began again, ricocheting through Lash's mind as he backed away from the worm and into the house with his gun drawn. He was all the way inside and halfway across the floor before he realized he had his back to the door of the room in which Casey was being kept. He crouched and spun. Heart pounding and slightly breathless, he aimed the gun at the middle of the door.

It took a bit for him to calm down. And when he did, he went to the door, rattling the knob just enough to let her know he was coming.

The tone of his voice took on a high, singsong pitch. "Here I come, ready or not."

He opened the door, saw her standing across the room, and stepped inside, right into the puddle of lotion.

One second Lash was looking at Casey and the next he was staring at the ceiling and struggling to breathe. He clutched his chest with a groan and rolled as air began to fill his deflated lungs.

"Damn you," he gasped, crawling to his feet just in time to duck an object that came flying through the air. Although he knew it wasn't Casey, he pulled the trigger in self-defense, then gasped as something splattered all over his face. He looked down at himself in disbelief. Beans? He'd shot a can of beans?

For Casey, the two shots outside the door were unexpected. But when total silence followed, Casey suspected her worst fears were about to come true. Not only was Lash capable of killing her, but she'd bet her last dollar he'd just done away with Bernie and Skeet. It figured. He wasn't the kind of man to leave loose ends untied. Lash was nothing if not neat.

She backed against the far wall, and when his voice taunted at her through the door, she traded the dagger in her right hand for the can of beans, then held her breath and waited.

The door opened, and to her undying relief, Lash hit the oil slick of lotion and fell flat on his back. While he was struggling for breath, she hauled back and sent the beans sailing, then ducked when his shot went wild.

While he was still brushing at the thick sauce and beans splattering his coat, she came at him. It was only through an inborn sense of self-preservation that he looked up in time to see her coming, but he didn't move in time to save himself from the dagger's sharp thrust.

He swung at her head with the butt of his gun just as the pain began to burn through his chest. Casey went limp, slumping to the floor at his feet as Lash stared at the familiar silver shaft sticking out of his chest.

The drumbeat got louder. He kept thinking of the dagger sticking out of that fat rat's body, and now it was in him. The analogy was as sickening as the nausea rolling in his belly.

By now, the drumbeat was so loud in his head that he couldn't hear himself scream. And yet the soft patois of the French-speaking slave, warning—predicting—promising, could still be heard above the drum.

Sharp like a serpent's tooth, it will spill your blood and your flesh will be eaten by the worms of the earth.

In a wild kind of panic, he yanked at the handle, ignoring the pain, losing sight of the fact that, with Casey Justice unconscious and helpless at his feet, his goal was well within reach. Blood welled then poured out of the wound, and Lash staggered from the shock of seeing his life spilling on Casey's legs.

And then he heard her groan, and a certainty came upon him. *Kill her now, before it's too late.*

He wiped at the sweat beading on his brow and aimed the gun. He had to do it now while she was unconscious. He no longer had the guts to let her witness her own death. Not anymore.

He leaned down, jabbing the barrel of the gun at her head as the room began to spin around him. And then footsteps sounded on the porch outside and he turned and froze. A gourd rattled, like a rattlesnake's warning, and the drumbeat grew louder, hammering—hammering—in what was left of his mind.

Crazed with pain and the impending vision of his own mortality, he lifted his gun, his wild gaze drawn to the shadow crossing the floor ahead of the man coming in.

When the first two shots came within seconds of each other, Ryder panicked. He tightened his grip on the gun Roman had given him and picked up his pace as he moved through the marsh beyond the old house. Brush caught on his blue jeans and tore at his shirt. Limbs slapped at his face and stung his eyelids and eyes. Water splashed up his legs to the tops of his knees and he kept on running, assuming that whatever was in his path would have to move of its own accord. His focus was on the house just visible in the distance, and the small white car parked nearby.

A hundred yards from the house, he saw the bodies of two men sprawled upon the porch and fear lent fresh speed to his steps. That explained the two shots. Water splashed a bit to his right and he knew that Roman was there on his heels as they ran out of the marsh and into the clearing.

Another shot rang out and Ryder almost stumbled. Dear God, it wasn't possible that they'd come this far just to be too late. He couldn't let himself believe that God would do that to him...not twice.

Two seconds, then ten seconds, and Ryder was up on the porch. He cleared Bernie Pike's body in a smooth, single leap and came in the front door on the run.

"Dammit, Ryder, look out."

Roman's warning came late, but it would not have slowed his intent. He kept thinking of that blip on the computer screen.

Had his wife's heart stopped when it had, too?

He saw them both at the same time. Marlow was straddling Casey's body with his gun aimed at Ryder's heart. And the knowledge that he'd come too late filled his soul. Despair shattered his focus. Rage clouded any caution he might have used.

His mind was screaming out her name as he pointed the gun
at Marlow's chest.

"You lying son of a bitch."

They were the last words Lash Marlow would hear as Ryder
pulled the trigger.

Lash's shot went wild as Ryder's bullet struck Marlow in
the chest. He bucked upon impact, and Ryder fired again, then
emptied his gun in him just to see him dance.

Roman was only seconds behind. He came through the door
with his gun ready, the echo of Ryder's last shot roaring in
his ears. But hope died as he saw the woman on the floor and
Marlow lying nearby. It looked as if Ryder would have his
revenge, but little else.

Ryder's gun was clicking on empty chambers when Roman
took it out of his hand. Ryder jerked, then groaned and let it
go. The pain in his chest was spilling out into his legs and
into his mind. He couldn't think past the sight of her battered
and broken body lying still upon the floor.

Roman started toward the two bodies but Ryder stopped
him. With tears streaming down his face, he grabbed his
brother's arm. "No. Let me."

Roman ached for his brother's pain as he stepped aside, and
Ryder walked into the room, absorbing the filth and degra-
dation of the place in which she'd been kept. Dropping to his
knees, he lifted her from the filth on the floor and into his
arms.

Blood ran down her legs as her head lolled against his
shoulder, and then he couldn't see her face for his tears. His
heart broke as he cradled her against his chest.

His voice broke along with his heart. "No more! No more!"
Laying his head near her cheek, he choked on a cry. "Ah,
God, I can't take anymore!"

His shoulders hunched as he bent from the burden of living
when those he loved kept dying around him.

Roman knelt at his side, sharing his brother's pain. He
glanced at the woman in Ryder's arms. Even through the
bruises and dirt, her beauty was plain to see. Years ago, he'd
shut himself off from this kind of loss. He'd seen so much
death and too much misery to let himself be hurt by it anymore, but this was too close to home. This woman, Ryder's

wife, was gone too soon. He reached out, lifted her hair from the blood on her face, and as he did, his finger brushed the curve of her neck.

His eyes widened as he tensed and shoved Ryder's hand aside. When he felt the pulse beating strong and sure, he rocked back on his heels. A miracle! That's what it was. A heaven-sent miracle.

Ryder choked on a sob. "Don't, Roman. Just leave us alone."

Roman grabbed his brother's hand, his voice shaking as he pressed it at the pulse point on Casey's neck. "She's alive, Ryder. I swear to God, your wife is alive!"

At that same moment in the Ruban household many miles away, Matilda Bass heard a whisper. She froze, and then tilted her head, straining to hear. As suddenly as the whisper had come, it was gone, and Tilly's body went limp. She leaned against the cabinet as the bowl she was holding slipped out of her hands and onto the floor, shattering into a thousand tiny pieces, just like the weight that had been on her heart.

Joshua spun, wide-eyed and startled. And then he saw her face.

"Tilly?"

"They found her, they found her. My baby girl is alive."

Epilogue

From below, the shiny black helicopter flying high above the earth resembled an oversize dragonfly charging through the air. From up above, the earth resembled a vast crazy quilt in varying shades of greens and browns that covered the landscape over which they were flying.

As if at some unseen signpost up in the sky, the pilot suddenly shifted course and soon, a long black rooftop became visible in the distance, along with the roofs of several outbuildings, connected together with a chain stitch of holding pens and corrals.

Casey leaned forward, grabbing at Ryder's leg as her eyes lit with excitement. "Is that it? Is that the Justice ranch?"

Ryder grinned at her. "That's it, darlin'. All seven thousand acres."

Her smile was nervous as she glanced at him. "I'm a little anxious about meeting your family."

"Easy now, you know they're going to love you."

She sighed. "I wish I could have promised you the same thing when I took you home to mine."

Ryder laughed. "At least they like me now."

"Like! Oh, Ryder, in their eyes, you are the next best thing to sliced bread and you know it."

His grin widened. "Only because Miles's new girlfriend keeps him too busy to meddle in our affairs."

Casey nodded in agreement. "And who would have thought that Erica would go on vacation and come home with a husband?"

"Yeah, and he has a job, which was more than you could say for me when you dumped me in their laps. Dora is walking in tall cotton over the fact that they are moving to Atlanta and taking her with them."

Casey laughed aloud. "Gran will miss you. You were the best chauffeur we ever had."

"Dora and I understand each other," he said. "But let's be honest, I was the worst chauffeur, and you know it. However, now that I have moved my planes and the charter service to Ruban Crossing, I have become a bona fide, acceptable businessman."

She patted his leg in a tender gesture. "Tilly was right all along. Somehow she knew you belonged. You are the best thing that ever happened to my family." Her voice broke. "And to me."

Ryder gave her a quick, nervous glance. A few months ago he'd cradled her body on the floor of Fostoria Biggers's bedroom, certain that his world had just come to an end. Sometimes at night he still lay awake just to watch her sleep. What she had endured was beyond his understanding; that she had endured it at all was a miracle in itself.

Now, most of the time she was fine. But once in a while, when things got too quiet, he saw her soul slip into a shadow and he knew she was fighting a dark demon of her own. He knew from experience that it would take time, and a whole lot of love, for the memories of what she'd endured to recede.

"I love you," he said softly.

Casey shivered, as if struck by an unexplained chill, and then she lifted her head and smiled and Ryder relaxed. For now, Casey was back in the light.

"I love you, too, wild man. Now take me home. I have a need to feel Texas under my feet."

Relieved that the moment had passed, he grinned. "Royal

is going to love hearing you say that. He's a real homebody
He lives for his daughter and the ranch, and I can tell yo
right now that, except for a remarkable resemblance which w
all share, Royal is nothing like Roman.''

A small shudder rippled through Casey's body, but she re
fused to deny it access. Remembering Roman also meant re
membering when they'd first met. Of waking up and seein
Ryder—of being lifted into the helicopter and looking up
an echo of her husband's face as Ryder laid her in Roman'
arms—of helicopters and hospitals—of police and FBI. O
fearing the dark and doctors and needles. Of Tilly's hand o
her cheek and Joshie's kiss on her brow. And always, over
shadowing everything and everyone, was Ryder. Ever presen
ever faithful, everlasting.

She turned to look out the other side of the helicopter, mar
veling at the size of the cattle herds in the far distance. From
up here, the cattle looked like so many ants. Finally, she wa
able to say what she thought.

''Roman will always have a special place in my heart. I lik
him a lot.''

Ryder's grin slid a little off center as his emotions betraye
him. ''Oh, hell, honey, I like him, too. He's my brother. An
I owe him more than I will ever be able to repay.''

The look they shared was brief, but it was enough to re
member they had a lot for which to be thankful.

Moments later, Ryder shoved the controls of the helicopte
forward and it started to descend, aiming for a wide, flat are
behind some barns like a horsefly heading for the rump of
steer.

That night, and long after Royal and Maddie had gone t
bed, Ryder walked the halls of the house in which he'd bee
raised, visiting the ghosts that had driven him away. Unabl
to sleep, he'd checked on Casey one last time and then gon
outside to the wide front porch to listen to the night.

It was spring, and the air was sweet and cool. The scent o
flowers in the nearby flower bed reminded him of Casey. To
him, she would always be a fresh breath of spring. She'd bee
his savior in so many ways that he couldn't begin to take

count, and they'd come too close to losing that which made life worth living. That day in Fostoria Biggers's house, when he'd touched her skin and felt the pulse of her life beating beneath his fingertips, he'd known then that they'd been given a second chance.

A night owl hooted from a nearby tree and Ryder paused, listening to the familiar sound. A cow lowed in a nearby pasture, calling for her baby. Moments later, a plaintive bawl announced the baby's location, and all was well. Ryder took a deep breath, absorbing the peace of home and the assurance that he'd done the right thing by bringing Casey here to visit.

A quick breeze came up, lifting the hair away from his forehead and brushing against his chest like a lover's fingers. He glanced up at the sky and then to the faint wisps of clouds overhead, judging the possibility of a rain before morning.

And while he was looking at stars, the breeze seemed to shift, and the skin on his flesh tightened in warning. A sound came out of the night, like a whisper, or a memory, but it was there in his mind. And he knew who it was that his heart finally heard.

Welcome home, son.

He turned toward the house. But it wasn't Micah who came out of the door.

Casey came off of the porch and out into the dew-damp grass to stand beside him. She lifted her hand to his cheek, feeling, rather than seeing the tears that had started to fall.

"Sweetheart, are you all right?"

Ryder wrapped his arms around her, holding her close until he could feel the even beat of her heart. He buried his face in the curve of her neck and took a deep breath. Flowers. She always smelled like flowers.

"Now that you're here, I'm more than all right."

Casey sighed, and held him even closer. "Come to bed, Ryder. I can't sleep without you."

He lifted her into his arms. "Then buckle up, darlin', and I'll take you to dreamland."

* * * * *

Share in the joy of yuletide romance with brand-new
stories by two of the genre's most beloved writers

DIANA PALMER

and

JOAN JOHNSTON

in

LONE STAR
CHRISTMAS

Diana Palmer and Joan Johnston share their favorite
Christmas anecdotes and personal stories in this
special hardbound edition.

Diana Palmer delivers an irresistible spin-off of her
LONG, TALL TEXANS series and Joan Johnston crafts an
unforgettable new chapter to **HAWK'S WAY** in this wonderful
keepsake edition celebrating the holiday season. So
perfect for gift giving, you'll want one for yourself...and
one to give to a special friend!

Available in November at your favorite retail outlet!

Only from

V *Silhouette* ®

Look us up on-line at: http://www.romance.net   JJDPXMAS

Take 4 bestselling love stories FREE

Plus get a FREE surprise gift!

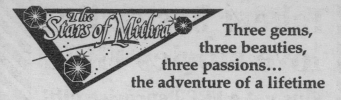

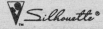